RISE OF A DYNASTY

SINS Series Book 3

EMMA SLATE

This book is a work of fiction. Names, characters, places, and incidents are the product of the author's imagination or are used fictitiously. Any resemblance to actual events, locales, or persons, living or dead, is coincidental.

©2016 by Emma Slate. All rights reserved, including the right to reproduce, distribute or transmit in any form or by any means.

One year later

Chapter 1

The late summer breeze caressed my skin as I reclined in the lounge chair by the private pool. The secluded villa was tucked away in the Italian countryside, twenty minutes outside of San Gimignano. The air smelled of ripe fruit and earth.

I reached for the cool glass of white wine on the table next to me, my eyes drifting to my cell phone.

"Don't do it," came my husband's deep voice.

He was in the lounge chair next to mine, his muscular chest glistening with sun and sweat. Flynn angled his head, and though I couldn't see his eyes behind his sunglasses, I knew they were an intense shade of cobalt, and no doubt lit with humor.

"Don't do what?" I asked.

A smile cracked his beautiful lips. The man wasn't handsome by traditional standards. He was too raw, too rugged. He was perfect—and all mine.

"They're fine."

"I know they're fine," I protested weakly.

He made a Scottish noise—a cross between a growl and a grunt—of disbelief in the back of his throat; it was a noise I would never be able to replicate no matter how long I lived in Scotland.

"I promised you a honeymoon," he said. "A honeymoon doesn't include children."

"Probably because a honeymoon is supposed to happen *before* the children are even in the picture. Our honeymoon is long overdue—we can make up our own rules. One call," I pleaded.

"We'll call tonight to check in."

"Do I have to remind you what happened the last time I left Hawk?" I still had nightmares about Hawk's kidnapping. Not frequently, but enough that I could never forget what had happened.

"I remember." Flynn's voice was a gruff whisper.

"And it's not just Hawk. We have the twins, now, too."

"Barrett, they're fine. There's nothing to worry about. Arlington is in prison. Winters is dead. There are no more threats."

"I just can't help but think the other shoe hasn't dropped yet."

"It's been a year, hen."

"A year is nothing," I muttered. "Besides, I barely remember this past year since I've been completely preoccupied with our children. I've been in a baby coma."

"Which is why you should be glad we're here, just the two of us. You get to drink wine, eat fresh seafood, spend time with me. If you're nice, I'll even let you make love to me."

I let out a laugh.

"I know it's hard, but can we try to remember that we're not just parents? The bairns are old enough that they don't need you every moment of every day. I'm just trying to give you some perspective."

"I'll show you perspective." My hand reached up to pull the bow behind my neck holding my bikini top in place.

"What are you doing?" he asked.

The scrap of material fell away. "I don't want any tan lines," I feigned in sham innocence.

Flynn lowered his sunglasses, cobalt eyes gleaming with desire. "You're too far away."

The villa was surrounded by an eight-foot wall, and the trees along the wall were even higher. We had complete and utter privacy, and there was no chance of anyone seeing us.

"And you have too many clothes on," I teased.

Flynn yanked down his navy-blue swimsuit, his eyes hot. He sprang free, proud, ready, and waiting for my hands and mouth. I stood up and went to him. His hand grazed along my outer thigh, tugging on my bikini briefs.

"Come here," he whispered huskily.

I swung my legs over the lounge chair so my naked body straddled his. My fingers trailed across the column of his neck, and I leaned over to press my lips to his chest. Flynn inhaled sharply as my tongue traced the lines of his pecs. I moved lower, nipping his belly, enjoying the strained tension in his limbs.

"You're killing me," he gritted.

"I'm taking my time," I said with a wide smile. "I finally have you all to myself."

He leaned his head back against the lounge chair and closed his eyes. I tormented him with light touches and soft kisses. Grazing my breasts along his thighs, I scooted down until I was at the heat of him. I grasped him in my hand, gently squeezing him. Flynn's breathing became labored, and raspy and a moan escaped his parted lips when I took him into my mouth. He was throbbing, ready. My auburn hair fell over his lap, shielding me from his view.

"Enough," he commanded. "I need to be inside of you."

I let him haul me up by my arms until I was sitting astride him. I held him, positioning him at my entrance. I slid onto him slowly, reveling in our desire, in our connection. We fit together perfectly. He wrapped his arms around me as I rocked against him, taking him slow and deep. Our mouths sought each other, fusing together. Any hope of taking it slow vanished. He gripped my hips, spurring me on to ride him harder, faster. Clasping his shoulders, I let my eyes close as pleasure snaked through me. I glided against him, skin flushed and slick.

"Barrett," he growled against my mouth.

I slammed down on top of him and came hard. My nails dug into his shoulders as his hands left my hips to grab my hair. I stared into his eyes as Flynn bucked beneath me, his strong muscular legs solid strength. One of his hands stroked my back, urging me to lean forward. He took a nipple into his mouth, pulling it deep into the warmth of him. He sucked me hard, on the verge of pain, but it sent a jolt of lust to my core.

He grunted and moaned when I clenched around him. My second release swept through me with the force of a tsunami, slaying everything in its path. With a shout, Flynn speared up into me and came.

I collapsed onto his chest, our skin sticky and sweaty. The late afternoon sun brushed my back in a warm caress. Closing my eyes, I reveled in the quick pace of Flynn's heartbeat.

"Is it me," I whispered, "or does it keep getting better?"

"Aye." His hands slid along the small of my back before resting low on my tailbone. "Any better and you might just kill me."

Before the sun completely sank into the horizon, Flynn and I managed to untangle ourselves. We hopped into the pool, the cool water washing away the heat of our coupling. Though we were sated, we still found reasons to remain close and touch one another. An ember of desire always flickered low, easily fanned into a fire that consumed. Wanting him hadn't stopped. Not even after three children and the exhaustion they brought.

Flynn scratched at his chin, the dark shadow of a beard beginning to sprout. He made a face. "I need to shave."

"Why?" I demanded, my own hand coming out of the water to trace his cheek. I loved the raspy feel of his skin.

"It itches."

"You could let it grow."

He raised an eyebrow. "You think I'd look good with a beard?"

"I think you'd look great with a beard."

I rested my hands on his shoulders while my legs wrapped around his waist. He traced a drop of water from my shoulder down the slope of a breast.

"These"—he cupped my breasts in his large hands—"are fantastic."

I snorted. "They used to look a lot better."

"Ah, love," he teased with a roguish grin. "I didn't take you as the vain type."

"I'm not vain," I said. "I just kind of wish things looked like they did before the babies. Is that wrong?"

"No. It's not wrong, but it's wishful thinking. You still look amazing. You run every morning," he reminded me. "You've got a nice round arse. If you'd like, I'd be glad to pay homage to it."

I smacked his shoulder playfully and laughed. His eyes darkened with serious intensity. The sun had finally set; the colors of twilight sprinkled the sky and highlighted his strong jaw.

"Have I thanked you?" he asked.

"For?" My arms wrapped around his neck, and I pushed myself closer.

"Everything."

I sighed and brushed my mouth against his. "I should be thanking you."

"Why?" he asked with genuine wonder.

"Because you gave me the family I didn't know I needed."

He smiled gently. "So you're no longer mad at me?"

"Mad? Why would I be mad at you?"

"Where should I start? How about when I took you in form of payment for your brother's debt?"

"Took me?" I repeated, aghast.

He grinned. "Or what about when I didn't tell you I ran an illegal brothel and casino, and you confronted me after getting drunk with Ash?"

"I wasn't drunk."

He raised his eyebrows in disbelief.

"Fine, I was tipsy, but I was still in charge of all my faculties."

"Hmmm. All right. Let's see, what else?"

"Quit while you still have all your working man parts," I said, causing him to laugh. It turned into a groan when I reached between us to caress him. He was hard again.

"Will you put my working man parts to use?" he demanded, his mouth already coming to take mine in a consuming kiss.

"I plan on putting them to use the rest of the night."

Chapter 2

"I'm starving," I said, rolling away from Flynn before he had a chance to engage me in another round.

"Me too," he said roughly.

I laughed, dodging his wandering hands. I switched on the bedside lamp before reaching for Flynn's discarded white undershirt and throwing it on.

"You're gorgeous," he said, propping himself up on one elbow to look at me. "And putting on my clothes only makes you hotter."

I turned my backside to him and flashed him my bare bum. "You're pretty good at this husband business, Flynn Campbell."

"I aim to please," he said, finally getting up.

"This was a really good idea," I said while I watched him pull on a pair of gray boxer briefs.

"What? Getting out of bed? I completely disagree."

"No, I mean, just you and me, here, without the bairns."

"You miss them, though, aye?"

"Well, sure. But it's a nice reminder that before them, it was just you and me."

"It wasn't you and me for very long." He took my hand

and led me out of the bedroom. We walked down the hallway and into the living room of the villa. It was cool tawny stone floors and whitewashed walls, open and airy, with an incredible view of the Italian countryside, which was a smattering of rich sienna, ochre, and green.

"Any regrets?" I asked as we entered the rustic kitchen.

Flynn opened the bottle of red that rested on the long wooden table. I went to the refrigerator to pull out the pot of seafood stew that had been left for us upon our arrival that morning.

"Regrets?" Flynn asked, pouring two glasses.

I turned the burner on low. "Yeah, regrets on how things worked out."

"Not really," he admitted, taking a seat.

I snorted.

"Guess you haven't forgiven me for the twins, aye?" he asked with a knowing grin.

"Oh, I've forgiven you."

"Because I got the vasectomy."

"I didn't think you'd actually go through with it," I admitted with a wry smile.

"I thought our family was complete—besides I was afraid for my life if I didn't go through with it."

"Well, with our luck, if we hadn't taken measures, we would've had another baby. And I would now be insane," I remarked dryly. "I don't even remember those first few months after Iain and Noah were born." It had all been a blur, even with the help of two nannies. Hawk had become a full-time handful since he'd been close to walking—and even though he was young, he'd understood that he wasn't the center of attention anymore, causing him to become quite the troublemaker.

"Question," Flynn asked, handing me a glass of wine.

"Shoot."

"Let's say you hadn't gotten pregnant with the twins. Would we have stopped at one?"

"It would've been nice," I admitted. "Having just a bit more time with Hawk by himself—before Iain and Noah—but no. I would've wanted Hawk to have siblings."

Flynn smiled, looking a bit relieved.

"Have we never really talked about this?" I asked, checking the soup.

"I think we've been a bit preoccupied this last year," he said.

"Truth," I agreed. Though things with the SINS were good, three young children accounted for the insanity along with Flynn constructing another Rex Hotel in Las Vegas. The opening was in a few weeks, and he'd been spending the last few months flying back and forth from Dornoch to Las Vegas. But we were finally getting our bearings, and Flynn and I were reconnecting.

Turning off the burner, I poured the soup into the waiting bowl, adding a dash of pepper and two spoons. I brought it to the table and set it down in front of Flynn.

"Smells good," he admitted.

My stomach rumbled. "It does."

I grabbed my glass of wine and took a seat. Flynn scooped up a spoonful, blew on its contents for a moment before giving me the first taste.

Brine, tomato, and clam all hit my tongue. I closed my eyes as I savored it. "Oh God. This is incredible."

Flynn took the next bite and whole-heartedly agreed. "We should hire an Italian chef."

"Then my arse really will get rounder."

"I wouldn't complain," Flynn said with a roguish grin. He kept his gaze on me when he asked, "Did you want a girl?"

"Did you?" I asked just as softly.

"I wouldn't know the first thing about raising a girl. Boys—boys I ken. I was one."

"I've heard some stories from Ramsey and Duncan," I reminded him. "I'm aware of just how much trouble you were."

"Aye, well, now it seems fate is paying me back three-fold. Three boys."

"Who will one day be teenagers," I reminded him. "We're going to have to lock the liquor cabinet."

He laughed. "When they think they're men enough to handle their scotch, I'll get them nice and pissed. They'll live through a hangover and vow moderation from then on."

I raised an eyebrow. "Oh? And that worked for you?"

Flynn paused. "We might need to lock the liquor cabinet."

Late the next morning, Flynn and I finally managed to leave our bed. We showered and got dressed, ready for a day in town.

Time had stood still in the little Tuscan village of San Gimignano. We walked hand in hand along the brick walkways, taking in the stone towers and buildings. There was a distinctly medieval feel with the many churches and markets. Because we didn't want to spend time inside, we bypassed the museums. Maybe we'd get to them later, maybe not. We were only there for a week, and I wanted to relax, see the town, and spend the rest of the time holed up in the villa with Flynn. Naked.

After we'd walked around for a few hours, we took a seat at one of the many outdoor cafés and split a carafe of white wine and a cheese plate.

"Best honeymoon ever," I teased him as I spread a glob of goat cheese onto a little piece of focaccia toast.

"Better late than never, aye?" Flynn asked.

I fed him the bite of cheese, watching his tongue dart out to catch a crumb on his lip. My insides shook with desire.

"I still owe you that island vacation," he reminded me.

"Maybe when the boys are older and we can travel farther for longer than a week," I said.

"Valid point, love."

We finished our light supper and then continued our meandering through the town. Shops closed, and the bars began to open. The town transformed. Young adults swarmed the streets, laughing and carousing.

I briefly remembered the time, not so long ago, when I was nothing more than a history scholar, living in a pre-war studio apartment, happy and content. And then I'd met Flynn, and everything I thought I knew about life—and love—had been challenged.

"Hen?" he asked, noticing that I'd fallen silent. "You all right?"

I nodded. "Just thinking."

"About?"

"How different my life was not that long ago."

"Ah, so we're in that mood, are we?" he teased, wrapping his arm around my shoulder and pulling me into the crook of his body.

"Don't joke," I said. "I'm being serious."

"Sorry. What can I do to help?"

"Just listen." I looked up at him and he nodded. "I want to go back to work. The twins are weaned, and though being a mother is great, I'm more than that. You have the SINS, and you have a purpose outside of our family. I need a purpose, or I might go insane."

He raised his eyebrows. "You mean, being the mother of my children isn't enough of an identity for you?"

I playfully elbowed him in the ribs, and he pretended to wince. He captured one of my hands and brought it to his lips. "Any ideas where you could get a job like the one you had in New York?" he asked.

I shook my head. "No. I did go to Inverness and meet with

the history chair department of the university there, but he didn't have anything to offer me. But that was a while ago. I might try again."

"Did you tell him who you were—who we were?"

"No."

"Why not?"

"Because at the time, I thought using the power of the Campbell name was cheating."

"And now?"

"And now, I think, if I go to one more baby-mommy yoga class, I'm going to kill myself."

"Well, at least you're not dramatic."

"Beast."

He chuckled. "I think I have a solution to your problem."

"I'm all ears."

"There's a library connected to Dornoch Cathedral. Father Brooks is going out of his mind because everything is out of order and nothing is catalogued properly."

"Oh, yeah?" I asked in surprise.

Flynn nodded. "Aye. He's been meaning to hire someone to get to it, but I said I knew just the person who would enjoy dusty books, hard to read handwriting, and someone who didn't mind getting lost for hours in the stacks, and stacks, and stacks of shelves."

I turned to Flynn and wrapped my arms around him. "You're perfect."

He grinned. "You think so?"

"I do. You're so perfect I want to have your babies. Oops. Too late."

Chapter 3

"You're really taking this 'no tan lines' seriously," Flynn said, strolling across the stone patio, ready for another leisurely afternoon by the villa's private pool.

I lifted my head from the lounge chair and grinned at him. "Sunbathing completely nude has its perks."

"I agree." He leaned down to kiss me. He nibbled on my bottom lip for a moment before pulling back, eyes dark with desire.

"I'm ready for sunscreen, though. Otherwise I might crisp—and that would not be good."

He set his towel on the lounge chair next to mine and then got comfortable, patting the seat in front of him. I got up, glad that his eyes followed my naked body as I sauntered toward him. I tossed him the tube of sunscreen and then perched in front of him, giving him my back.

"Be thorough," I commanded.

Flynn chuckled. "Woman, there isn't a swatch of your skin I won't get. Trust me."

He massaged my backside, completely ignoring the sunscreen. His lips followed the curve of my shoulder and up my neck. My skin hummed from his touch.

"Lean back against me," he said softly into my ear.

I did as commanded, and then his hands were trailing down my body to the apex of my thighs.

"Spread your legs."

Tingles of desire shot through my belly as his fingers danced across my skin, playing with the dampness between my thighs.

"God," I moaned.

Flynn gently bit my ear as his finger entered me. I opened wider, wanting more, wanting it deeper. He obliged and added another finger. Squirming against his hand, I panted in earnest. Flynn's free hand went to my breast, kneading it until the nipple stood at attention.

I was primed and eager, a bow ready to release. Flynn murmured Gaelic words in my ear—I didn't know their actual meaning, but the seductive intent was unmistakable.

"That's it, love." His fingers were inside me, and he took his thumb and pressed it between my folds. I let out a strangled cry. I shook with rapture, gripping Flynn's thighs, hard enough to gouge him with my nails.

Flynn eased out of me as I tried to catch my breath. His hands languorously slid down my body, caressing and petting, promising me more.

A cell phone rang from inside the villa. Neither one of us moved to answer it. Whoever it was could wait. We checked in every night with the two nannies that were staying with the boys, so I didn't think for a moment it was one of them. The phone quieted and then started up again.

"I should get that," Flynn said.

I moved off him and reached for his towel, wrapping it around me. "I'll get it." I leaned over to give him a gentle kiss before heading inside the villa. Both our cell phones were on the coffee table, but it was Flynn's that was ringing. Ramsey's name flashed across the screen. I picked it up.

"Hey, it's Barrett," I said.

"Hi, lass," he greeted. "I'm sorry to bother you on your last night in Italy."

"You sound tired."

"I am tired. Jane dragged me to another one of her events last night."

I chuckled. "You fell in love with a society girl," I reminded him. "Formal wear and mingling with uppity people are part of the package. But I know you didn't call to talk about your fiancée. SINS business or personal business?" I began to walk back to the patio with the phone.

"SINS business."

I strolled across the stone walkway, drawing Flynn's attention. I held out the phone to him. "Ramsey."

He put the cell to his ear, and then a moment later put the phone on speaker. "We're both here," Flynn said.

"Arlington's dead," Ramsey said without preamble.

"Dead?" I repeated, my eyes darting to Flynn. His jaw was clenched and his eyes were cold.

"Killed in prison," Ramsey explained.

"By?" Flynn demanded.

"Not sure yet. Still getting information. I'll call when I have more." Ramsey clicked off and the phone went silent.

"This isn't bad news, is it?" I asked when the silence had gone on for long enough.

"Don't know," Flynn admitted. "It wasn't us, though."

"The SINS, you mean?"

He nodded. "Can't say I'm upset by it. Arlington was a greedy bastard."

"Yeah, I won't mourn him." The man had aided in the kidnapping of Hawk when he was only a few weeks old. I still couldn't think about Arlington without wanting to go homicidal.

"Could be nothing," Flynn said slowly. "Could be a coincidence."

"Right. He could've made an enemy in prison. That's a logical conclusion."

We were quiet for a moment and then I asked, "You don't really believe that, do you?"

"No, I don't." He leaned forward and placed his elbows on his thighs.

"So, you didn't give the order and Duncan didn't give the order, so it came from someone else. Or another rogue SINS member."

"Oh God, anything but that," Flynn grumbled.

"Who else did Arlington piss off?" I wondered.

"The million-dollar question. Ramsey is in London and will do some scouting."

"And just when I thought the other shoe wasn't going to drop…"

"It drops with a loud thump," he said with a wry smile.

"Guess this means the honeymoon is truly over."

"So it would seem." He reached out and touched my cheek in a tender gesture.

"Pack?" I asked.

He nodded and stood. "Pack."

I opened the front door to our home in Dornoch and was immediately assaulted by mayhem. A full-grown sheep ran to welcome us, bleating loudly. Betty nudged my leg in greeting, and I absently patted her while trying to figure out what the hell was going on. There was crying, yelling, and the sound of something crashing against the wall. The house was in complete disarray. Piles of clothes were strewn about the floor, baby toys littered the staircase, and there was one wall of the hallway hand printed in what looked like chocolate syrup.

"This is our house, right?" Flynn wondered, coming in behind me.

"Yes."

"What happened?"

"I don't know." I headed for the staircase. "Anna? Beth?" I called out, hoping the two nannies might be able to clue us into what was going on. There was no answer as Flynn and I moved forward. We stood in the doorway of the nursery and found the source of all the noise. Or sources, as it were.

Hawk stood in his crib, holding onto the bars, tears streaming down his cheeks. He howled like a baying animal, and Flynn immediately went to pick him up. Anna had Iain on the changing table and was trying to get his diaper on, but he wasn't having any of it. He kicked his legs, and then I saw a geyser of urine spraying upward. Anna cursed in Gaelic, trying to keep everything under wraps.

"Anna?" I asked, heading to the crib the twins shared. Noah sat quietly, his hands clutched around a toy. I ran a hand down his auburn hair, and he looked up at me and gave me a gummy smile.

"That's it!" Anna yelled, picking up a half-naked Iain and bringing him to me. She unceremoniously dropped him into my arms before glaring at both Flynn and me. Her face quivered in anger.

"Where's Beth?" I asked her.

"Beth quit four days ago. It wouldn't have been so awful except the housekeeper had to leave due to a family emergency. I've been fielding this alone the last few days. Now that you're both back, I'm quitting too!"

"Don't quit," I protested. "Please?"

She pointed to Hawk who had calmed the moment Flynn picked him up. "Your son will not sit still. He runs around and I have to chase him."

"He has a bump on his head," Flynn said.

"Let me see," I demanded, shuffling Iain while trying to examine Hawk. There was a small red lump on the side of his head. "What happened?"

"He climbed up onto the couch and jumped off it. This was after he decided to paint the walls with maple syrup. That's the day Beth quit," she explained. "Whenever I put Hawk in his cot, he screamed and screamed until I let him out."

"Why didn't you call someone for help? Why didn't you call Ash? Or call us? We would've come home," I said.

Anna's mouth pressed into a firm line. "I did call Mrs. Buchanan. She told me I wasn't allowed to call you unless your children were in mortal danger. She gave me a bonus. She sent people to help, but as you can see, I'm alone. No one stayed. I'm leaving, too."

Before Flynn or I could say anything to dissuade her, she zoomed past us, leaving us to clean up the destruction.

"They scared off two plus nannies within a week," Flynn said. "I think we underestimated our children."

A disgusting smell coming from Iain had me grimacing. I gently lifted him away from me so that he could finish his business.

"If they weren't ours, I'd be scared off too," I remarked dryly.

Chapter 4

Three days later, we had two new nannies, the maple wall had been cleaned and repainted, and Hawk had been moved into his own room. He had a unique influence on his younger brothers—his mood set the tone and it was never calm.

We had a welcome home dinner with Ash and Duncan and their six-month-old daughter Carys. She was as angelic as our boys were demonic. And she looked just like Ash—bright blue eyes, strawberries and cream complexion, and blond hair.

Ramsey called, but there was nothing new to report. We discussed contacting Don Archer, my FBI contact, to see if he had any knowledge on the subject, but we quickly shut down that idea. The last few years taught me that if we could keep information within the family, it was better that way.

By the end of the week, we were finally back in our routine. I woke up before Flynn and got the boys changed and fed. By the time Evie, one of the new nannies arrived, Flynn was finally awake. Pouring a cup of coffee, he sleepily kissed me and then headed off to his study. Ash showed up for our usual morning jog, blond ponytail high on her head.

"Town today?" she asked.

"No," I said. "I want to stay close to home."

Ash pouted. "If we go to town, we can have tea with Glenna."

I smiled. "You don't want tea—you want her homemade cookies."

"I love those cookies."

The jog was scenic as we passed heather in full bloom, strips of purple everywhere. The Highlands were gorgeous, in every season, but late summer was my favorite. The sunshine and lack of rain made it easier to run; I'd done my fair share of jogging through mud and even snow.

"What are you wearing to the opening?" Ash asked when we got back to the house.

"I haven't even thought about it," I said truthfully. The crazy of the last few days had made me completely forget about the Las Vegas Rex Hotel opening.

She smiled in gentle understanding.

"I'm just gonna get something when I'm there."

"You? Shopping?" Ash asked, raising her eyebrows.

I put my arm to the doorframe so I could grasp my leg to stretch it out. "Flynn has assured me that I'll find something in one of the many boutiques in the new hotel. He's already called with my measurements. I just have to go try stuff on. Very minimal effort involved."

"Ah, that makes more sense. This is going to be the biggest and grandest Rex Hotel yet."

I nodded. The hotel had to contend with others of its size and grandeur, and it was Las Vegas. Each establishment tried to outdo its competition. The one thing The Rex Hotel brand did better than any other empire was grandeur and old-world opulence without being tacky or garish.

"It's going to be incredible," I said. "I've only seen photos in different stages of construction, but I'm excited to see it at its completion.

"Are you bringing the kids?" she asked.

"Would I be a terrible mother if I said no? Hawk can't sit

still, and the last thing I want to do is bring babies across an ocean for a three-day trip."

She frowned. "I thought Flynn was staying in Vegas longer."

"He is," I agreed. "But I'll fly back after the grand opening. He'll only be staying a few extra days, anyway."

"And then he'll be home full-time?" she asked.

"For a while. Until he gets restless and needs a new project."

"Most women would resent their husbands for spending so much time away from home and their family."

"Most women don't understand the men they married," I said.

"Still, this last year hasn't been easy on you."

"Most of this last year was spent sleep-deprived and attempting to get my body back. Half the time Flynn was home, I wasn't even aware he was here. I don't blame him for throwing himself into opening a new hotel." I looked at her pointedly. "Italy was perfect—we reconnected, and I remembered how much I loved Flynn."

"You forgot you loved your husband?" she asked with a soft chuckle.

"No," I said with a knowing smile. "I just remembered what it's like to have an adult conversation that doesn't revolve around children."

"And sex. You remembered that you really like sex."

I shook my head. "I remembered that I really *love* sex."

She sighed, her face going all dreamy. "Yeah, sex is good."

"Makes the world go 'round." I set my foot down and picked up the other.

"Don't kill me," she began.

"What did you do?"

"Nothing. Yet." She sighed. "I'm not going to the opening."

"Why not?"

"I don't want to fly that long for a few days. I don't want to be separated from Carys. And besides, I've got the gallery. I don't want to leave it just as I went back to work."

My smile was slow, and I shook my head.

"What?" she demanded, pulling out her messy blond ponytail and running her finger through the snarled locks.

"I never thought I'd see the day when Ashby Rhodes decided to bow out of a very good party."

She rolled her eyes. "It's Ashby Rhodes Buchanan—and you should know that anything is possible. Especially after the life you've been living these past few years."

I laughed. "Valid point, Ash."

After I showered, I checked in on the boys in the playroom. They were having fun and the nannies didn't look overly harassed, which seemed to be a miracle. Who knew what sort of crazy Hawk would get into next?

I headed downstairs to find Flynn. He was in his office and in the middle of a phone call. When he saw me hovering in the doorway, he waved me in and gestured for me to close the door. He ended the call and set the cell down on his desk. It landed with a decisive thud.

"Who was that?" I asked, walking to him and placing my hand on his arm.

Flynn ran a hand across his chin, scratching at the stubble that was rapidly becoming a beard. "Ramsey."

"News about Arlington?"

"Aye. There are photos of Arlington's body. Ramsey sent them in an email."

"Gruesome?"

He frowned. "That's what's so weird. They're not."

"No?"

"No. The body wasn't disfigured. They did an autopsy, and the pathologist said Arlington died of asphyxiation."

"Asphyxiation," I repeated. "So, he was strangled? Or smothered?"

"There were no signs of struggle."

"What did the tox screen say?"

"Clean."

"No."

Flynn clenched his strong jaw. "Aye." He leaned over his desk and pressed the spacebar of his laptop. The black screen flashed with color, and then I was staring at a cropped photo of Arlington's neck, specifically the swatch of skin behind his ear.

I leaned in closer. "Is that…"

Flynn pressed a few buttons, and the photo zoomed in so I could see the white ink tattoo better. It was no bigger than a dime, a bird with open wings.

"Arlington never struck me as the type of guy that had a tattoo," I said.

"It was a calling card," Flynn said. "Someone wanted to take credit for this without being obvious about it."

"That's weird. Why wouldn't someone just fess up?"

"I don't know the answer to that." He looked at me. "What are you thinking?"

I continued to stare at the computer screen. "I'm not sure yet."

"Something nagging at you?"

"How d'you know?"

"Because I know you—and you've got this intense, scholarly furrowed brow."

I smiled and reached out to touch his cheek. "I love that someone knows me so well." My hand dropped. "Why now?"

"What?"

"Why didn't Arlington die during the proceedings? Or during his trial? Why within the first few weeks in prison?"

"Probably so it wouldn't draw as much attention," Flynn mused. "People tend to forget the headlines pretty quickly. Arlington dying in prison only affects the few that remember him. Try not to worry too much about it, love. Not at the moment."

"Why worry about something you can't change," I stated.

"Exactly." He watched me carefully, as if he already knew what I was thinking—that I wasn't torn up about the fact that Arlington was dead.

"Maybe we should consider this a blessing," I suggested. "The last link to The Pretender is gone, and now it's wrapped up. Done. Finished. We can truly move on with our lives."

Flynn's cobalt eyes gleamed like precious jewels. "It's been weighing on you?"

"Has it been weighing on you?" I asked back.

"I didn't like that we gave Arlington to the Brits to let them handle it. I would've preferred—"

"Yeah, I know what you would've preferred. But cutting that deal was the right thing to do." I shook my head. "Okay, I can't talk about this right now. I'm headed into Dornoch. I wanted to speak to Father Brooks today about cataloguing the library."

He kissed me softly. "I have to talk with Duncan."

"Late dinner?" I asked.

"Probably."

"Wine?" I asked.

"Most definitely."

"Sex on the kitchen table?" I teased.

He grinned. "Absolutely."

Chapter 5

Dornoch Library was a Gothic stone building with high-winged arches, sitting on a parcel of land just behind the cathedral. It was three floors of cobwebs, dust, and books that needed cataloguing and organization. It was exactly the kind of project I couldn't wait to tackle.

Father Brooks gave me a set of keys and free reign. I could come and go as I pleased. He was actually quite happy to be rid of the overwhelming undertaking.

"Weel," he said in his thick brogue. "I'll leave you to sort out this mess." With the energy of a man half his age, he sprinted out of the austere and dark building, leaving me alone.

The first order of business was to get a new light design put in, otherwise I'd strain my eyes and go blind trying to read all the small printed titles on the leather-bound books. I'd have to get a cleaning crew in there to give the place a thorough dusting or I'd be sneezing every five minutes.

I wandered around the library for the better part of an hour, trying to understand the layout and make sense of the disorder. There was no way I was going to be able to find anything until I pulled out all the books and began rearranging them.

As the sun set, I reluctantly locked up the library. I was excited and eager to dive in, but it would have to wait. When I got home, I briefly checked in on the twins, but they were bathed and ready for bed. I headed to the den, finding Flynn with Hawk on his lap.

"He's sitting still," I commented with a smile, leaning down to kiss Flynn.

The toddler began to squirm as soon as I said it. Flynn set him down in front of me, and Hawk wrapped his arms around my legs, peering up at me with a cute, impish grin.

"Come here, devil," I teased, picking him up.

"You cursed it," Flynn said. He got up and headed toward the bar. "Want a drink?"

"Scotch, please," I said as I carried Hawk and sat down on the couch, setting him down to stand between my legs.

Flynn poured us two glasses and then set mine down on a coaster on the coffee table. Hawk saw it and immediately went for it. "Mine."

I threw Flynn a look. "Should we?" I asked with a grin, holding the glass out of reach so Hawk wouldn't spill Balvenie Triple Cask all over the carpet.

"He doesn't seem to know when to quit," Flynn said with an amused glance. "I say we give him a taste and see what happens."

I dipped my finger into the glass and then touched Hawk's teething gums. He smacked his lips together and his brow furrowed in confusion. He glanced at his father and then back at me. And then like a tiny baby bird, he opened his mouth and demanded more.

"That had the opposite reaction I was going for," I said, setting my glass down so I could lift Hawk onto my lap. I cradled him against me and rubbed his back.

Flynn shot me an amused look. "We may have opened the door to Hawk's love of scotch."

I brushed back the dark hair off his forehead to reveal the bump that was healing. "Yeah, I think Hawk is smarter than both of us. It totally backfired. Let's just hope the twins are easier to wrangle."

"Aye," Flynn agreed.

Hawk's nanny came into the den and asked if she could take him for his bath. Demonstrative in his affection, Hawk gave me a noisy kiss before letting his nanny lead him out of the den.

I picked up my glass and took a sip of scotch. "Nice time with Duncan?"

"We were discussing our next move with the SINS. It's difficult, you know? We're entrenched with the FBI. We're watched and our illegal activities are monitored."

"Don Archer leaves us alone," I reminded him.

"Aye, in exchange for information about other illegal groups causing trouble in the United States."

I smiled in understanding. "You feel like a nark."

"A nark?"

"A snitch."

Flynn shook his head and then grinned. "Pretty much."

I pat the couch seat next to me, and Flynn got up from his chair and came over. Fitting myself into the nook of his body, I rested my head on his chest. We enjoyed our scotches in silence until we heard Hawk fighting his nanny.

I looked up at Flynn and grinned. "No rest for the wicked."

"Don't I know it," he said.

Hoisting Hawk higher on my hip, I knocked on Barnabas's front door. A crop of white hair appeared the moment the door flew open. Hawk squealed in excitement, attempting to lunge out of my arms.

"Do you want to see the puppies?" Barnabas asked as he took Hawk from me.

"I do," I said. I leaned up to kiss Barnabas's weathered cheek.

"Come in, come in," he said with a grin. "You're looking tan."

I laughed. "Liar."

"How was Italy?" Barnabas asked as we walked through his old stone cottage toward the back.

"Gorgeous, restful, perfect. Glad to be back, though. Now where are these adorable puppies?"

Barnabas opened the door to the pantry to reveal Nan, a black and white Border Collie resting on a pile of old blankets. Her litter of eight puppies nuzzled against her eagerly.

I crouched down onto the floor and petted Nan. Her ears flattened against her head as she leaned into my hand. Barnabas handed me Hawk, whom I settled onto my lap.

"You say hi to Mama first," I said to him, taking his hand and petting Nan's silky ear. Nan licked Hawk who giggled. He crawled off my lap and scooted toward the month-old puppies.

"Gentle," I said to Hawk.

"You want to hold one, laddie?" Barnabas asked. He crouched down and tenderly lifted a puppy and set it in Hawk's lap. The look on Hawk's face was priceless.

"Every lad needs a good dog," Barnabas said with a grin.

"He's got a sheep."

"Not the same."

~

The next morning, I was drinking coffee and eating a slice of toast at the kitchen table when Flynn walked in. He was dressed in a navy sweater and dark slacks, his hair styled.

"What's your mood like?" Flynn asked.

I looked up from my list of what I needed to do to make the library presentable. "My mood is good. The twins had a good night's sleep, and they're not crabby, and Hawk is at Barnabas's farm."

"Again? You were both there yesterday."

"He likes the puppies."

"No," Flynn said.

"No what?" I demanded.

"No, he better not come home with a dog. We have a sheep that lives in the house. That's enough."

"She gets bathed regularly, so I really don't know what your issue is." I got up to refill my cup of coffee.

"Because she—can we not talk about Betty?"

"Sure. What's going on?"

"I have to go to Las Vegas earlier than I planned."

I raised my eyebrows. "Earlier when exactly?"

"Tomorrow."

"What happened?" I demanded.

"Nothing. Yet."

"Oh, I get it. You think your mere presence will ensure that everything goes accordingly for the opening and nothing would dare go wrong."

"Pretty much."

"I think it's a solid plan and I support it," I said. "So you take the jet and I'll take a commercial flight."

Flynn's smile was slow and full of amusement. "Ah, hen. You do make me laugh."

"I didn't know I was so funny."

"I was going to ask if you wanted to come with me tomorrow instead of flying out later. Let's bring the boys with us," he suggested. "The penthouse is more than big enough for us, and there's a connecting suite for the nannies."

"You've thought of everything," I marveled.

He grinned. "I try. Think about it. While I'm running around like a maniac, you can hang out by the pool."

"That's all well and good," I said, "but it's not fun to drink and sunbathe alone."

"Ash will be there."

I shook my head. "No, I don't think so. She doesn't want to leave Carys and besides, she's got stuff to do at the gallery."

"She'll come," he promised. "I'll get Duncan to talk to her."

"She's in a place."

"What place?"

"You know, the baby place. Where you can't see straight or think straight and everything revolves around that."

He made a noise in the back of his throat.

"You're a man," I said with a smile. "So you don't get what having a baby does to your brain. You don't make rational choices, and logic flies out the window."

Flynn looked at me thoughtfully for a moment. "I have an idea. Didn't you do something so foolhardy as to meet with Winters without vetting the situation first?"

I didn't like that reminder. "I was stupid. And hormonal. I wasn't thinking clearly."

"Hey," Flynn said, coming to me. He took the coffee cup out of my hand and set it aside before pulling me to him. "I didn't mean to make you—"

"I know," I assured him. I hugged him back, breathing in the clean smell of his shirt, the hint of him beneath.

"Can you believe it?" he asked.

"Believe what?"

"Believe that we made it through all we made it through?"

I leaned my head back. "Sometimes I think we're characters in a book and shit just keeps happening to us."

He let out a chuckle as his hands cradled my cheeks. He

leaned down to kiss me, and just as he attempted to end it, I refused to let him, demanding that he deepen it.

"I have a minute," he whispered against my lips.

"Just a minute?" I teased.

"Like you need more than a minute," he quipped.

"What can I say? We fit together really well. And when it works, it works."

"Amen to that," he said, tugging me toward the privacy of the back porch.

Chapter 6

The Las Vegas Rex Hotel wasn't on the strip but twenty minutes outside of town, surrounded by the browns and greens of the desert. The Rex was meant to be its own entity so that guests could shop, go to the spa, attend shows, gamble in the casinos, eat and drink in the restaurants, all without having to leave the resort. There was also a golf course and a high-class brothel. Because prostitution was illegal in parts of Nevada, Flynn still had to bribe the right people to get them to look the other way.

The expansive lobby was white marble and gold accents; the decor and design of the hotel had been inspired by Versailles. Overwhelming opulence was around every corner and even Ash, who'd grown up with money, gaped.

Unfortunately, we were exhausted from traveling so we didn't get time to explore or take it in. We all headed up to the private penthouse floor, juggling tired, crabby children who were ready for bed.

"Breakfast tomorrow?" I asked Ash as the nannies took the children from our arms and swept them away toward their beds.

"Yes."

"Duncan and I have an early business meeting," Flynn said. "So it will just be you ladies."

"Mimosa breakfast. Excellent," I teased. We said goodnight and then went to check in with the nannies and tuck in the boys. They were already conked out in their cribs, and I sent up a small prayer that they'd sleep through the night.

I planned on heading to the master bedroom, but Flynn took my hand and led me out of the room and into the hallway.

"Where are we going?" I asked.

He shot me a grin but didn't reply as he pushed the elevator button. We got in and he inserted a brass key. The elevator ascended, and we were quiet. Our silences had long ago become comfortable.

The doors opened, and I was greeted by the sultry desert night and a panoramic view of the inky sky and stars. Off in the far distance, I could see the garish bright lights of the Vegas strip.

"What's this?" I asked, taking in the long rectangular pool, lounge chairs, and umbrellas.

"This," Flynn said. "Is our private pool. Only we have access to it."

"Really?"

"Did you think I'd build a hotel and then not have a private pool for our own use?"

"You do spoil me," I remarked.

"It's the other way around, love," Flynn said, his eyes heated with desire and joy. "Come here."

He pulled me into his arms and we began to sway like we were dancing, only there wasn't any music. We didn't need any.

After breakfast the next morning, Ash and I left our children in the care of three nannies and went down to a dress boutique in the lobby of the hotel. Everything was ready to wear, one of a kind. If they didn't have it in your size, you were shit out of luck. Just another example that The Rex experience was elite and exclusive.

I picked out a floor-length, off-the-shoulder white gown. It showed a bit of cleavage, but Ash convinced me I could pull it off with the right bra. I didn't believe her at first, but the boutique attendant agreed with her. Ash chose a black cocktail dress in the flapper style with a matching black sequined headband.

When I made a move to look at jewelry, the boutique attendant stopped me, which meant only one thing: Flynn had already bought me something and he wanted to surprise me. Usually, I just wore the diamond studs he'd given me on our wedding day. They were classy, elegant, and went with everything.

When we finished shopping, Ash and I headed back up to our suites to change into our swimsuits so we could laze by the private rooftop pool. We were still in the midst of jet lag and didn't yet have the energy to explore the sumptuous hotel.

"Duncan hasn't called. Think they're still in their business meeting?" Ash asked, adjusting the brim of her straw hat.

I slathered on sunscreen even though I'd opted for shade under the umbrella. It was already obvious that it was going to be a hot dry day in the desert, and it wasn't even noon yet.

"Meeting—or drinking scotch on the golf course?" I asked.

"No. You think?"

I gave her a look.

"Okay, maybe their business meeting took place on the golf course."

"That's probably far more likely," I said with a grin.

The elevator doors chimed open, and I turned my head.

Flynn and Duncan stepped out of the elevator, already dressed in their swimsuits, sunglasses perched on their noses.

I always seemed to falter a bit at the sight of Flynn's bare chest. He was chiseled and completely masculine. I sighed in feminine appreciation. I heard Ash let out her own little breath when she took in Duncan's form. Though he was also in amazing shape, he was shorter and a bit bulkier than Flynn.

"Gentlemen," I greeted.

"Ladies," Flynn said back.

"How was the morning meeting?" Ash asked, lowering her sunglasses as she surveyed her husband.

"A lot was accomplished," Duncan said.

I looked at Flynn. "Got a lot done, huh?"

He nodded. "Aye."

Ash laughed. "You're a rotten liar, Duncan Buchanan. Just admit you guys were playing golf and you wanted it to be boys only."

"We weren't playing golf," Flynn lied.

"The back of Duncan's neck is burned," Ash stated.

Duncan sighed. "We were playing golf."

"Thank you," Ash said in exasperation.

"Sorry we didn't invite you," Flynn said.

I shrugged. "I hate golf. I don't feel slighted."

"Well, I don't like golf either but being asked is always nice," Ash reprimanded.

"I'll get up with Carys tonight," Duncan volunteered.

Ash raised an eyebrow.

"Fine, I'll get up with her every night this week," Duncan relented.

Ash grinned. "You are forgiven."

Flynn and Duncan pulled lounge chairs close to us and settled in. "Let's order lunch," Flynn said.

"Good idea, I'm starving," I answered.

While Flynn saw to our food, I called Evie and had her bring Hawk to the pool. I wanted the twins to stay inside since it was scorching out, and I was worried that they'd get heatstroke.

Hawk looked like a miniature version of Flynn in his navy swim trunks. I slathered him in sunscreen, and he squawked and protested. Scooping him up, I headed to the steps of the pool. I gently lowered Hawk into the water, and he shrieked in excitement, struggling to get out of my arms.

"Patience, you little devil," I said with a wry grin.

"That kid is all you," I heard Ash say to Flynn.

"God, I hope not," Flynn muttered.

By sunset we were all exhausted, including Hawk who was struggling to stay awake. We left the pool and headed back to our suites. Instead of eating in one of the many restaurants, we opted for room service and then crashed.

The next day, Ash and I finally got our tour of the hotel. We took a golf cart out and drove around the grounds, passing the outdoor pools and golf course. That evening, the flame-throwing acrobats were rehearsing, so we were able to catch their show. We ate dinner in one of the high-end restaurants. Flynn left in the middle to take a phone call, which I assumed had something to do with hotel business. When he returned, he was quiet and his smile was forced, but he didn't volunteer any information. The mood at dinner had been disturbed, and tension seeped into the meager conversation.

By tacit agreement, we skipped dessert and said goodnight. We checked in on the boys; Hawk was awake but strangely quiet. He started to make noise when he saw us, and then I had to spend the better part of an hour quieting him down. At least he had his own room so that the twins weren't disturbed.

By the time I got Hawk to bed, it was past midnight, and I hadn't seen Flynn for an hour. I checked the master bedroom wondering if he'd gotten ready for bed without me, but he wasn't there. I found him in his office, sitting in his chair and staring out the large window.

"Flynn?" I asked softly, pushing the door open.

"Hmm?"

"Can I come in?"

"Aye."

I entered and closed the door to lean against it. "What's wrong?"

"Ramsey called while we were at dinner. Lord Birmingham was found dead in his home."

I frowned. "Lord Birmingham?"

"Another member of the House of Lords," he explained.

"Any connection to Lord Arlington?"

"I'm assuming, but I don't know for sure."

"White ink tattoo?" I asked.

"Don't know that yet either."

"But if you had to guess?" I pressed.

"I'd guess there's a connection." He sighed and ran a hand through his disheveled hair. "I have Ramsey on background detail. Lord Birmingham's name never came up when we were dealing with Arlington and The Pretender."

I let out a stream of Gaelic curses. Flynn raised his eyebrows and smirked. "I see you've learned the most important words, aye?"

"Aye," I mocked. "I learned from the best."

I moved away from the door and settled onto his lap. Flynn ran a hand up my lower back and pressed his face into my chest. "It still has nothing to do with us—or the SINS. Officially anyway."

"But things have a way of spilling over onto us, right?" I said, running my fingers through his hair and gently rubbing his scalp.

"Aye, they do. I don't think these will be the only deaths."

"Guess we'll know more if we discover that Birmingham's body has a white ink tattoo. What's worse? Finding out these deaths are related or finding out they're not?"

"I need a scotch," Flynn muttered.

Chapter 7

The night of the opening arrived. Ash and I spent the afternoon in the spa, getting the works and then having our hair styled. I went with long sleek waves, reminiscent of 1950s Hollywood glamour. Ash had her hair done in the classic flapper style, complete with the black headband across her forehead.

"I love that we look completely different," she said with a red smile. She went for bold makeup while I settled for elegant.

"Me too. And there's no jealousy involved. It keeps our friendship competition free," I said in a teasing tone.

"You know, before you, I never really had girlfriends," she said.

Ash and I had met our freshmen year in college at Columbia, and we'd been boon companions immediately. We were so different—she'd been the fashionable socialite with cold parents, and I'd been the tomboy orphan with a resentful older brother.

"Girls are mean," I said. "And I'm just glad you were in the market for a best friend."

"Funny how things work out, huh?" she asked in

amusement.

"Very funny."

Married to Scotsmen, we had become expatriates, choosing to make our homes in another country. Our children were growing up together. She was family, and I thanked my lucky stars that I had a friend like Ash who stood by me, even when she knew the ugliness of my recent past.

We left the spa and parted ways at the elevator. I entered the penthouse suite and found the twins playing together on a blanket in the living room while Hawk sat on Evie's lap. She was reading him a book, but the moment he saw me, he wiggled off her and darted for my legs. Hawk wrapped his arms around my calves before raising his arms. "Dup!" he called, wiggling his fingers in demand to being picked up.

I spent a few minutes with him before gently urging him back to Evie. Iain began to cry and then Noah followed suit. Wondering what had set them off, I crouched down next to them on their blanket. They immediately crawled toward me, and I settled them into my lap. I brushed my lips across Iain's forehead and then Noah's.

The door opened. "What's going on?"

I glanced at Flynn. "Iain's warm. I think he has a fever."

Flynn frowned and came down to sit next to me. He set his hand on Iain's head and then nodded. "Aye. He's warm."

"Just cutting a tooth," Evie said absently. "Nothing to worry about."

"Maybe I shouldn't go to the party," I said.

"He's not sick, hen," Flynn said gently. "Evie and Jennifer will take good care of him."

Watching my son cry had tears forming in my eyes. I knew it was hormonal and biology, but watching him in any kind of pain, pained me. I cradled Iain against me and stood up. Flynn picked up Noah so he wouldn't feel left out, but then Hawk wanted in on the attention and began to fret in Evie's lap.

I took Iain into the room he shared with Noah. I felt completely torn in two. I wanted to go to the opening with Flynn, but how was I supposed to leave Iain when he wasn't feeling well?

Flynn followed me into the nursery, softly closing the door to drown out Hawk's wailing. Noah cuddled up against his father's chest, seemingly unaware of the surrounding noise.

I couldn't think straight at the moment. Though I was hardly the most maternal woman in the world, I still never forgot that I had children. Thoughts of them were always close to the front of my mind, but I'd only just begun to resurface from the baby brain affliction. Multitasking was difficult; it took an effort to remember there was life outside of my children.

Iain's cries turned to whimpers, and it was like daggers slicing my heart. I sent Flynn a pleading look.

"Can you go to the party without me? I can join you later."

"He's just teething, Barrett," he said. "We went through this with Hawk, remember? It was nothing."

I couldn't explain why I felt so split. Teething wasn't a life or death situation. If Iain had an ear infection or Strep, then it would make more sense to stay. I rubbed a hand down his back and looked at him.

"Come on, love," Flynn said. "Come to the party with me. Iain will be all right."

Nodding, I set Iain into his crib. He shoved a fist into his mouth and began to gnaw on it. I rubbed his belly, hoping my touch soothed him.

"Why don't you go get ready," I said to Flynn. "I'll stay with Iain for a bit longer and then I'll change. I'll be fast."

Flynn came to stand next to me at the crib, brushing his hand across Iain's dark hair. Flynn kissed my cheek and left with Noah.

Iain fell asleep almost immediately, and I slipped away.

Heading back to the living room, I told Evie that if his temperature spiked, I wanted to know even if I had to be pulled away from the party. Hawk was having a bath, and it was the perfect time to duck into the bedroom to change. I kissed Noah who was perfectly content alone on the blanket, and then escaped.

Flynn was in the middle of tying his bowtie when I opened the door to the master bedroom. He stood in front of the full-length mirror as his fingers deftly tied an intricate knot. He'd already donned the Campbell plaid.

"You, my love, are like a fine scotch. You just get better with age," I teased, trying to get into the party mood. He turned and grinned, his smile a white curve in the dark beard that had finally filled in.

"You're good at compliments," he remarked. He turned back to the mirror and finished tying his tie and then shrugged into his tuxedo jacket.

"Thank you, I try," I said, scooting past him to enter the closet, passing my reflection in the mirror.

"Oops," I said with a sigh.

"Oops what?" he asked.

My hands went to my hair. All the stylist's work had been for naught. Due to the mayhem of kids, I was lucky to make it out with only messed up hair.

"Before you restore order, I want to give you something," Flynn said. He went to the bedside table and opened the drawer, pulling out a jewelry box.

"Ah, I had a feeling," I said. "The boutique assistant wouldn't let me try on any jewelry."

He winked as he brought the box to me. I flipped it open to find a pair of pearl and diamond drop earrings. They were elegant and demure—the perfect accessory to my dress and the only jewelry aside from my wedding band that I'd wear that evening.

"Oh," I said on a sigh. "These are lovely." He held the box

for me so I could put on the earrings. The pearls complimented my skin tone, the diamonds sparkled, and I couldn't wait to see the full effect when I put on the dress.

Flynn zipped up my gown and then his hands lingered on the expanse of my bare shoulders, his fingers grazing my collarbones. "You're stunning."

I smiled up at him, our gazes colliding in the mirror. Banked desire flared to life in his startling blue eyes. My breath hitched. Flynn reluctantly moved away, taking the heat and promise with him.

He stood by while I fixed my hair. I gathered the messy waves and loosely braided them before pinning it into a low bun. "Well?" I asked, looking at Flynn.

"Call me crazy, but I like what you did far more than what you got done at the salon."

His cell phone buzzed and he answered it. "Aye. Meet you down there. We had a situation." He smiled at me. "No, nothing serious. See you in five." He hung up and placed his cell phone in the pocket inside his tuxedo jacket.

"Duncan and Ash are already in the lobby," he explained.

I grabbed my white clutch that only had lipstick and a cell phone in it. "I told Evie to call me if Iain's temp spiked."

Flynn nodded and held out his hand to me. Evie was feeding Noah a bottle, and I was just about to go over and say one last goodbye, but Flynn tugged me out of the suite before I could get waylaid again.

We met Ash and Duncan in the lobby. I chuckled when I saw Duncan in the Buchanan plaid; I loved the way Flynn and Duncan chose to do things. It was always so uniquely different from everyone else. They both were striking in their kilts.

"What happened to your hair?" Ash asked in lieu of greeting.

I sighed. "Children."

Chapter 8

The antique crystal chandelier that had once been part of the French court glowed brightly from the center of the high ceiling. Exclusive guests, including politicians and celebrities, mingled about the gold damask ballroom. Eventually, we'd move the party to the casino, and then there would be a show with flame-throwing acrobats.

Flynn and I worked the room, welcoming people, talking and laughing and exchanging light conversation. I heard the snap of a camera and turned, expecting to find a member of the paparazzi. A genuine grin of happiness spread across my face when I realized it wasn't the paparazzi but a good friend.

"I am so glad you're here," I said.

Lacey smiled. "Yes, well, I've been there for every Rex Hotel opening. I wasn't going to miss this one just because I was in Cambodia."

"Cambodia? Last we talked you were in Vietnam," I said. 'Talk' was a loose term. I got random emails from Lacey as she was currently globetrotting, taking photos and enjoying her life.

"I can't be bothered with technology," she quipped. She looked at Flynn. "Hiya, Mr. Campbell."

Flynn laughed and embraced her. "You look good."

She did. Her skin had a healthy golden tan, and she'd put on about ten pounds. Lacey had always been willowy and thin, but a lot of that had been because of her rigorous work schedule when she managed The Rex burlesque club in New York. Now that she was a little more relaxed, she looked happier. That might've had something to do with the handsome young blond guy standing next to her, his arm at her waist.

"Babe," he said.

"Sorry," Lacey said with an absent smile. "Barrett, Flynn, this is Chase."

"Chase," Flynn repeated, holding out his hand. The two men shook hands.

"Nice to meet you," I said.

"Can I get you something stronger than champagne?" Flynn asked, leading Chase toward the bar.

"How did you know?" Chase asked with a wry grin.

As soon as they moved away, I said to Lacey, "Okay. What happened to Jeremy?"

"He got boring. I dumped him when I was in Japan."

"And you met Chase…" I pressed.

She scrunched up her nose. "About three hours after I dumped Jeremy."

I chuckled. "So you're having fun, huh?"

"So much fun. Chase is twenty-seven and a professional surfer."

"Shut up."

"It's true. Body like Poseidon," she said dreamily. "We're flying to Australia next week—he has a competition, and he asked me to go with him."

"Hard life," I remarked.

"Isn't it? So, how are the wee ones?"

I caught her up on the insanity but tried to keep it quick. They were my kids—Lacey was under no obligation to have the same feelings toward them as I did. Chase and Flynn returned, and then I saw Ash and Duncan through the crowd. They joined our group, which made everything more animated and lively. Chase was in the hot seat, but he handled questions with ease, intelligence, and humility. He wasn't at all what I expected a surfer to be. Appearances were deceiving, and I wondered when I'd remember that.

Things got a little awkward when Brad Shapiro arrived. Lacey and Brad had worked together for years and only recently they'd decided to try it as a couple. It hadn't worked out, but gathering the way Brad kept his eyes glued to Lacey, I imagined he was willing to try again. Unfortunately for him, Lacey was completely enthralled with her young surfer.

I gently excused myself, wanting to check my cell phone and see if there was a message from Evie. Heading to the corner of the room near one of the cocktail bars, I pulled out my phone. I was relieved to see there weren't any messages. Still, that didn't stop me from sending out a message of my own.

"Facebook or Twitter?" a voice asked.

I looked up into the handsome face of a man with honeyed colored skin and dark brown eyes. Rakish brown curls rested on his forehead, his smile wide and easy. Though he was a little over average height, I noticed that his body filled out a tux nicely.

"Neither," I said with an answering smile.

"Really?" he drawled, his hands still in his trouser pockets. "I find that hard to believe. Look at this place. People are going to be bragging on social media all night long."

"That's the hope." My phone buzzed with a response from Evie. Iain was fine, she assured me. The kids were asleep, and I should enjoy the party.

"Boyfriend?" my companion asked, pulling my attention away from my phone.

"Excuse me?"

"Are you texting your boyfriend about the great party he wasn't invited to?"

My lips trembled with wanting to smile. "No. No boyfriend."

"Shame."

"What is?" I asked.

"You don't have a boyfriend. I think that's a shame."

I couldn't help it—his overly flirtatious manner wasn't at all threatening or sleazy. I laughed. "I think my husband might be glad I don't have a boyfriend."

The man blinked. "Husband?"

I held out my hand. "Barrett Campbell. Nice to meet you."

"Campbell," the man muttered, taking my hand and giving it a hardy squeeze. "Your husband is Flynn Campbell. Owner of the Rex Hotel empire."

My hand dropped from his. "That would be correct. And you are?"

"Sorry," he said, deliberately not introducing himself.

I waved away his apology. "Don't be. It made my evening."

"You're just saying that," he said.

"Do I have the face of a liar?" I teased.

He cocked to his head to one side, pretending to study me. "Not a liar. Siren, for sure. A woman with the intent to lure men to their demise."

Though his words were teasing, something in his tone had the hairs on the back of my neck standing up.

"Well, Mr.—"

"Filippi. Alessandro Filippi," he introduced.

"Mr. Filippi. It was lovely meeting you, but I have to get back."

"To your husband. Ah, what a shame. You have a husband."

I walked past him, heading in the direction of Flynn and

the others. For some reason, I turned around. Alessandro Filippi's gaze was still on me, intense, and all traces of his humor were gone.

∼

"Everything okay?" Ash asked when I found our group again. Flynn was off somewhere, no doubt conversing with guests.

"Hmm?"

"Everything okay," she repeated. "With Iain?"

"Oh. Yeah. He's fine. The kids are asleep."

"Then what has you looking so worried?" she wondered.

I grasped her elbow to turn her away from Lacey and the group. "I had one of those moments."

She lifted her perfectly groomed eyebrows. "Moments?"

"You know, where something just happened and you don't really know what it was, but you know it's significant?"

"Ah," she said in understanding. "Moments. Yeah, gotcha."

I was in desperate need of a drink. Now that I was sure Iain was fine, I could imbibe just a bit. I decided to head to the other side of the room, far away from Alessandro Filippi. I wandered to another bar nestled in the opposite corner. There were a few people in line waiting for something stronger than champagne. I finally made it up to the bartender and asked for a glass of scotch.

"How can you drink that stuff?"

I turned, grinning. "Better than the swill you drink."

Sasha laughed and lifted his glass of clear liquid, which I knew was high-end vodka.

"That's how you say hello to me?" I demanded. "By insulting my drink of choice?"

Sasha opened his arms and embraced me. It was quick but strong.

"I'm so glad you're here," I said when I pulled back.

"Me too." Sasha surveyed the room with bright blue eyes. "I haven't seen Campbell yet to congratulate him."

"He's around here somewhere," I assured. "How's the suite?"

"Campbell outdid himself," he said.

"Your flight in was okay?"

"It was. I flew out of Boston."

I frowned. "Boston?"

He took a sip of his vodka. "Had some business to take care of before I came out."

I raised an eyebrow. "Business?"

Sasha smiled, all charm and rogue.

"Ha. I knew it. Did you bring her?"

"Her? Her who?" he feigned innocently.

"Oh, come on," I said, teasingly shoving his arm.

"Yes, I brought Quinn."

"I'm excited to finally meet her," I said. "You've hidden her from me long enough."

"I haven't been hiding her. You live in Scotland. It's not like you could come to Boston or New York for a quick cup of coffee."

"Valid point. So where is she?" I asked.

"Restroom. What's been going on with you? How are the boys?"

"The boys are good." I briefly told him about coming home from Italy to find that Hawk had maple syruped a wall and that both nannies had quit.

Sasha had a good laugh.

"It wasn't funny," I said, even though I was chuckling. "Hawk ruined the tranquility that I'd somehow gotten when on vacation. It lasted five minutes."

"And how did Campbell handle it?" he wondered.

"With his usual Flynn-ness. He took the crazy all in stride."

"You look really good, Barrett."

I smiled. "Thanks. So do you. I'm glad you're here. It wouldn't be the same without you."

"Really?" he asked with a winsome smile.

"Of course."

He paused. "We're good, right?"

My smile was wide. "We're perfect."

Chapter 9

Sasha's eyes slid from my face to focus on a spot behind me. I watched his gaze heat and his smile widen. I turned to find a raven haired, willowy woman walking toward us. As she drew closer, I registered the haughty set of her features—high cheekbones, and green eyes the color of Irish hills.

She effortlessly glided into Sasha's side, and his arm went around her slim waist. They made a striking picture, especially when Sasha leaned in and whispered something in her ear. She smiled, and it changed her face. I wondered if other women found her intimidating. Ash and I didn't have a lot of girlfriends for the same reason.

"Barrett Campbell, I'd like you to meet Quinn O'Malley," Sasha introduced.

I switched my glass of scotch to my left hand and held out my right. "It's nice to meet you," I greeted.

She grasped my palm. "It's nice to meet you, too."

Our clasp released, and we spent a moment studying one another the way women do. Sasha and I had a unique relationship. There was history and love and a lot of complication. Quinn was the first woman after me to mean something to him, and I wanted to make sure she was good enough.

Sasha dropped his arm from around her waist and reached into his trouser pocket to pull out his vibrating phone. He frowned. "Sorry, I have to take this." He gave Quinn his glass of vodka and then stalked away, phone to his ear.

"So, you're from Boston," I said, focusing on Quinn. "I've never been to Boston."

"It's old," she stated.

I blinked. "Yes. Old. I've heard it's lovely, though."

Quinn's unwavering green gaze held mine. "So you're the woman. The way he talks about you, it's painfully obvious."

I frowned. "Obvious?"

"That he's in love with you."

"I thought extreme bluntness was a Midwestern quality," I mused.

Quinn didn't crack a smile. "I thought it was important to cut to the chase."

"I don't know what he's told you—"

"Nothing," she interrupted. "He's told me nothing of your history, only that he's the godfather to one of your children."

What was I supposed to tell her? Hawk had been kidnapped, and Sasha had helped find him. There were so many other things the man had done for me. Not to mention we were linked because of Igor Dolinsky, and that was a can of worms I never wanted to open again.

"Sasha and I are close," I said slowly. "I'm sorry if that upsets you."

"You're married. Why do you need Sasha?"

This woman held no prisoners.

"Whatever he's told you—or hasn't told you—you need to know only one thing. I love Sasha. He's family to me, and I want him happy. That's it."

She rolled her eyes, all of a sudden looking much younger than I first thought. I could understand her jealousy. My relationship with Sasha was nothing you could put into a box and label. It didn't make sense half the time, but that was just the way we were.

"Why did you come here with him?" I pressed, holding her gaze and refusing to back down.

"I wanted to meet you," she said simply. "I wanted to see the woman I'm in competition with."

"For the love of—I'm married. I have three children. I'm ridiculously in love with my husband. If you want, I'd be glad to introduce you to Flynn."

She paused, all of a sudden looking a little hesitant, as if she was finally aware of her insane, blunt behavior.

"Just a piece of advice?" I went on. "Don't alienate those who would do anything for Sasha. If you've got an issue with him, take it up with *him*. This really has nothing to do with me. And I think you know that."

Before Quinn could reply, I stalked away, leaving her with her own concerns.

It was difficult to compose myself, but I managed to slap a smile on my face. I passed guests, some I recognized because they were famous; the others whom I didn't recognize, I knew were more influential and had billion-dollar companies.

Finding Flynn, I sidled up to him. He was talking business with a group of powerful men and women and I pulled him away.

"I saw you with Sasha briefly. Where did he go?" Flynn asked, placing his hand on the back of my neck. His touch was warm and soothing.

"He had to take a phone call."

He frowned. "What's wrong?"

"I finally met the girl."

"Ah."

"Ah? What does that mean?"

"You hate her," he said with a knowing grin.

"I don't."

"You do," he insisted.

"No one's good enough for him," I muttered. "He deserves the best."

"He can't have the best, hen. So he'll have to settle."

I sighed. "I think she might really love him."

"Then why do you sound so depressed?"

"Because she was kind of a bitch," I said.

"Barrett—"

"Seriously, Flynn. She was cold and haughty and when Sasha left us alone, she had all the tact of a storm trooper."

Flynn sighed and shook his head. "You've got incredible timing, you know that?"

I frowned in confusion. "What do you—"

He gestured behind me. I turned, coming face to face with Sasha. "How much did you hear?" I demanded.

"Enough," he said, glowering. He looked past me to my husband, holding out his hand. "Good to see you, Campbell."

"Good to see you, Petrovich," Flynn greeted, shaking his hand. "I'm going to let you guys sort this out." With a sympathetic glance at me, Flynn left.

I winced when I looked at Sasha. I opened my mouth to say something, but a group of people came up to greet me. If Sasha and I were going to be able to talk uninterrupted, then we were going to have to leave the party.

"Let's get out of here," I said to him.

He nodded. "I'm going to talk to Quinn, and then I'll meet you in the lobby."

On my way out, I was waylaid by Ash. I told her where I was going and that I'd tell her everything later. Sasha was already waiting for me when I made it out to the lobby. We walked through the hotel and ducked into one of my favorite bars in the place. It was modeled after an aristocratic old library. The couches were leather and comfortable, the bar and bookshelves were dark wood, and the lighting was low.

I greeted the bartender by name—the employees knew me by sight, and I'd met a good deal of them and made it a mission to remember their names. After ordering two glasses of vodka, Sasha and I sat down in leather chairs that were angled toward each other.

"What does she know about me?" I asked him.

"About us?"

"Only that we have history."

"So she doesn't know why you're Hawk's godfather?"

"You mean did I tell her that your son was kidnapped? No."

"Does she know how we met?" I asked pointedly. We rarely spoke of Dolinsky. It was a dark time for both of us.

"No." His eyes met mine. "What did you say to her?"

"I told her you were my family and that she should get over whatever it was that was eating her."

"Barrett—"

"She was mean to me first!" I accused.

He tried not to smile and failed. "She's intimidated by you. And if you knew Quinn, you'd know that never happens."

"Why did you keep her away?" I asked. "By not introducing us sooner, she thinks she has a reason to be jealous of me."

He sighed. "I wasn't ready to share her yet."

"Does she make you happy?" I asked.

"I think she could make me happy."

We fell silent and I took a moment to enjoy my drink. Finally, he spoke again. "I didn't tell her much about our history because your story isn't mine to share."

"Listen, I know we have a complicated back-story. And, yeah, I'm not a fan of a near stranger knowing some of my most terrible moments, but if she matters to you, then you need to tell her. Use your judgment, but don't keep it from her just because you're worried about my part in all of this."

Sasha let out a sigh and then swallowed the rest of his drink. "I guess I can do that."

"You trust her?" I asked.

He nodded. "She knows about my affiliations—and her father is a predominant businessman in Boston."

I knew what 'businessman' really meant. "Quinn O'Malley. Irish."

"Yes."

"How does her father feel about his daughter's involvement with a Russian?"

Sasha smirked. "He's already said he wants to pay for the wedding."

"Wedding?"

"Don't worry. I'm not there yet."

"Right. Okay," I teased.

"Do you really hate Quinn?" he asked suddenly.

"If I did, would it change how you felt about her?" I asked instead of answering.

"No. It wouldn't."

"I don't know Quinn," I said truthfully. "I was hoping to get to know her, but she said…"

"What? What did she say to you?"

"She said she could tell that you were in love with me by the way you talked about me. You're not, though, right? Not anymore."

"I'm not in love with you anymore, Barrett," Sasha said with a soft smile.

I grinned. "Do you promise?"

"I promise."

"Then maybe you should tell Quinn?"

"Yeah, I should probably talk to her."

"If I were you, I'd pull her out of the party and talk to her now. And then tomorrow night, you both will have dinner with Flynn and me. Quinn can meet the boys and maybe she and I can start over."

Sasha reached out, and I gave him my hand. He squeezed it. "Thank you."

"Any time."

My clutch buzzed.

"Sorry, let me look at this," I said, digging around for my cell. I looked at my phone to see a message from Flynn telling me the party had been moved to the casino.

"Come on," I said, pulling Sasha along. "Let's find Quinn and then gamble away a lot of money."

Chapter 10

I found Flynn at a high-stakes poker table with four other men, one of whom was Duncan. The lowest table limit was five thousand dollars, so in reality, every table was a high-stakes game.

"Call," the man next to Flynn said.

The men put their cards on the table, one by one. With a grin, Flynn set his cards down and with a straight flush, won the jackpot in the middle.

Duncan groaned. "I knew I shouldn't have sat at the same table as you."

"Blame Barrett," Flynn said, looking up at me with a teasing grin. "She's always been good luck." He scooped up his winnings and rose from the table.

"Don't forget," he said. "Tonight's winnings are being donated to charity. So have fun and even if you lose, know that your money is going to a good cause."

"Where's Ash?" I asked Duncan as Flynn went to a cashier to cash out his chips.

"Last I checked, she was at the slots," Duncan said, turning his attention back to the table.

"Okay, thanks," I said, knowing he was getting sucked

back into the game. "Good luck, gents." I walked toward Flynn, who turned to me with a smile.

"You cheated, didn't you?" I whispered.

He pretended to look offended, but there was a definite twinkle in his eyes. "No, I didn't cheat."

"Uh huh."

"You settle everything with Sasha?"

"Think so," I said. The moment we'd gotten to the casino, Sasha had left my side to try to find Quinn. I hoped they were speaking to one another and clearing everything up.

"We're having dinner with Quinn and Sasha tomorrow," I told him.

"Yes, dear," he chimed, taking my elbow and escorting me around the dim casino. The sounds of laughter and slot machines cashing out hit my ears. A slight headache had formed at my temples. I wasn't used to crowds anymore.

We found Ash at one of the slot machines, and she was thoroughly enjoying herself. She threw me a wide grin.

I looked at Flynn who was about to say something just as his phone vibrated. He growled. "This is my fifth phone call tonight." He put the phone to his ear, shot me an apologetic look, and turned away.

"Be my date?" I asked Ash with a wry smile.

"Sure. My husband ditched me to play poker," she said.

"I saw."

"So are you just going to stand there, or are you going to sit next to me and gamble?"

I plopped down at the slot machine next to Ash, and then my clutch vibrated. "Ah, crap," I said when I looked at my phone.

"What?" she asked.

"It's Evie."

"Is Iain worse?"

"No. But apparently Noah and Hawk now have fevers too."

"That's not teething," she said.

"Nope." With a sigh, I hopped up from my seat. "I guess this is the part where I say goodnight."

"Good luck," she said with an understanding smile.

I walked out of the casino and headed down the expansive corridor lined with boutiques and restaurants. I texted Flynn to let him know what was going on and that I was headed up to the penthouse.

Finally making it to the rows of elevators, I pressed the up button. While I waited, my gaze wandered across the relatively quiet lobby since most of the guests were currently in the casino. I frowned when I saw a scene taking place by the exit.

A gorgeous woman with light blond hair pressed herself against a man. He was angled so that his lower body was shielded by a large Ficus, but I could tell he was tall and broad. Suddenly, the man moved, the light catching the threads of his kilt. And that's when I realized the man was my husband.

The elevator doors dinged open, but I didn't step inside. The doors closed. Instead, I kept my eyes riveted to the scene playing out across the lobby.

Flynn roughly shoved the woman away from him. She clawed at his face, but he deftly managed to grab her wrists and hold them in one of his hands. Two men, one of whom was Brad Shapiro, swooped in to relieve Flynn of the angry woman.

I was too far away to hear what she yelled at him as Brad and the other security man escorted her out of The Rex. Flynn's head drooped for a moment, and then he swiveled his gaze. Our eyes collided, and his jaw clenched.

I pressed the elevator button again, wanting to escape. I knew what I'd seen.

Flynn had spent a lot of time away from Dornoch the last few months, focused on The Rex and its construction. And when he had been home, we hadn't prioritized time to connect with one another. Could I blame him if he'd cheated?

"Barrett!" he yelled, the sound of his footsteps coming closer as he ran across the marble floor.

I refused to look at him, willing the elevator to come.

"Hen," he began.

"Don't," I clipped.

"It's not what you think."

"You don't know what I think," I said, still refusing to look at him. The elevator opened and a crowd of people spilled out, drunk and excited for the night to continue. I dashed inside the elevator car, Flynn hot on my heels.

Before I could even press the PH button and find my key, Flynn pushed the button that locked the elevator, ensuring I couldn't escape. Flynn stalked toward me, pressing me against the wall of the elevator, pinning me with his body.

"Look at me."

"No."

He growled. "Barrett, if you give me thirty seconds I can explain." When I refused to meet his gaze, he said softly, "I never took you for a coward."

My gaze snapped up to meet his. "How dare you?"

"No," he boomed. "How dare *you*! Do you really think that after all we've been through I would be unfaithful to you?"

"I wouldn't begrudge you, Flynn."

His face darkened with anger. "You wouldn't *begrudge* me? What the fuck, Barrett?" His hands shot up to land on either side of my face, bringing him even closer.

"I'm saying I'd understand if you strayed," I said. "I've been occupied. You've been out of town. Things happen."

"You've been occupied?" he repeated. "By occupied, you mean raising our children? You think just because our marriage has been a little neglected that gives me grounds for cheating?"

I swallowed and lowered my eyes in shame.

"You think because of what happened between you and Dolinsky, I deserve a free pass?" he said, voice lowering.

"Well, yeah."

We were quiet a moment and then I asked, "So who is she?"

Flynn took one of his hands off the elevator wall to lift my chin so that I was forced to meet his gaze. "Burlesque dancer. I wasn't in charge of hiring her—I left that to the club manager. Anyway, she was always late to rehearsal and completely unreliable. So I fired her."

I frowned. "That's not all of it. She did not look like a disgruntled employee."

"She came on to me a few times."

"Oh," I said in understanding.

"She came back to make a scene, cause trouble. Security caught her before she could get to the casino. I was dealing with her."

Flynn's fingers skimmed over my cheeks, down my neck to dust across my exposed shoulders. "Do you believe me, hen?"

"Yes," I said on a sigh. Flynn's hands were wandering, eliciting chills on my skin.

"Do you believe I only want you? That I'll always want you?" His lips grazed the curve of my cheek and then drifted down to linger at the corner of my mouth.

"Yes," I breathed when his hands hiked up my dress to my hips. "What are you doing?"

"I think you need proof," he said, sinking down to his knees.

"Proof?" I squeaked when his hot breath teased the inside of my thighs. "We can't do this here."

"Why not?" His fingers began to migrate.

"Because there's a camera."

"When have you ever been shy?"

"But—" I gasped when I felt Flynn's hot mouth through my white lace underwear. He dragged his tongue across damp material, teasing me, prodding me. He bunched my dress in his hands as he kept his face between my thighs.

I lifted one of my legs and placed it on his shoulder, spreading myself so he could devour me. Nudging the fabric aside, his tongue touched my bare skin, sending sparks of excitement through my belly. My hands gripped his hair as I roughly held him against me. His relentless tongue held me prisoner, the whiskers of his beard a beautiful torture. When he added a finger to his ministrations, I fell apart, coming hard against his mouth. I trembled in the aftermath as Flynn slowly removed my leg from his shoulder. My dress fell down, the sound of swishing fabric in my ears.

Flynn stood and blatantly adjusted his bulging erection, his own breathing labored. He pulled me into his arms. "Are we okay?"

"Yes. More than okay."

"Then we should probably get back to the casino. People will notice if we're gone."

I finally remembered the reason I'd left the party to begin with. "Evie texted. The kids are sick. They all have fevers."

He frowned. "Should I—"

"No. You have to go back to the party. I'll text you and let you know."

"You sure?" he asked, his hand cradling my cheek.

"I'm sure."

Chapter 11

Pandemonium reigned. The nannies were frazzled, my children were in tears, and the penthouse was a mess. There was no way to comfort all the kids at the same time, and I briefly thought about calling Flynn to help. But he'd been waiting for this day, and I wouldn't be the reason he didn't get to celebrate the opening of his new hotel.

"A pediatrician is on the way," Jen said, holding Noah close to her body and rubbing his back in a soothing gesture. "He should be here soon."

Evie's attention had been pulled between Hawk and Iain, but she gave me a smile of relief when I took Hawk off her hands.

Hawk's forehead blazed with fever. He stuck his thumb in his mouth, whimpering against my chest. "When did all this start?" I asked, trying to remain calm.

"Iain's temp spiked about an hour ago and the other two began to feel warm around that time," Evie explained. "Jen called down to the front desk and had the concierge track down a pediatrician."

I brushed my hand across Hawk's forehead. "It's just got to be a bug, right? I mean, that makes the most sense."

"I'm sure it's nothing to be concerned about," Jen said.

There was a knock on the suite door, and I went to answer it. A middle-aged-man with gray hair at the temples stood at the threshold, carrying a black leather bag.

"Mrs. Campbell?" he asked.

"Yes. Hi. You're the doctor?"

He nodded and stepped inside. "I'm Dr. Patrick." His eyes dropped to Hawk, and with a gentle smile he asked, "Is this the sick one?"

"They're all sick," I blurted out.

He blinked brown eyes but didn't appear alarmed. "Tell me what happened."

"Iain got sick first," I began. By the time I was done explaining the situation, Dr. Patrick was finished examining Iain and had moved on to Noah.

"Do you think it's just a bug?" I asked.

Dr. Patrick pulled up Noah's onesie, and then he gestured to Hawk. "Can you lift his shirt and show me his belly?"

I frowned but nodded. Adjusting Hawk, I raised his T-shirt despite his squirming protest.

"They don't have a bug," Dr. Patrick said after a quick examination.

"They don't? What do they have?"

"I'm sorry, Mrs. Campbell," the pediatrician said with a sympathetic smile. "Your children have the chickenpox."

"All of them?" I blurted out. "But they don't have rashes."

"They do have rashes—along the scalp. It will spread to the rest of their bodies in a few days. Don't worry. They should be fine in about a week. Maybe ten days."

"Chickenpox." My head spun. Three children under the age of two with chickenpox. The universe was totally laughing at me.

"Thank you so much for coming," I said, showing him to the door.

"Not a problem," he assured me.

"Have the bill sent here, okay?" I closed the door after him and spent the next hour helping Jen and Evie get the kids to bed. By the time they were asleep, the nannies and I were exhausted. I sent them off to their own beds, thanking them profusely.

In the throes of all that had been going on, I'd forgotten to text Flynn. I knew he wouldn't be up to bed until after dawn. The party had been going strong when I'd left; no doubt everyone was having a great time.

Everyone except me.

I was still in my formal dress but my hair had come down. A nightcap was in order. I poured myself a glass of scotch and was about to text Flynn when the door to the penthouse opened. My husband strolled in, immediately shrugging out of his tuxedo jacket.

"Hi," I said in confusion. "What are you doing here? Aren't you supposed to be watching limber, flame-throwing acrobats?"

He shook his head and removed the bowtie from around his neck. "One of the acrobats fell and broke her ankle. That put a damper on the show."

"Oh my God! Is she okay?"

"She went to the hospital, but she should make a full recovery." He flung both discarded items onto a chair.

"Rough night," I muttered.

"Aye. How are the boys? They okay?"

I laughed into my glass of scotch before I downed the rest of it. "Yeah. Fine. Except for the chickenpox."

Flynn groaned. "No. Seriously?"

"Seriously."

"Pour me some of that scotch, would you? I need it after tonight."

"Get your own bottle," I teased. "This one's all mine."

The next morning, I woke up to a fevered husband. "Well, love," I said, taking the thermometer out of Flynn's mouth. "You have a fever of one hundred and one. There's no way you're getting out of bed."

"I feel fine," he lied obviously.

"Yeah, I might believe that if you weren't shivering," I said, tucking the covers up under his neck. "Face it. You've got the chickenpox."

"But I don't have a rash."

"Not yet. But you will."

"I've already had the chickenpox," he protested.

"Well, apparently you're getting them again."

"I have meetings—"

"I'll cancel them."

He glared at me. I unplugged the hotel phone and grabbed Flynn's cell phone. "What are you doing?" he demanded.

"You need to rest," I said. "And I know you won't get any rest if your cell phone is near you. If anything monumental happens, I'll let you know."

I leaned over and kissed his forehead. "Love you."

He mumbled something in Gaelic under his breath. I didn't for a second believe it was anything flattering. I closed the bedroom door and took a deep breath before going to see to my sick children.

By midafternoon, I was ready for a drink. Between taking care of the kids and tending to Flynn, who was acting like a big baby, I was exhausted. Duncan popped his head in while everyone was napping.

"How are you holding up?" he asked, taking a seat on the couch.

"Flynn is whiny when he's sick," I said. "But please don't tell him that."

Duncan chuckled. "I'm not surprised. Ash said the same thing about me when I was laid up in bed."

"You had good reason," I said. Duncan had taken a bullet to the chest and almost died. "Do you mind going to some of Flynn's meetings? Answering his phone calls?"

"No, I don't mind."

I tossed him Flynn's cell phone. "Thanks. I appreciate it. I don't think there's anything urgent at the moment."

He nodded absently, looking at the phone in his hands as he leaned forward.

"Okay, what's up?" I asked.

"What do you mean?"

"You're acting weird."

"Are the nannies here?"

I nodded. "They're napping. Which is what I should be doing," I added.

"Can we go out onto the balcony?"

"Sure."

Once we were settled on the balcony, the beautiful warm air caressing my skin, I turned to him. The sliding glass doors were closed, so we had complete privacy.

"Has Ash been acting differently?" he asked bluntly.

I frowned. "Differently? Differently how?"

"I don't know. Something just seems off lately. I wanted to know if you noticed, or if she talked to you about anything."

"You didn't ask her?"

"Of course I asked her. She said there was nothing wrong."

I held up my hands. "I don't really know what to tell you then."

He sighed. "I guess I'll talk to her again."

"Word of advice? Don't ask the best friend if she knows anything."

"So you wouldn't tell me anything even if you knew?"

"Would you tell me something that Flynn told you in confidence?"

"Point taken. I don't know though, Barrett. Something's off with Ash."

"Ash works things out in her own time," I reminded him. "She's probably processing and when she's done, she'll come to you. I wouldn't worry about it though."

"You're right." He looked relieved but still pensive. "I'll give her some time."

The sliding glass doors opened, and Jen popped her head out. "Sorry to interrupt, but Mr. Campbell is asking for you."

"Okay, tell him I'll be right there," I replied.

"Oh," Jen said, cheeks flaming pink. "I meant he wanted to see Mr. Buchanan."

I faced Duncan. "Better you than me."

Chapter 12

"This is all your fault," Ash said to me without any real heat.

I raised my eyebrows. "My fault? Carys would've gotten the chickenpox at some point in her childhood."

"Yes," she agreed. "Probably true. But don't take this the wrong way—your children—"

"Spawn of the devil?"

"Pretty much."

Poor Carys had come down with the chickenpox a few days after the boys. We currently had four children covered in Calamine lotion, mittens on their hands so they couldn't scratch, and a routine of oatmeal baths. I had a photo of Flynn in the tub, surrounded by our three boys, all of them covered in oatmeal. I'd tried not to laugh while I was taking the photo, but it was just too good. I was thinking of having it blown up and framed.

The kids had gone down for the night about an hour ago and Flynn was in bed, dozing to a movie. Ash and I finally had a moment to ourselves.

I stared at her.

"What?" she asked.

"Anything you want to tell me?"

"No. I don't think so."

"You sure?"

She frowned. "Uh, yeah. Why are you asking me this?"

I paused just a moment before saying, "Duncan asked me if there was anything going on with you."

"And what did you say?" she wondered.

"I said that you hadn't confided anything in me, but if you had, I wouldn't betray your confidence."

"Really?"

"Really. Best-friend clause. I love Duncan, but we've got history, Ash."

"We do," she agreed. "Doesn't always mean what it should mean."

We were quiet for a spell and then I asked, "Are you okay?"

"I don't know," she said softly.

"It's okay, you know. Not to be okay right now."

She nodded. "Most of the time, I'm really glad we're so close. Other times—"

"You hate that there's someone who knows you so well that they can see through all your crap?"

"Exactly," she said with a laugh.

I took a sip of wine and changed the subject. "So, Lacey's new boyfriend…"

"Chase Youngston. Damn. Girl has good taste."

"Yeah, he's hot," I agreed.

"You missed a lot of good stuff while you were talking to Sasha."

"Oh, yeah?" I wondered. "Like what?"

"Well, Brad pretended that Chase wasn't there and then couldn't take his eyes off of Lacey."

"This is better than a soap opera," I said. "So how did Lacey act?"

"She blatantly ignored Brad. I don't think they're done with each other."

"It's painfully obvious they're not," I agreed.

"But why are they fighting it?"

"Because it didn't work the first time around," I said easily.

"So? Circumstances are different this time. They no longer work together."

"But she's enjoying her life—traveling and taking photos."

"And hooking up with young hot surfers along the way," Ash added. "Yeah, I can't see her giving that up any time soon."

"As long as she's happy, I'm happy," I said. "It will be interesting to see how that all plays out."

"Hmm," she said in agreement. "How did your talk with Sasha go?"

"It was fine," I said. "We cleared the air."

"And her? Did you make peace with her?"

"Ah, no. I wasn't able to."

"Why not?"

"Because Quinn left the night of the opening and Sasha chased after her. We never got to have dinner and start over."

"Wow. What did you say to her?" she demanded.

"Nothing she didn't deserve. I told her Sasha was family, and all I cared about was his happiness. I might've also said that alienating those that loved him wasn't the best way to go about this."

"Jeez. That's blunt, even for you."

"She started it."

"You sound like a five-year-old."

"Look, I can't be responsible for everyone else's feelings," I said.

"Can you blame her?" Ash wondered.

"It's not my fault that Sasha and I—"

"How do you think it makes Flynn feel?" she interjected, her own temper fraying. "Don't you remember how difficult it was for him? Let's assume this girl is falling for Sasha. She knows next to nothing about you except that you guys have a complicated history."

"She's got nothing to worry about," I said.

Ash nodded. "You know that, Sasha knows that, Flynn knows that, but Quinn doesn't."

I leaned back and closed my eyes briefly. "I told him he could tell her as much as he wants about our shared history."

"That will either push her away or pull her closer."

"It's all in the telling," I said. "It's for Sasha to explain to her."

Ash sighed. "You just seem to forget—"

"I don't," I said. "But Sasha has finally moved past his feelings for me. Our relationship is now completely platonic—and deeper, if that's even possible."

Ash held up her hands in supplication. "I've said my peace. I'm done."

"Okay," I said with a nod.

"I'm trying hard not to fall asleep on your couch, so I'm going to head to bed." She stood up.

"Ash? Thanks for being straight with me."

She grinned. There were lines of fatigue at her eyes and mouth. "Always."

I cleaned up, at least putting the dirty glasses in the sink. Exhaustion tugged at my eyelids, and I headed for my own bed. The TV was still on, softly playing the movie, but Flynn was asleep. I reached for the remote and shut it off.

I took a moment to study him. True love was not being physically repulsed by your husband when he was covered in blisters. I put a hand to his forehead, relieved that his fever was down.

"Barrett?" he whispered, turning his head to me.

"Go back to sleep," I said quietly, removing my hand from his face.

"Love you," he murmured before his breath evened out.

I smiled into the dark. "Love you, too."

My eyes widened when Duncan told me the news. "You can't tell Flynn," I stated.

"I have to," Duncan said. "He'd want to know."

"The moment you tell him, he'll want to head to New York—and he's not well enough yet." I glanced at the closed bedroom door, sure that Flynn could hear us even though our tones were low.

"That's not the only thing. Ramsey called," Duncan went on.

I threaded my fingers through my hair. "I'm not going to like this, am I?"

He shook his head.

"Birmingham?"

"Aye."

"White bird tattoo?"

"Aye."

"I'll tell Flynn. About everything," I said.

"You sure?"

I nodded. "It's better if it comes from me."

"You mean you have ways of making him stay?" he asked with a slight smile.

"Exactly."

He cleared his throat. "Thank you."

"For what? Being the one that's going to tell him?"

"No. Whatever you said to Ash last night."

I raised my eyebrows. "Oh?"

"Don't play dumb. I know you guys talked."

"Does that mean *you* guys talked?"

"Not exactly. But she was acting like her old self. So whatever you said, thanks."

"You're welcome." I looked to the bedroom door again. "Might as well get this over with."

"Good luck," he said.

I waved to him as he headed out of the suite. Taking a deep breath, I went to the bedroom and quietly opened the door. Flynn was propped up in bed, reading a book. He smiled at me.

"Hi," I greeted, closing the door. "How are you feeling?"

"Better," he said.

"You lying?"

He shook his head. "Still tired, throat is still sore, and I itch like hell. But I don't think I have a fever anymore."

I went to him and pressed my lips to his forehead. "I think you're right."

"How are the boys?"

I wrinkled my nose. "Scabby. Finally."

He chuckled and then cocked his head to the side. "What's going on?"

"It seems Lord Birmingham has a white ink tattoo on his body. Exactly like the one found on Arlington."

"Did Ramsey call you?"

"No. He called Duncan."

"You need to give me my cell phone back," he said. "I can't be out of the loop like this."

I grimaced. "There's more."

"Go on."

"Brad called Duncan earlier this morning. There's been a fire at The Rex Burlesque in New York."

"What?" Flynn yelled.

"Calm down."

Flynn threw off the comforter and swung his legs over the side of the bed. "I need to call Brad. Now."

"Get back into bed," I commanded.

"Barrett, I'm fine," he stated, even as he wobbled.

I went to him and gently put a hand to his chest, pushing him back. He fell over immediately, his face ashen. He was weaker than he'd thought.

"No one was hurt," I said. "Now get back under the

covers. I'll give you back your cell phone, but you're not flying out there. Not yet."

"How did you know that's what I'd want to do?" he grumbled.

"Because I know you."

Chapter 13

After tucking Flynn back into bed, knowing he wouldn't stay there, I went for a run around The Rex property. I breathed in the fresh morning air as I passed the golf course, including the manmade lake. I couldn't remember the last time I'd been outdoors. The past week or so had been spent cooped up in the penthouse suite, surrounded by sick children and a sick husband. Thankfully, everyone was on the mend and dispositions were improving. So was my morale.

When I got back to the penthouse, I found Flynn on the couch. The phone was to his ear, and he shot me a smile when he saw me come in.

"No," he said to someone on the other end of the phone. "Don't release a statement yet. I'll talk to the press when I'm there. Okay. Bye."

"Brad?" I asked when he hung up.

"Aye. Just giving me an update about the club. The fire was worse than originally thought, and it's going to have to close for a few weeks for repairs."

"That sucks," I said, heading for the refrigerator and grabbing a bottle of water.

"It does," he agreed.

"So when are you leaving?" I asked.

"Tonight. I feel okay and all my pox are gone."

I sighed. "I was hoping to get the boys home. I'm ready to get back to a routine."

"I completely understand. I was thinking I'd take a commercial flight out tonight, spend about a week in New York, depending on how bad it is, and then come home."

"That works."

"You're not mad at me?"

"Why would I be mad at you?"

He smiled, relieved. "No reason."

"Need some help packing?" I asked.

Flynn stood up and walked over to me. His hand snaked out to grab my waist, pulling me toward him.

"Later," he murmured.

"Later," I agreed as his mouth covered mine.

Flynn was on his way to New York a few hours later. Though I was used to spending time apart, there always seemed to be an adjustment period. I hung out with the boys, tried to read Hawk a story, but he was back to his old antics of not sitting still. He was making up for lost time, clearly.

Ash poked her head in late that afternoon. "How ya doing?"

"Okay," I said. "I miss Flynn even though he's only been gone for a little while."

"I figured. Let's go out tonight. Just you and me."

"Yeah?" I asked in excitement.

"Yeah. I can't remember the last time it was just the two of us. No husbands, no kids, no responsibilities."

I was ashamed to admit I couldn't remember, either.

"I'm in," I said. "How about dinner here, but then we head to the strip? I haven't even been this time around."

"Perfect," Ash agreed. "But before dinner, I say we hit the spa."

As we got pampered, we sipped on mimosas. By the time we changed for dinner, we were more than a little tipsy. Ash's face was pink and her smile was wide, and whatever had been weighing heavily on her seemed to have disappeared.

At dinner, we split a bottle of wine. When we climbed into a waiting car that would take us to the strip, I was feeling light and excited. Flynn called to let me know he landed in New York, but our conversation was brief. He told me to have fun and that he'd check in tomorrow. I hung up, vowing not to be tethered to my phone the rest of the evening. I just wanted to be myself, out on the town with my oldest friend in the world.

"I think Jack is in love," Ash said to me when the car was on the way toward the strip.

"Oh, yeah? What makes you say that?"

"Because I've never heard him sound so enraptured and so frustrated by a woman all in the same breath."

"Who is she?"

"She works part time at his firm. Apparently, she's an art student."

"What? No."

Ash nodded. "She won't go out with him. He's tried everything. Flowers, chocolate, flirting, ignoring. Nothing is working."

"Has he tried sincerity?"

Ash paused. "I don't think so. He's so used to getting his way because he's a Rhodes."

"And this girl isn't impressed."

"Not in the least."

"Poor bastard," I said with a winsome smile.

"Seriously. But I feel bad for her too. I mean, when Jack wants something, he goes after it."

"So now we have to wait and see who's more stubborn? This is going to be fun."

Our car pulled to a stop outside the MGM. Ash looked out the window and smiled. "Are we going to walk the yellow brick road?"

I grinned. "I'm game if you are."

"I suck at this game!" Ash wailed when she busted yet again.

"You're not thoughtful enough," I told her. "You go all in and you don't think before you ask for a hit."

"Well, you're too conservative," she shot back.

"Too conservative?" I scoffed. I pushed all of my chips forward, causing the other players to gasp.

"How much is in there?" one woman asked, her eyes nervous for me.

"About ten grand," I said. I blamed the alcohol for my boldness, or stupidity, depending on how this turned out.

When all the bets were in, the dealer dealt the first round of cards face down. I took a peek and then waited for the dealer to deal the second round of cards face up. I had an ace in the hole, but my shielded card was a six. I had a seven or a seventeen—neither would secure me a win. When the dealer stopped at me, I tapped the table signaling that I wanted another card. He flipped over a five. Now I had a twelve. I tapped the table again. The dealer flipped a card to reveal a nine.

I made it to twenty-one.

"I'll stay," I murmured.

The dealer moved on, and then when he got back to his hand, he stayed. He flipped over his under card, revealing a ten. His top card was a jack. Twenty was hard to beat. Two of the people at our table busted, and one lost with a sixteen. Ash had twenty, so she got to keep her chips.

With a little flare, I revealed my winning hand. Everyone at the table erupted into cheers.

"That's the most incredible thing I've ever seen," a voice said.

I turned to see Alessandro Filippi standing behind me. Something about his smile made me pause.

"You saw that?" I asked.

"If you ladies aren't going to bet, you need to leave the table," the dealer said, pulling my attention.

"There's nowhere to go but down," I said to Ash. "Let's cash out."

She nodded in agreement, her eyes darting from me to Filippi. Ash and I gathered up our chips and stepped away from the table. I tipped the dealer, giving him a thousand-dollar chip. He thanked me generously.

Filippi followed us to the cashier window.

"Have you guys met?" I asked.

"Don't think so," Ash said, holding out her hand.

"Mr. Filippi was at The Rex opening," I explained.

Ash stepped up to the window, and I turned back to Filippi. "What are you doing here?"

He grinned. "I imagine the same thing you are."

I rolled my eyes. "No, I meant, what are you still doing in Las Vegas? The hotel opening was days ago. Or do you live here?"

"No, I live in New York," Filippi said. "But I have a business deal going through, so I stayed."

"Oh," I said. "Good luck with that." Ash stepped away from the window, and it was my turn to cash out.

"It was good to see you again, Barrett. Enjoy the rest of your evening."

He nodded at Ash and then turned to walk away.

I watched him depart, a frown marring my face. "Was it me, or was he kind of..."

"Overfamiliar?" Ash supplied.

I nodded. "Yeah, overfamiliar."

Of all the casinos in Las Vegas, Alessandro Filippi had

been at the MGM at the same time as me. And he'd watched me win big. I couldn't shake the feeling that it wasn't a coincidence.

After I cashed out, Ash and I found a bar lounge. The sounds of the casino were muted; instead we were treated to the gentle murmurs of low conversations. We located an empty table and sat down. Seeing Filippi had jarred me sober. I couldn't shake the feeling that there was something I was missing.

Ash ordered an apple martini, and I decided to go for a scotch.

"So, that was interesting," Ash remarked, sipping on her newly delivered cocktail.

"Me winning all that money? Yeah, that was strange."

She shook her head. "No, I mean meeting that guy— Alessandro Filippi. I feel like I've seen him before, but I don't know where."

"Well, he is from New York. Maybe he ran in your circle."

"Maybe," she said with a shake of her head. "This is going to bug me."

"You'll probably put the pieces together when you're sober," I teased.

She laughed. "You're totally right."

Chapter 14

The night wore on, and Ash continued to drink. I stopped after two glasses of scotch, but she kept downing apple martinis like they were water. I hadn't seen her drink like this since we were in college. I thought it was nothing except her letting loose, but when her smile turned brittle and her eyes became glassy, I knew something was up.

"Ash? What is it?"

She stared into the green liquid of her cocktail and took a shaky breath. "It's too horrible to admit."

I reached out across the table to grasp her hand. "I highly doubt that."

Ash didn't even smile at my teasing tone.

"It's just you and me here," I said quietly.

She nodded, finally lifting her eyes to meet mine. "I was pregnant," she whispered. "I found out when you were on your honeymoon in Italy." She fell silent, gathering her thoughts.

"I wasn't happy about it, Barrett," she said. "I wasn't ready for another baby. I don't even know if I want another one."

"Did you…"

"No. I didn't have an abortion."

"Then what—"

"I had a miscarriage."

"Oh, sweetie, that's not your fault," I said.

"I know that." Her eyes met mine. "But I was relieved."

She felt guilty. It wasn't rational, it was emotional. I understood that, better than most.

"You have nothing to be ashamed about," I said. "Your feelings are your feelings."

"That's what my therapist said."

"Therapist?"

"I was seeing a therapist back in Scotland—not in Dornoch," she clarified.

"Which is why you were able to keep it a secret."

"Yeah," she said tiredly. "I like my life the way it is. I love Carys and I love that I don't have to divide my time between children. I have enough time to be at the gallery and still feel like I'm not ignoring Duncan. If we had another baby, then…"

I smiled sadly. "Then your life would look kind of like mine."

"You know I didn't mean it like that," she said.

"I know. But it's true. I love my children, but I'm just now resurfacing. I just now feel like I'm getting *me* back. It's okay, Ash. However you feel."

"Thanks, Barrett," she said, sounding relieved.

"Can I ask? Have you told Duncan yet?"

"No."

"Why not?"

"What if he gets mad? He wants more kids." She bit down on her lip, looking worried.

I shrugged. "You won't know until you talk about it. And I bet you, if you talk to Duncan, you won't need a shrink to help you work out your feelings."

"I went to a shrink because I wanted to talk to someone who didn't know me. Who could be objective."

"Sorry, I was trying to lighten the mood."

"I know."

"Did it work?"

"Kind of." She smiled. "You mind if I step out and make a call?"

"You're not calling Duncan and telling him all this now, are you?"

She laughed. "No. I just wanted to check in and see how Carys is doing."

"We could just go back," I suggested.

"You kidding? This is our last night in Vegas. I'm not letting you go home until dawn."

Ash threw me a grin and then stood. She walked out of the lounge on steady legs, not at all appearing like she'd had too much to drink. Somehow, the woman held her liquor.

I sat by myself at the table, contemplating ordering another scotch. I was coming down from being tipsy, and I knew tiredness would set in, so I knew I had to keep going.

While I waited for the cocktail waitress to come around, I had a moment to study the casino bar. There was the usual mix—people just out for a good time and then others that drank with obliteration in mind. Vegas, with all its bright lights and excitement, was actually depressing. You could be on top of the world and then, with the turn of a card, plummet into extreme hopelessness.

The waitress who had been taking care of us all evening came up to the table and set a glass of scotch in front of me.

"Oh, I didn't order this."

She smiled, showing white teeth. "It's from the gentleman at the bar."

I looked around her to see Alessandro Filippi, his dark brown curls resting casually against his forehead, his chocolatey eyes glittering in the low light. He smiled when he saw me watching him.

"Thank you," I told the cocktail waitress. She nodded and then moved along to another table.

With deliberate purpose, I rose slowly, picking up the glass of scotch. I approached Filippi, who angled his body toward me. I set the glass of scotch down in front of him.

"I can't accept this."

"Why not?" he wondered.

I stared at him for a long moment, holding his gaze. "What are you doing?"

He cocked his head to one side, showing off the strong lines of his neck. He smiled faintly. "I thought it was obvious."

"I'm married."

"Happily?"

"Yes, happily," I snapped.

He shrugged. "Doesn't look that way to me."

"And how did you ever come to that conclusion?"

Filippi paused. "Your husband hasn't been honest with you."

"And let me guess. You're here to tell me what secrets Flynn has been hiding?"

"The night of the opening," he began. "Did he leave the party to attend to something—someone—who was trying to ruin the evening?"

Cold fear washed down my back, but I somehow managed to keep my face passive.

He grinned, but it was cruel and mocking. "You don't know anything, do you?" he pressed. "He flies across the world, spending months on end opening a new hotel, while you sit at home with his children."

I refused to engage, refused to give him an answer that would only inflame the situation more. I believed Flynn, I trusted Flynn, but Filippi's statement reached the part of me I could no longer ignore.

The resentful part of me.

I'd given up a lot to be with Flynn, to make a family with him. I had been the one to stay home and be with the children. I didn't even recognize the person I'd become.

"How did you know?" I asked finally. "About the woman?"

"It's my business to know," he replied.

Who was this man? Mysterious, calculating, a dichotomy of charm and ruthlessness?

It had been so long since I'd had to be anything but Barrett Campbell, wife to Flynn, mother of his three children. But I was still a woman, and if I wanted information, I had to play the part. I was rusty at it, but hopefully, I still had weapons in my arsenal.

As I slid onto the stool next to him, I made sure my leg grazed his. Not enough for it to mean anything, but it was a shrewd move.

Filippi pushed the rejected glass of scotch toward me. I shook my head and pushed it away.

"You still won't accept it?"

"I only accept drinks from those I trust, and I don't trust you."

Filippi let out a laugh, a genuine sound of amusement. "Smart."

"Not really. It's just common sense."

"I've heard common sense isn't so common."

"I've heard that too." I opened my clutch and pulled out my cell phone.

"What are you doing?" he asked.

"Texting Ash and telling her to take the driver and go back to The Rex," I said honestly. I met his dark brown eyes. At one point in time, I might've found his penetrating gaze intriguing. Now I knew better. Filippi was a viper, dangerous because I didn't know how or when he was going to strike.

I set my phone aside and turned back to the man whose leg was slowly inching toward mine.

"Start over?" I asked pleasantly, holding out my hand.

He grasped it, bringing it to his lips. "You are gorgeous."

My smile was wide. "I know."

Filippi let out a laugh as he boldly rested our entwined hands on his thigh.

"May I buy you a drink?" he asked.

"Maybe," I allowed. "I still don't accept drinks from strangers. And you're still a stranger."

He gently let go of my hand, but I continued to let it rest on his thigh. Filippi reached for his glass of clear liquid, which I assumed, was vodka. He handed it to me.

"What is it?" I asked with a delicate sniff. The intense aroma hit my nose. Curious, I took a tiny sip. It was candied sweetness with succulent citrus.

"Oh," I said in surprise.

Filippi smiled. "It's called Solerno. It's made from Sicilian blood oranges."

I looked at him with fresh eyes. Dark hair, dark eyes, his name. I pulled my hand back from his leg in sudden understanding. "You're Italian."

"I am."

"You're from New York."

He smiled, showing his viper teeth. "Keep going. You're almost there."

"You're the head of the Italian—"

"Barrett?" came Ash's voice. "What the hell are you doing?"

Chapter 15

I jumped off the stool, grasped Ash's elbow, and tugged her a few feet from the bar. "It's not what you think."

She glared down at me. "Not what I think? I come back to find you with your hand on a man's leg. A man who is not your husband. A man who is clearly stalking you."

"Ash," I begged. "Please trust me."

"I think our evening has come to an end," Filippi said, sidling up next to me. He handed me my clutch and cell phone. "Ladies. It's been a pleasure." With a cock of his head, he sauntered out of the lounge bar, leaving Ash to gape after him.

"What the fuck did I just miss?" she asked softly.

"Let's get out of here."

I dragged her from the lounge back into the casino, looking around to see if Filippi had disappeared. We had just been getting somewhere, and Ash's presence had derailed it.

"Didn't you get my text?" I demanded when we finally made it out to the sidewalk. I'd forgotten to call our driver, so we stood there, two women dressed in bright sequined dresses, no doubt appearing like we were ready to party.

I pulled out my phone but before I could call Billy to swing by and get us, I noticed I had a text from a number I didn't recognize.

We aren't finished.

A shiver of fear worked its way down my spine. The buzz of Ash's voice was in my ear, and I finally turned to look at her. "What did you say?"

"I said that I didn't get your text until I was already back in the lounge. Now it's your turn to explain."

Explain? Explain what, exactly? I didn't even know what *that* was.

"Are you cheating on Flynn?" she demanded.

"No."

"Didn't look that way to me."

"You've had a lot to drink," I said. "You don't know what you saw."

"Don't do that," she commanded. "Don't put this back on me. Just tell me."

"Not here," I said. "Not on the sidewalk and definitely not in the car."

"But you'll tell me?"

I nodded. I needed to confide in someone; I needed to talk this out with someone who wasn't Flynn because he might flip out and do something drastic.

I got Billy on the phone, and he said he was ten minutes away. When he pulled up to the curb, I opened the passenger door and waved Ash inside.

"Back to The Rex?" Billy asked.

"Uh, no," I said, looking out the window, seeing the Eiffel Tower glowing against the sky. "Paris, please." I looked at Ash who nodded.

"It's been so long since I've been to Paris," Ash joked, but it fell flat.

A few minutes later, the car dropped us off. Entering the

lobby, I went right for the reservation desk, asking for a room for the night. The woman smiled and took my credit card before handing me a key and pointing toward the elevators.

"Why couldn't we go back to The Rex?" Ash asked when we were zooming toward the fifteenth floor.

"Because I wanted privacy."

"Ah," Ash said.

The doors dinged open and we turned right. Walking down the long hallway, I found our room. I'd gotten a standard, nothing fancy. It was just so that Ash and I could sit and talk, no casino sounds around us, no other distractions.

She kicked off her heels and plopped down onto one of the beds and made herself comfortable. She took down her hair and ran her fingers through the curls that had been sprayed and shellacked.

"How drunk are you?" I asked.

"On a scale of one to shit-faced? I'm right on the verge of tipsy."

I nodded. "Okay. Tipsy is okay." I began to pace across the carpeted floor, trying to make order of the swirling thoughts in my mind.

"I guess I should start with the night of The Rex opening," I began. I told Ash what I'd seen in the lobby, Flynn with the nameless woman who had tried to cause a scene, the familiarity between them that could be misinterpreted as more.

"What does that have to do with Filippi?" she asked.

"Filippi mentioned it in our conversation. He knew about it. Said Flynn wasn't telling me the truth about who she was—that she wasn't an angry ex-employee."

"Then who was she?" Ash demanded. "Because she's obviously important."

"Don't know. I might've been able to find out if you hadn't—well, whatever, it's done now." I sighed.

"So, what was going on with you and Filippi? I saw your hand on his leg. Were you…ya know?"

"'Ya know'?" I raised my eyebrows. "Care to explain that?"

"Were you doing what you know how to do? Enticing him, making him think he stood a chance if he gave you information?"

I went to my clutch and pulled out my cell phone. Opening it to the text from Filippi, I tossed the phone at Ash who read the screen.

"Oh, shit."

"There's more," I said.

"Of course there is." She looked at me and waited. "Well?"

"Alessandro Filippi is the head of the Italian Mafia in New York City."

Ash's eyes widened. "How?"

"I don't know."

"I thought Flynn and Duncan took care of—"

"They did," I said, my tone bleak.

"What's Filippi's end game?"

"I don't know."

"Does he want to kill Flynn?"

"I don't know."

After a stunned moment of silence, she said, "This was supposed to be a straightforward fun girls' night out."

"Yeah. It's all been shot to shit, hasn't it?"

"So what do we do?" Ash asked, her head stuck in in the minibar.

"We?"

She looked at me and frowned. "Of course *we*. Why not *we*?"

"You don't have to get dragged into this," I said. "You can stay out of it."

"Like hell I can." She opened a mini bottle of tequila and took a swig before offering it to me. "You need me, and we're best friends."

I took the mini bottle but didn't drink yet. "I've put you in some untenable positions. Asking you to keep my confidence, telling you about some of the ugliest things I've ever done."

My mind flashed back to my time with Dolinsky. I went from hostage to killer. And then in the basement of that house in Edinburgh with Fred Winters; I'd gone from killer to torturer.

"Barrett?" Ash asked, jarring me back into the present.

I washed down the memories with tequila. "I have to tell Flynn."

"What are you going to tell him? Be on your guard? Filippi might want to kill you? He's got a bodyguard. If Filippi wanted Flynn dead, wouldn't there have already been an attempted hit?"

"It's a conversation I want to have with him in person. And soon," I said. "I don't trust Filippi. He says I don't know the truth about Flynn and that woman."

"Do you believe him? Flynn?" she clarified.

"He didn't cheat, but it was damning—the picture they made, from what I saw in the lobby. And I…" I trailed off, swallowing, "believed the worst in him. I would've forgiven him for it."

"Because you love him," she stated. "And one mistake shouldn't be the reason you walk away."

"Yeah," I murmured. "But he's forgiven me for a lot worse. Many times over. Could I have really punished him for being human?"

"Well, at least it's not something you have to actually feel through, because Flynn didn't cheat. Okay," she said, switching gears, "what are we going to do about all of this? How are we going to find out who this woman is?"

"She's not important right now. I need to know everything there is to know about Alessandro Filippi, and there's only one person I trust to get me the information."

"Who's that?" she asked.

I grinned at her. "Your brother."

Chapter 16

I woke up the next morning completely confused. Looking around the bedroom, I saw Ash sprawled out on the other double bed and realized we were still in the Paris Hotel suite.

We'd fallen asleep sometime around dawn after raiding the minibar and deciding not to call Jack until we were sober.

We were leaving Las Vegas today. We were supposed to fly back to Dornoch, but I was going to change the plan and meet Flynn in New York. We needed to talk face to face.

When I got out of the bathroom, I saw that Ash was awake. She smiled, but it turned into a wince. "I think I drank all the tequila in Las Vegas."

"Not to mention you'd been downing apple martinis before that," I pointed out. "Never mix your liquors."

"My sorority sisters would be ashamed of me." She sat up slowly, gathering her tangled hair into a messy bun, using the hotel pen to hold it in place.

"I was going to call Jack and then we should probably get back to The Rex," I said.

"Good idea. I kind of forgot to text Duncan and tell him we were crashing here."

"Think he's worried?"

"Nah, he knew we planned to stay out all night. If anything, he can ask Billy what we were up to."

"Poor Billy," I said with a smile. "Probably asleep in the limo still waiting for us."

"Let me just use the loo and then we can get out of here."

After I called Billy and woke him up, I phoned Jack's cell and left a message. I shoved my feet into my heels, and then I groaned in protest.

"Okay," Ash said, coming out of the bathroom. "I've made myself look less raccoon."

I laughed. "We look like we're doing the walk of shame."

We linked arms and headed out. A disheveled, wrinkled Billy met us when we got out of the hotel. I promised him a hot breakfast when we were back at The Rex. The drive was quiet, but at some point, Ash reached over to clasp my hand. She gave it a little squeeze, and I took comfort in her presence. She'd always been more sister than friend. I trusted her with my life, I trusted her with my secrets.

"I texted Duncan, but he hasn't replied. He's probably still asleep," she said.

"I should call Evie and Jen. Tell them to make sure the boys are packed. I need to see Flynn."

I walked in the front door of the suite to see every piece of luggage packed and ready to go. Hawk was playing on the carpet, cartoons blaring from the TV. Scrambling up from his spot on the floor, he righted himself before running over to greet me.

I scooped him up into my arms and pressed a kiss to his nose. He smelled like little boy and sugar.

"They've all had their breakfast," Jen said from the couch. "Evie is with the twins, cleaning them up."

"Thanks," I said.

"You and Mrs. Buchanan must've had a fun night—if you're just now getting in."

"Fun. That sums it up," I said. What was I supposed to tell the nanny?

I took Hawk into Noah and Iain's room, and I spent some time with them even though all I wanted to do was shower and eat.

Room service and two missed calls waited for me when I got out of the bathroom. I returned Jack's call first.

"I hear you're in love," I said when I had him on the line.

"My sister can't keep her mouth shut," Jack moaned.

"Not when it comes to your love life. It's too good not to share."

"I know you didn't call to talk about my dating life."

"I could've called to talk about your dating life," I stated.

"What do you really want, Barrett?" he asked. I could hear the smile in his voice, so I knew he wasn't angry.

"I need a huge favor. And by favor, I mean I'll pay your exorbitant fee because I know your time is money."

"What do you need?"

I told him.

"Give me a few days," he said and then hung up.

I returned Flynn's phone call next. "I heard you didn't get home until after dawn," he said.

"Already spoke to Duncan, huh?"

"Maybe." He laughed. "I miss you and the boys."

"You've only been gone a day."

"And you miss me too."

"I do," I admitted. "So I have an idea. What if the boys and I come to New York for a little while instead of heading straight home to Dornoch?"

"But what about your life?" he asked. "What about getting the Dornoch Library in order?"

"It'll keep. Besides, it's autumn in New York. Would be a shame to miss it. Don't you think?"

"I'll meet you guys at the car," I said to Evie who had Hawk on her hip. Jen had the twins in a stroller and was wheeling them toward the elevator. Two bellmen had already come and taken our luggage down.

When I was sure I was alone, I pulled out my phone and dialed Alessandro Filippi.

"I was wondering when I was going to hear from you," he stated.

"I'm leaving Las Vegas," I said. "I'm headed to New York to spend some time with my husband."

"Noted," he said.

I hung up, my heart thumping hard in my chest. With a deep breath, I looked around the suite, making sure I had everything before closing the door behind me. When I got to the lobby, I thanked the concierge staff and left a stack of envelopes for them. I found my sunglasses, ready to put them on the moment I stepped outside.

As I rushed through the lobby, I nearly plowed into a woman. I reared back before any damage was done. "I'm sorry," I said absently, barely sparing her a glance.

"Mrs. Campbell?" she asked.

"Yes?" I finally took a moment to look at her. She was the blonde who'd pressed her voluptuous body against my husband the night of The Rex Hotel opening.

She was dressed in an empire waist black dress that displayed a lot of cleavage, but the hemline hit just above the knee.

Her eyes met mine. "You don't know me. My name is Lila St. James."

"I'm in a bit of a hurry. What can I do for you, Ms. St. James?" I asked distractedly. My phone began to buzz, and it was probably Ash asking what was taking me so long. I rudely searched through my purse to look for my cell.

"I'm so sorry to approach you like this, but I feel it's my duty—as a woman—to tell you what your husband has been up to."

I stopped hunting for my phone and slowly looked up to meet her cornflower blue gaze.

"What can I do for you?" I asked again, my voice cold.

"Can we go somewhere more private and talk?" she pressed. "I really don't want to say any of this out in the open."

"No need for pretenses," I said, grinding my jaw. "Say what you want to say."

She took a deep breath. "I've been having an affair with your husband."

"For how long?"

"Five months," she said without pause.

"Where did you meet?"

"The Bellagio," she said. "I was a performer there. Five months ago, he came to see the show I was in, and he stayed after to talk to me. He bought me a drink and then asked me to come up to his hotel room. I went."

Well, the girl knew Flynn's habits of where he stayed when he was in Vegas during the completion of The Rex. I'd give her that.

"I'm so sorry," she said.

"For?"

"For sleeping with your husband."

"Thank you for telling me," I said politely.

She frowned in confusion. "You're welcome."

I adjusted my stance, somehow appearing taller, like a queen surveying an unworthy subject. "What is it you want, Ms. St. James?"

Her eyes narrowed. "I don't want anything."

"Then why did you ambush me in the middle of a hotel lobby to tell me of my husband's infidelity?" I demanded.

"I told you I wanted to speak privately," she said, glancing around her as other guests zoomed past us. No one was paying the slightest bit of attention to our drama.

"I'm leaving for the airport, so you have exactly twenty seconds to tell me what it is you want."

"Money," she spat, finally giving in.

"How much?"

"Five hundred thousand," she said without taking a breath.

"Did you ask Flynn for it?"

An ugly sneer overtook her face. "Of course I asked him for it."

"The night of the opening," I realized. "He wouldn't give it to you, so you were making a scene. What makes you think I'd give it to you if Flynn wouldn't?"

She didn't reply.

"You think I'd be a weaker mark," I realized. This woman had no idea whom she was dealing with. "What happens if you don't get the money?"

"Then I go to the press."

"And tell them what?"

She pulled her loose dress taut around her middle so that I could finally see what she'd been concealing.

Lila's smile was triumphant and ruthless. "I'll tell everyone that your husband knocked me up and told me to have an abortion."

Chapter 17

Violent, volcanic rage erupted in my veins turning my vision red. Somewhere in the back of my mind, I registered Lila St. James taking a quick step back, her beautiful face flashing in fear.

I wanted to strangle her. I wanted to reach out, take her throat in my hands, and choke the life out of her. I wanted to mar her flawless skin with bruises and pain.

"Get out of my hotel," I gritted.

She swallowed. "Five days," Lila said before turning to leave. "Five days to get me the money or I go to the press."

I watched her walk out. Everything around me seemed to be moving in slow motion. Suddenly I was running toward one of the Ficus plants in the lobby, and then I was throwing up in the Ficus plant in the lobby.

"Barrett? I was just coming to see if—oh my God! Are you okay?" Ash asked from somewhere behind me.

"Fine," I mumbled, discreetly wiping my mouth.

"You just threw up," Ash murmured quietly, stepping to my side.

I tilted my head up to look at her. Her eyebrows were raised, and she was asking a question without asking it.

"I'm not pregnant," I assured her.

"You could be. Vasectomies fail all the time."

Despite the swirling anger and nausea in my belly, I grinned. "How reassuring."

"If you're not pregnant, then are you sick? Still hungover from last night?"

"No."

"Then what—"

"I can't talk about it. Not right now." I slowly righted myself and picked up my bag that I'd dropped.

"Okay," Ash said. "We should probably get going."

"I need a minute."

"Do you want me to go with—"

I shook my head. "I'll be out in a bit, okay?" I didn't even give Ash a chance to respond before I was striding across the lobby to the women's restroom. Opening the door, I breathed a sigh of relief when I saw that it was empty. I went into a stall and locked myself inside. All I wanted to do was scream, let it out, free the hatred and the ugly, the violence.

I wanted Lila St. James to burn. But first I wanted her to suffer. The woman claimed to be carrying my husband's child. The swell of her belly was damning evidence. When Flynn told me Lila was an ex-employee, he never told me her name. Had that been on purpose? Had he evaded the truth so I wouldn't question things further? He knew I would dig. Dig and dig and dig until I got to the bottom of it. The bottom of his alleged affair. Had he lied to my face about having an affair while making me come in an elevator?

No. He hadn't lied. He would've confessed to me. Or he would've cleaned up his mess so there would've been no bloody trail to follow.

No. Flynn hadn't cheated. Flynn hadn't lied about getting someone pregnant.

My husband had honor and loyalty, but he also had his own moral code. Flynn hadn't been unfaithful, but he was still keeping secrets from me. And I'd warned him what would happen if he ever lied to me again.

"Can I get you something to drink? Mrs. Campbell?"

"Hmm?" I asked, pulling my gaze from the airplane window. Puffy white clouds scattered across the blue sky, obstructing the view below.

"Can I get you something to drink?" the young flight attendant repeated patiently.

"No, thank you. Wait," I said when she started to move down the aisle. "I'll have a scotch."

"A little early, isn't it?" Duncan asked.

I smiled, but it was thin. "Hair of the dog, you know?"

Duncan nodded in understanding. Ash stared at me, and I turned away from her prying eyes. I graciously accepted the glass of scotch and took a healthy swallow. I hadn't wanted to drink this early in the day in a very long time.

We landed in New York just after sunset. I'd been in a pensive fog all day, and it didn't lift even as I strode through the familiar lobby of The Rex Hotel. Greeted by staff that knew me, I waved and smiled absently, playing the role of tired passenger. I was anything but.

Flynn wasn't in the suite to greet us, so I told Evie and Jen to get the boys settled while I went in search of him. But before I did that, I needed to vent some steam. I changed into workout clothes and then headed to the gym. I ran five miles, but instead of exhausting myself, I only found renewed strength. My anger wasn't going anywhere. It was time for kickboxing.

Sweat poured off me as I beat the sandbag. My muscles strained, felt like they were on fire, and still I didn't give up. I hated Lila St. James. I hated everything about her. I hated her effortless beauty. I hated that she spoke of Flynn with authority. I hated that she made me feel stupid and inconsequential.

"I've been looking everywhere for you."

I yelped and whirled to glare at Flynn. "You don't sneak up on a person."

He frowned. "I didn't sneak. I called your name three times, and you didn't hear me. Are you okay?"

"Fine."

"Whenever a man asks a woman how she is and she answers 'fine,' that's code for 'go fuck yourself.'"

I went back to hitting the sandbag and didn't answer him. Flynn moved to stand in my sight line. "What's going on?"

My tired arms dropped. "Why didn't you tell me Lila St. James was attempting to extort money from you?"

He paused. "How do you know about that?"

"Ah, Flynn Campbell," my voice went hard, "you've been keeping things from me."

"Aye," he admitted.

"Why didn't you tell me?" I demanded.

"Because it's being handled."

"Like hell it is," I nearly yelled. "She accosted me in our hotel, Flynn. It's like she was waiting for me. She spun quite the story about how you seduced her, got her pregnant, and then told her to have an abortion."

Flynn cursed in Gaelic and I went on, "She asked me for five hundred thousand dollars in exchange for her silence, otherwise she's going to the press. What were you planning on doing?"

He didn't reply.

"Whatever you're planning, you expected to leave me out of it. Why?"

Again, he didn't reply.

"I'm thinking the worst here. You realize that, don't you? Is that why you didn't tell me the whole story? I feel blindsided you didn't give me all the information about her."

"I can't ask you to trust me?"

"It's not a matter of trust," I said. "Of course I trust you. But how were you planning on keeping Lila quiet? Paying her off is a gamble."

"As is everything."

"So you *were* going to pay her off, weren't you?" I demanded.

"Since when have you ever known me to be backed into a corner?"

I paused. "She's pregnant."

"I'm aware."

"Does that change how you're planning on dealing with her?"

"Aye. For now."

"Why didn't you really tell me the truth about her?"

"You haven't been…present."

"Present," I repeated. "The kids, you mean."

"You've had a hard time—multitasking," he said slowly.

"So you shut me out," I stated.

"No, I—"

"Just admit it," I snapped. "You think all of my priorities have shifted because I became a mother."

"You're different," he said calmly. "It's not good or bad, it's just different. We're different."

"You still feel neglected."

"What am I, a child?" he grumbled. "You think my not telling you about Lila extorting money was to get back at you because my feelings are hurt?"

"I don't know what to think because you kept this from me! And I don't believe you planned on telling me the truth. Ever."

"Why would I?" he demanded. "So you have something else to worry about? I know what you've given up to be with me, what you've given up for our family. I wanted to shield you from all of this. From Lila's accusations, from her lies—"

"I haven't needed shielding since I took down a mob boss for you."

His gaze darkened. "Don't. Don't pretend you killed Dolinsky solely for my sake. You did that for yourself."

"Yes," I spat. "Yes, I did. Because men like Dolinsky, men like Winters, men like *you*, Flynn Campbell, will always think women are weak."

"I am not like those bastards. I don't think you're weak and you know it."

"No, I don't. Because if you thought I was as strong as you, you would've told me the moment you thought Lila St. James was going to be a problem." My eyes turned from his. "Go away, Flynn."

"As much as I want to give you space to cool off, we've got a bigger problem at the moment."

Chapter 18

"Ramsey did *what?*" Ash yelled, jumping up off the couch.

Duncan calmly looked at his wife when he repeated, "Stole Birmingham's body."

"He's insane," Ash went on, pacing across the floor of the penthouse suite.

I stood on the opposite side of the room, far away from Flynn. "How?" I asked. "I mean—yeah, how?"

"Forget how," Ash interrupted. "Why? Why did he do it?"

"Because he didn't believe what was in the autopsy," Duncan said, explaining away his brother's behavior.

"There was nothing *in* the autopsy," Ash went on. "There was no obvious cause of death. No struggle."

"Just like Arlington," Flynn said. "Both have the white bird tattoo at their necks, both tox reports came back clean, and both autopsies revealed that neither of them struggled."

"So Ramsey's bright idea was to steal Lord Birmingham's body and do what exactly?" I asked.

"Have our own man look at the corpse," Flynn answered. "And it wasn't his idea. It was mine. I told him to do it."

"Our own man?" Ash squeaked. "Are you kidding?

Stealing a corpse is a felony. At least it is in the U.S. I'm not sure about in England."

"I'm gonna go with it's a crime to steal bodies in any country," I said, trying very hard and failing not to smile. I caught Ash's eye and her mouth began to twitch. And then suddenly, we burst into laughter.

"Oh God," Ash said, wiping the tears from her eyes. "No one would believe me if I told them."

"They still act surprised," Duncan said to Flynn. "You think they'd be used to this kind of stuff by now."

Getting myself under control, I said, "Are we done here? I'd like to shower." I was still in my exercise clothes, having walked into our penthouse suite to an impromptu meeting.

"We're done," Flynn said, his eyes finding mine.

I didn't hold his gaze as I strode toward the master bedroom. I whipped my grimy shirt over my head and entered the bathroom. I turned on the shower and while I was adjusting the temperature, the bathroom door opened.

"What are you doing?" I demanded when Flynn closed the door and began stripping off his suit.

"Showering with you."

"No. We're in a fight."

"Why?"

I straightened. "Are you serious right now?"

"Completely," he stated. "I don't want to be in a fight, but you won't talk to me. We'll talk in the shower."

"It's times like these when I wish we hadn't sold our New York apartment."

"Why? So we can use it as the proverbial doghouse?"

"So I can have space away from you to clear my head."

"Hen, please, can we just—"

"I'm showering," I said. "But I'm not talking."

Turning away, I stepped under the spray. I wasn't done being upset, but I didn't want to yell it out anymore. Nothing good came from yelling. It was exhausting and fruitless. I closed my eyes and let the spray bathe my face. I felt Flynn behind me, but he didn't touch me.

"I know you're not weak," he said softly. "Far from it. I saw what you did to Winters. A weak woman doesn't do that. You're fierce, you're protective, you're incredible."

I reached for the bar of soap, pretending to ignore him, pretending I wasn't hanging on his every word.

"I've seen what this life—my life—has done to you, Barrett. I know the things you've done, and I don't judge you for them, just like you don't judge me for my past. You've found a way to live with what you've done. You've made your peace with it. But, hen"—he gently reached out to grasp my chin and forced me to look at him—"there are some ghosts you never lay to rest. There are some moments that change your life forever and there's no going back. You're not the same woman I met a few years ago. You're different. You're harder."

I stared into his blazing blue eyes, the heat of the water pounding my shoulder blades, the pulse of my heart loud in my ears. "You were protecting me from myself, weren't you?" I asked quietly. "Afraid what I might do, could do to that woman—a pregnant woman..."

It sickened me to think about it. I'd killed three men in cold blood. But killing a woman and her unborn child... I'd fantasized about choking Lila St. James. What had stopped me aside from the fact that we were in public? Would I have really gone through with it? Killed Lila, condemning her innocent child to the same fate?

I sank down into the tub and pulled my knees to my chest. How could have I fantasized about killing another mother?

Flynn sat in front of me, wrapping his large hands around my ankles. Water dripped down the sides of his face, his dark beard covering the angular cut of his jaw.

"Do you believe we have souls?" I asked him softly.

"I don't know."

"I do," I whispered. "I believe we have them. And mine is black." I pressed my forehead to my knees so I wouldn't have to look into my husband's eyes. I knew the truth. And so did he.

I wouldn't kill a pregnant woman. But I could.

I was capable of terrifying things. We all were.

We dried off, our skin wrinkled from being in the shower so long. Flynn and I hadn't spoken since he pulled me up from the tub and I resumed scrubbing my body. I was exhausted. Anger had run its course, replaced by guilt.

"She shouldn't have been able to get into the hotel," Flynn said, finally breaking the silence.

I went to the dresser in the bedroom and pulled out a pair of underwear. "Well, she got into the hotel. Oh. I might've forgotten to mention that she said I had five days to pay her five-hundred thousand dollars, or she was going to the press."

"She's not going to the press," Flynn said. "She knows the minute she talks, she'll get sued for slander and I'll bury her."

"Then why did she come after me?"

"That, I don't know. Maybe because she thought you were an easy mark, a woman who didn't want her husband's indiscretions known to the world."

"But it's not true."

"She probably banked on you believing it. I don't know how she was able to get to you in the hotel. Security was supposed to monitor and watch for her. If she showed up, she was supposed to be physically removed."

"Seems someone fell down on the job," I quipped.

"Or it seems one of my employees isn't as loyal as I thought." He pulled on a pair of boxer briefs, but left his chest and torso tantalizingly bare as he strolled across the room to retrieve his cell phone.

"Do you mind if I make a call?"

I shook my head and proceeded to get dressed. I didn't listen to his conversation with Brad, not wanting to hear Lila's name spoken. The woman disgusted me.

The penthouse suite's door opened.

"Snack!" Hawk cried.

His boisterous demand set off the twins who became equally as vocal. They reminded me of little wolf cubs. My children were hungry after a day in the park with Jen and Evie. My heart lurched with guilt. I couldn't stand to see them. They were pure and innocent, and I wasn't. The things I'd done, the things I kept locked away so tightly were struggling to break free. Flynn was right. I was no longer the woman he'd married. Somewhere along the way, it hadn't just become about protecting Flynn, protecting my sons. It had become about the rage. I had so much rage it threatened to choke me.

I hated Dolinsky. He'd kidnapped me, kept me a prisoner in his gorgeous mansion, seduced me with power and charm. He'd seen something in me that I hadn't known existed. I hated that he'd uncovered my secret wants and needs. He'd rearranged the moral makeup of me.

The old me had died when Vlad did. And when I'd killed Dolinsky, I'd changed again. Power had rushed through me like lava. Liquid heat—and when it cooled, it had become something else entirely. The Barrett of now was cold, calculating, a weapon of mass destruction.

Weapons of mass destruction didn't feel guilty. They destroyed. They annihilated. And that's exactly what I was going to do to Lila St. James.

Chapter 19

It was two o'clock in the morning and I was sipping on a glass of scotch, looking through Lila St. James's file. The children were asleep and so was Flynn.

"Find anything?"

I turned my head and saw Flynn standing in the doorway of the bedroom. His chest was bare and the flannel pajama bottoms sat low on his hips. I felt a coil of desire snake low in my belly. Anger and desire. It would always come back to anger and desire.

"No, I didn't find anything. But you knew that already."

Flynn pushed away from the doorjamb and entered the living room. He took a seat next to me on the couch, resting his arm on the top of the cushions, but he didn't touch me.

"You haven't forgiven me yet," he said quietly. "For not telling you the truth about Lila and what she wanted."

"No, I haven't forgiven you. You think I'm out of control. You think I would've killed a—Jesus, Flynn, I still have morals. I still have a code of ethics."

He looked at me, blue eyes intense and raw. "Who are you trying to convince, hen?"

"Would you still love me?"

"Yes."

I paused, staring at the glass of scotch in my hands. "I hate this woman," I said softly. "I hate that she wants to destroy you, us. But she's pregnant. And one thing I don't do is murder the innocent."

I slammed back the rest of my drink and finally looked at him. "You know that. You know me. So what I don't understand is why you're using me as the excuse, as the reason, for not telling me that Lila wanted money."

Flynn remained steadfastly silent.

"What are you hiding from me, Flynn?" I asked softly. "It's yours, isn't it? The baby."

He got up off the couch and went to pour himself a glass of scotch. His silence was deafening. The sick feeling in the pit of my stomach swelled until I thought I was going to be ill.

"Not mine," he said, retaking his seat.

"Then whose?" I whispered.

He sighed.

And then I knew. "Oh God."

"You can't tell her."

My eyes widened. "You can't be serious."

"Barrett, this is why I didn't want to tell you."

"My best friend's husband knocked up another woman," I hissed in low tones. "And you want me to be able to look Ash in the eye and pretend I don't know anything? How the fuck did this happen? If you tell me it was a one-time slip up, I'll hit you."

"It was, though," Flynn said. "Duncan came out to visit and one morning he woke up in bed next to Lila. Six weeks later I get a call from her because she wanted to track down Duncan to tell him she was pregnant. I asked her what it would take to keep it quiet. I gave her money, and she signed an NDA."

"Does Duncan know?" I asked quietly.

"Yes."

"The night of The Rex opening, she was there for Duncan, not you."

"Yes."

I looked at him, understanding coming to me. "You would've been prepared to take the fall for his indiscretion. And he would've let you. Why?"

"Because this will destroy Ash and Duncan. She's not like you, hen."

"You might be surprised," I said. "Ash has stuck by me through a lot—"

"You and I both know marriage is different from friendship."

"She's my family."

"And Duncan is mine."

I sighed. "You really were trying to protect me—from having to lie to my best friend."

"I'm sorry," he said. "I'm sorry for making you doubt yourself, or doubt me."

"She's still going to go to the press," I said, interrupting his apology.

"I know," he said quietly. "Money won't silence her. A lawsuit threat won't stop her."

"But why go to the press and claim you as the father?"

"Because I'm in the public eye and going after me will do serious damage. To my reputation, to my business…"

"So if it's not money she wants," I said. "What is it?"

"That I still haven't figured out."

"Well, we have four days to figure it out otherwise she goes public and our lives blow up."

"I'm working on it." He moved a fraction closer to me and rested his hand on my thigh.

"Don't touch me," I said.

"What? Why?"

I shook my head, a slight smile on my lips, but there was nothing funny about the situation. "You lied to me. Manipulated me. Kept secrets from me. Because you put Duncan first."

"You wouldn't have done the same thing for Ash?" he demanded. "You wouldn't have kept things from me if it meant protecting Ash?"

"I would've trusted you with everything, Flynn," I said quietly. "Because we are a team. But you can't be on a team by yourself."

I stood up slowly, his hand falling from my leg. "When did we stop being a team?"

Flynn went back to bed, and I left the hotel. I walked the streets of Manhattan. The early morning was quiet except for the sounds of delivery trucks. Bars had been closed for hours. Everything felt lifeless, dead. I would never be able to look Ash in the face, and she would know something was wrong. I wanted to maim Duncan. I hated that he'd stepped out on Ash. I hated that a child had been conceived, and there was physical proof of a one-night stand.

I understood why Flynn had wanted to keep me in the dark—so I wouldn't have had to lie to Ash and pretend I knew nothing about the secret love child her husband had created with an opportunistic gold digger. While Ash had been dealing with a miscarriage, Duncan and Flynn had been covering up Duncan's mistake.

As the sun rose, I found myself at a coffee shop in the Meatpacking District. I ordered a scone and an Americano and sat in the corner. It was quiet except for the grinding of beans for the occasional espresso. It was still too early for most of the city to be awake and there wasn't even a trickle of steady customers yet.

He walked in at a quarter to seven dressed in exercise clothes. His blond hair had grown out, long enough to fall across his forehead. With a smile and few bucks in the tip jar, he took his to-go cup of coffee. Just as he turned to leave, he saw me.

Shaking his head, he walked over and took a seat across from me. "You're far from the Upper East Side—and it's not even seven o'clock."

"Your coffee shop has good pastries," I said.

"So does The Rex Hotel." Sasha took a sip of his coffee and then filched my untouched scone.

"Did Quinn stay the night with you?"

"Quinn's in Boston and she isn't speaking to me right now," he said.

"You don't sound concerned about it."

"I told her everything."

"Everything," I repeated. "Jeez."

"Not just about you and me and Dolinsky. But about my childhood. Things I never talk about."

"I don't know anything about your childhood," I said. "And I never thought to ask."

"I never thought to confide." He shrugged. "Quinn asked for space to think about it all. Your turn."

"My turn?"

"Why are you here?"

"I told you. The pastries."

He gave me a knowing look. "Flynn?"

I nodded.

"What did he do?"

I shrugged.

"Want to talk about it?"

"I don't think I can. It's not just about us."

"SINS business?"

I shook my head.

"Personal business?" he tried again.

"Yeah. Sort of. It's weird. And complicated."

"Is it forgivable?"

"In time. I think."

The coffee shop was picking up in customers, and I knew the morning rush was well on its way. It prevented me from asking questions not meant to be asked in public.

"How long are you going to be in town?" he asked.

"A few weeks probably," I said. "Flynn wants to be here while the burlesque club gets repaired."

"You should check out my new lounge. You and Campbell."

"I'd like that," I said.

"And I'll come by and see the boys. After I drink a lot of caffeine and eat a lot of sugar."

I laughed. "Right? Welcome to my world." I looked at my phone and saw that I had a few missed calls from Flynn. "I need to get back."

We headed out of the coffee shop and were met with street traffic and bright sunlight. Sasha embraced me, kissing the top of my head.

"Lunch this week?" he asked.

"Yes, definitely."

I stepped away from him and lifted my arm to hail a cab. "Thank you," I said to him.

"For?"

I smiled and for the first time since last night, it was genuine. "For being you."

Chapter 20

Flynn was having breakfast when I got back to the penthouse. He was dressed in a three-piece suit and he'd shaved. His beard was gone.

It felt like a slap. He knew how much I loved the beard. Flynn was back to looking like a dominant hotel mogul. We were a long way from Dornoch where Flynn dressed in trousers and wool sweaters. His persona was in place, and for some reason, it made me sad. Incredibly sad.

"Hi," I said, my eyes raking over him. I moved into the kitchen and poured myself a cup of coffee. "The children?"

"At the park. You never came to bed," he said.

"I walked around the city. I needed time to think."

Flynn looked up from his plate of scrambled eggs. "Figure anything out?"

I shrugged.

"Where were you?"

I leaned against the counter and gripped my mug. "You know where I was."

"I have an idea. You always run to him when you're mad at me."

"I didn't run to Sasha," I protested.

"I won't do this with you, Barrett. I know we fight, I know we disagree, but when you feel I've wronged you, you go to him, because you know it guts me."

"It guts you? It *guts* you? In choosing Duncan, you didn't choose me. Somewhere, in your mind, you thought you were doing me a favor—"

"It was Duncan's mistake," he stated, shooting up from his chair. "It wasn't my secret to share. Why can't you understand that?"

"Oh, I understand that," I sneered, stalking toward him. "But you should've come clean with me the minute I told you Lila came to me for money. You didn't. Instead, you told me I was different, and you were worried for me about what I might do to that money-hungry bitch."

"I fucked up. Okay? I *fucked up*! I know I did. I'm sorry. I'm sorry I hurt you, I'm sorry I made you doubt yourself, I'm sorry I made you doubt me. Christ, am I sorry." His face was bleak, his eyes full of pain.

I set my cup of coffee on the counter and went to him. I threw myself into his arms and felt my strong husband tremble.

"Did I lose you?" he whispered against my hair. "Did I drive you away?"

Did I drive you into another man's arms, he didn't ask.

"No. Never," I vowed, pressing myself to his chest, trying to get closer, trying to burrow into him so we were one.

"I won't be able to handle it," he said. "If you went to him to get back at me."

I pulled away so I could look into his eyes. Tortured blue gems, startling in their intensity, their heartbreak. "I didn't go to Sasha to get back at you."

"Does he give you clarity?"

"I don't confide in Sasha anymore."

"No?"

I shook my head. "He's in love with someone else and our

relationship has changed. For the better. I did go to the coffee shop across from his apartment and we did talk. But I didn't tell him anything."

"It's Sasha. He knows you. He knows when something's going on with us."

"True. He didn't press." Reluctantly, I stepped away from Flynn. His arms dropped from me and he waited.

"I need to say something to you, and I really need you to hear me." When he nodded, I took a breath and went on, "You're loyal. It's both a blessing and a curse. It's why you kept Duncan's secret from me. Because it wasn't for me to know. It wasn't any of my business, Flynn. I know that—rationally. Emotionally, I felt like I was left out of the club. I behaved…well. You know."

"Barrett—"

"Let me apologize, Flynn. I apologize for ever making you feel like I'd be a vindictive bitch who'd go to some other man just to twist the knife in your belly. I won't do that to you, and I hope you know that."

He reached out to cradle my cheeks in his hands. "I do know that. This is my stuff, not yours."

"I'm here because I want to be. I choose you. I choose our life. I choose our sons." I inhaled a shaky breath. "The truth about Lila will come out. There's no way to stop it unless we take drastic measures, and we both know that's a line neither one of us will cross. Ash will find out. And when she does, she's going to realize that I knew the truth about Duncan, and she will hate me for it."

"Hen—"

"But I choose you, Flynn. I choose you first. Even over my oldest friend in the world."

"I never wanted you to be in this position in the first place."

"I know. But I am anyway." I sighed. "Now, what the hell are we going to do about it?"

Flynn and I were once again a united team. Whatever else went on in the world—my world—wasn't right if Flynn and I were at odds.

He leaned down to kiss me. His hands went to my ponytail and pulled it out of its tie. Flynn grabbed a handful of my auburn locks and tugged me toward him.

"Flynn," I whispered.

"You want me to stop?" he growled.

I nibbled on his bottom lip and then grinned. "No. I was going to tell you to carry me into the bedroom."

He lifted me into his arms, and I wrapped my legs around his waist. Our mouths fused together as he took me to our bedroom. The door shut. He lay me down on the bed, his body covering mine. He was being gentle and sweet. I didn't want gentle and sweet.

"I want it rough," I said against his mouth.

"Good."

Clothes ripped, shirts were ruined, and then we were skin to skin. My nails scraped his back, and he hissed in pain.

"You shaved." It came out as an accusation.

Flynn's fingers found my nipples. "Aye."

"You knew how much I loved the beard. You did it on purpose."

"I didn't." His mouth dipped lower to my bellybutton.

I let out a strangled laugh. "I don't believe you."

His tongue found my core and I gasped. Flynn continued to lick me, tormenting me. "I don't need a beard to make you come."

As if to prove it, he kept his face between my legs until I was moaning and trembling against him.

When I opened my eyes, I saw Flynn up on his elbows, smiling wickedly at me. "You think you're so clever," I teased.

"I am."

"Oh, yeah?" I asked, wiggling out from under him. He let me go and then flipped over onto his back. I straddled him and his hands went to my hips.

"I am clever," he said, his blue eyes heavy lidded with desire. "I got you to marry me, didn't I?"

"Extenuating circumstances," I said, leaning over and taking a nipple into my mouth.

Flynn's breath hitched. "I would've found a way to get you to marry me even if the FBI hadn't gotten involved."

I lifted my mouth from his skin. "You're still coherent. I must not be doing a good job."

Scooting down his body, I skimmed my fingertips along the planes of him. He was stunning, breathtaking, like a natural wonder that had been forged over thousands of years.

I grasped the length of him, watching his eyes roll back in his head as he enjoyed himself. I took him into the wet heat of my mouth, and then I took him into the wet heat of me. I rode him deep and fast. His hands gripped my hips hard enough to leave bruises—and still it wasn't enough. I wanted more.

More pain, more anger, more lust. Just more. So I took it from him, and he took it from me. We never made love, we screwed, we fucked, we were a devastating tornado. I screamed in pleasure until my throat was raw and still it wasn't enough.

"More," I demanded.

He flipped us over and slammed into me. He bent my leg back so I could take him deeper and harder.

"More," I commanded, even as I gasped. "Give it all to me."

He did. He didn't stop until I'd come so many times I'd lost count, until my body wept with pain, until my eyes wept tears. He didn't stop until he knew were back to being us. And then he gave it to me all over again.

Chapter 21

We popped out of our room when the nannies returned with the children. But once they were down for a nap, we went back into our room. By dusk, we were both starving. Flynn called for room service, and we had a naked picnic on our bed.

"This has been nice," I said.

"Nice?"

"Well, the fighting part, not so much. The reconciling part, uh yeah."

"It's better than nice."

I grinned. "Yes, Flynn, it's better than nice."

"We can't stay in this bubble for much longer."

"I know." I chewed a bite and swallowed. "Ash and Duncan have to go home to Dornoch. I can't look at them right now. Ash will know I'm hiding something from her and Duncan. I want to kill him."

"For cheating?"

I shook my head. "For making me have to lie to my best friend."

"I'll get Duncan to take her home," he said quietly.

We ate in silence for a few bites and then I asked, "So

what do we do about Lila?" When he continued to eat and didn't reply I said, "You've done something already, haven't you?"

"Maybe."

"Well?" I demanded. "Tell me."

He picked up a napkin to wipe his face. "I took a play from the Dolinsky handbook."

I frowned for a moment while I worked out what that meant and then I grinned. "You had her kidnapped."

"Aye. She won't be harmed."

"So we just keep her locked up until…"

"Until she comes to the correct conclusion."

"That could take months. I know we have no plans to hurt her, but can't we, I don't know, threaten her? What's the morality clause on that, do you think?"

Flynn laughed. "I wouldn't even know. I thought about threatening her, but what's the point? She'll realize that we're not planning to harm her, so really, what does she have to be afraid of?"

"Blackmailers," I muttered. "What I don't get is why she still wants to bring you down. I mean, if it were really about money, wouldn't she have asked for a huge sum up front from you and been done with it? She obviously knew that you'd pay her to keep quiet about Duncan. But she came to me, too. Why? I don't understand her motivation."

"I don't either," he admitted.

"Ah," I said. "I get it. I get what you've been doing."

"What's that?"

"You've been reactive, haven't you? She came at you, you dealt with her. She came at you again the night of the opening, you dealt with her. Band-Aids. I get it."

"What more can I do?" he wondered. "I have a file on her, we did a background check, nothing came up. I even had my guy dig a little deeper. Nothing."

"We need a legit hacker, Flynn. Someone who can find trails where there are no trails."

"You can't mean what I think you mean."

I nodded. "Yep. We need Don Archer. We need the FBI."

~

"Do I get a say in any of this?" Duncan asked.

My eyes blazed with anger, but it was Flynn who answered him. "No. You don't get a say in this."

"I messed up," he admitted, his tone contrite.

"Aye," Flynn said. "You're allowed to make mistakes, but now it falls to Barrett and me to clean this up."

"Especially if you don't want your wife knowing about your illegitimate love child," I snapped, unable to hold back any longer. We were in the penthouse suite, the children and the nannies were out for a day in the city, and Ash was packing. Duncan deserved my wrath, and I was ready to give it to him.

Duncan's contrition vanished, replaced by his own rage. "You don't think I know how terrible this is? That I—"

I leapt up from my spot on the couch and faced him. "No! You don't get to feel anything! Flynn kept your secret from me at a great cost to himself—and to our marriage. Not to mention, I'm now in this! I have to look my best friend in the eye and pretend her husband isn't a—"

"Love," Flynn said softly but with steel. "Don't add to the fire."

Whirling away from them, I stalked to the large glass windows and stared out at Central Park. "I know you feel badly," I said, unable to look at Duncan. "I know you both thought you were handling this in the right way. But now, you don't get a say. The mess didn't get cleaned up. It got worse, and it's still out there, not being taken care of." I finally turned, my gaze darting between the both of them. "I agreed to keep this from Ash. I'll take responsibility if she should ever find out. But now it's time for you to take your wife and daughter home. Flynn and I will stay and fix this."

Duncan stared at me, eyes forceful, and then he looked to Flynn, his brother in all ways but blood. Flynn nodded stiffly. Without a word, Duncan stalked from the penthouse suite, leaving me with Flynn. The air crackled with remaining tension. Flynn came to me and pulled me into his arms.

"Are we doing the right thing?" I asked against his chest.

"I don't know."

"Why are we stopping Lila?"

"Because you and I both know this will destroy them."

I burrowed my head into his shirt. "It's exhausting, Flynn. Trying to keep it all together."

"Aye."

"Sometimes I don't want to do it."

He gently tugged on my hair to get me to look at him. "But if we don't, the world just might fall apart."

"Our world anyway." Reluctantly, I moved away from him, and his hands dropped to his sides. "So we're in agreement, then? I'll ask Don Archer for a favor?"

He nodded. "We do this, then we have to give him something. Or owe him something."

"I don't know what more we can offer him. We're not running guns; he doesn't care that we've got the New York casino and brothel, what else is there?"

"Guess you'll ask him and see."

"Why do I have to talk to him?" I asked.

Flynn smiled. "Because he likes you better than he likes me. And you're more his type."

"Because I'm a woman. God, you men really are too easy. You know that, right?"

"I know." He lifted my hand to his mouth and kissed my

knuckles. "Before you call Archer, I thought I'd take you down to the club, show you how it's coming along."

"Yeah, I'd like to see it. After that, I should probably check in with Katherine. I've been here a few days, and I haven't even seen her. Glenna will want a full report on her granddaughter," I said with a grin. For the last year, Katherine had been living in the city in my old rent-controlled prewar apartment and working at The Rex Burlesque. Glenna wasn't happy that her granddaughter had fallen in love with New York City and chosen to make her home away from Dornoch, away from her family.

"I need to give Alia a buzz, too," I said, mentioning the current manager of The Rex Burlesque. "She'll kill me if I don't hang out with her at least once while I'm here."

We left the penthouse suite and headed down to the lobby. Flynn held my hand as we walked through the hotel, smiling and waving to the employees we recognized. The burlesque club's lights were on full blast, and there were men sanding down the stage.

"So it was the stage that caught fire?" I asked in confusion.

"No—it was the liquor room. I figured if we had to close for a few weeks to get everything cleaned up, safe, up to code, it made sense to redo the stage. I'm also having the bar redone."

"Look at you," I teased. "Silver lining kind of guy."

"That's me," he agreed with a grin and a glance at his watch. "We better get back upstairs."

And just like that, all my good humor fled.

"No, bring back the smile," Flynn said as we walked out of the club and into the lobby.

"Fine, but it's under extreme duress."

"All you have to do is get through the next ten minutes."

"And hope Ash believes the sky isn't falling. Lies can be good, right?" I asked him. "Tell me the lies that protect those we love are good."

He took my hand and gave it an understanding squeeze. "Come on, love, let's just get you through the next few minutes and then we can have a moral discussion."

"With scotch," I stated as he led me toward the elevators.

"With scotch," he agreed.

Chapter 22

The next morning, I awoke to Flynn's cold side of the bed. I knew he was already out of the suite and gone for a day of meetings. When Flynn was in New York, he always made the most of his time. I respected it and loathed it. But a man like Flynn didn't spend his time the way normal people did. He was never idle; he was always pushing toward something else. It made me worry when we were back in Dornoch. Would he ever be happy and content, or would he always want more?

I hadn't been incredibly ambitious in my career. I hadn't gotten off on all the politics and back-scratching that went along with academia, and I'd never had any plans to go for my PhD. I studied history because I loved it. History was my first true love. Falling in love with Flynn, choosing him, choosing secrets and lies, somewhere along the way it meant I didn't choose history. I didn't choose me.

Sighing, I rolled over to stare at the ceiling.

"Mam!" a young voice shrieked. I heard the sound of little hands pushing against the door, and then Hawk was in the bedroom, running toward me.

I leaned over the side of the bed and scooped him up, placing him on my belly. I lifted my legs to prop him up.

"I'm sorry!" Evie said from the doorway. "He got away from me."

I grinned at her. "It's okay. He hasn't seen much of me the last few days. I'll take him for a bit."

"You sure?"

"Yeah," I said, suddenly feeling a pang for my other children. "In fact, I'll take all of them for the day. You and Jen should take the day off."

Evie blinked. "Are you feeling okay?"

"I can spend the day with my children alone, Evie. I am their mother."

"I know that, ma'am, but they're a lot to handle. Even with the two of us, sometimes we have trouble. What if we give Jen the day off and I stay with you?"

"Fine," I said, my attention being pulled to Hawk who was struggling to lean over so he could press his face to mine.

"Do me a favor?" I asked. "Hand me my cell phone. It's on the nightstand."

Evie grabbed it and handed it to me. "I'll let Jen know she has the day off."

"Thanks."

Evie closed the door on her way out. I unlocked my phone while trying to keep Hawk from stealing it. I grasped his hand and brought it to my lips.

"I was wondering when I was going to hear from you," Alia said in way of greeting.

"You could've called if you knew I was in town."

"Let's not fight," she pled.

"Agreed. I'm calling you now. You busy this afternoon?"

"Nope."

"Great. How do you feel about going to The Met?"

Before she could answer, Hawk somehow managed to get my phone into his little paws and he hung up.

I sighed, leaning over and bumping my nose with his. "That wasn't very nice."

I sat on a bench in Central Park with my three children. They were in one stroller and for the moment, all of them were quiet. Perhaps it was because the twins were asleep. Though Evie was supposed to be with me, Jen had managed to get two last-minute tickets to a Broadway show the girls had been dying to see. I gave them both the day off, and I hoped they enjoyed themselves.

Flynn was currently in meetings, and I had plans to meet Alia in an hour on the steps of The Met. For the time being, I was enjoying the perfect autumn afternoon, and Hawk was sitting still. I was bribing his silence with Cheerios.

"You have beautiful children."

I tried not to stiffen. The smile on my face remained while I kept my attention on Hawk. "You shouldn't be here."

"You haven't called or texted since you left Las Vegas," Alessandro Filippi said.

"I've been a bit busy," I said, finally looking at him.

Filippi looked like an ancient Roman who once kept company with kings and Gods. His black waves fell over a patrician forehead, a high aquiline nose, and a mouth that would tempt even the most in love of women.

But the only man I wanted in my bed was my husband. I could live with his demons, his ghosts, his secrets, his danger. Flynn's and no one else's.

I hadn't spoken to Flynn yet about Filippi. Other things had been getting in the way. Jack hadn't called me with any information. I was on my own.

"This little one looks just like your husband," Filippi said with a smile in Hawk's direction.

"What do you want?" I demanded, not in the mood to play games.

"You were much nicer in Las Vegas."

"Don't pout. It's unattractive."

Filippi grinned. "There's the woman I know."

"You don't know me. Never think you do."

"I'll take that as a warning." Filippi leaned back against the bench and set a hand on his leg. He was dressed in dark slacks and a blue button-down, and he looked like one of the thousand other men who worked in an office in the city.

"I don't know you," he said softly, "but I know a lot about you."

"I'm sure you do. I'm sure a man like you has done his homework."

Hawk got a little testy when I stopped handing him cereal. The last thing I wanted him to do was cry and wake his brothers. I couldn't deal with them and Filippi at the same time. So I gave Hawk more Cheerios and waited for Filippi to tell me why he'd come to me, now, when I was in the park with my children.

"Is this about Flynn?" I asked. "Are you going after Flynn because he has something you want?"

Filippi began to laugh and shake his head. I frowned. "I don't know why that's so funny. It's a logical conclusion. Flynn has enemies. You wouldn't be the first."

"I have nothing against your husband," Filippi said when he finally got himself under control. "Actually, I admire him. Reigning supreme, king of the city. He has the respect of the criminals and the politicians—who, let's face it, are also criminals. The man is untouchable. And he has some powerful friends, some powerful allies."

"And let me guess, you want to be one of his powerful allies?"

"Ah, you're getting ahead of me." He had the audacity to chuck me under the chin. "Powerful allies. One of whom is Sasha Petrovich."

A feather could've knocked me over, and I didn't even bother hiding my surprise. "Sasha? This is about Sasha?"

"I know what happened on the docks with Fred Winters and Giovanni Marino."

"I don't—"

"Before you spit out a lie, let me tell you this: I know the night that Fred Winters killed Giovanni Marino, I know your husband was there with Petrovich. Petrovich took over Italian jurisdiction—my jurisdiction."

I frowned. "So you want justification for Marino's death?"

"Fuck no," Filippi spat. "Winters taking out Marino saved me the trouble. But I want my territory back."

"I can understand that," I began slowly, my mind a whirl. "But why can't you speak to Sasha about this? Why involve me at all?"

"Do you really think Petrovich is going to give up lucrative territory just because I asked for it back?"

"No." Not to mention, most of Sasha's enterprises now were legitimatized. The FBI was no longer on their backs, and the Russians funneled clean money to the SINS. Sasha losing territory hurt not just the Russians, but it hurt Flynn too. It hurt our cause for a free Scotland.

"Again, I ask, why involve me?"

"Your husband has his pride, no? As does Petrovich?"

Filippi seemed to want my agreement, so I just nodded.

"Right. So I figure, if I come to you, I have a better chance of being heard."

"I'm not involved in my husband's affairs," I lied.

Filippi smiled, that cool, calm, about-to-strike viper smile. "Fine. If that's the way you want to play it. Let me put it this way: you help me get back Italian territory, and I'll tell you who wants to destroy your husband."

"Destroy?" I asked faintly.

The air suddenly seemed colder.

"Yes."

"Lila St. James," I guessed. The woman was relentless and money hadn't silenced her.

"You're not only beautiful, you're actually smart. I like that in a woman."

I nibbled my top lip. "And if I don't help you and get Sasha to relinquish territory?"

Filippi's dark brown gaze held mine for a moment before sliding to the direction of the stroller. "It would be a shame, wouldn't it? If innocents were hurt?"

The acrid stench of fear rose up to meet my nose. It was the equivalent of a man shitting himself just before he died.

Filippi leaned over and brushed his lips across mine. "You have my number. Use it."

Chapter 23

"Are you ready to see The Met?" I asked, leaning down to kiss Hawk's nose.

He clapped his hands and then reached for the rest of the Cheerios. I forced myself not to look around because I knew Filippi had men in place watching me. It was the only reason I could think of for why he had known I was in the park. So I did what I had to do: I pretended I wasn't shaking on the inside.

Alessandro Filippi had threatened the lives of my children.

Fear morphed into anger, but I kept a lid on that, too. Otherwise I might just lose it in public.

Iain woke up and then so did Noah. Before I knew it, I had three cranky children, and my immediate attention was turned to caring for them. After giving the twins their bottles, I got us moving. I pushed the stroller along the sidewalk, trying to think of a way out of this.

It made sense that Lila was working with someone. If she'd been working alone, she would've taken the money and run, but she hadn't.

I nearly groaned aloud. Now Sasha was involved in all of this? He couldn't give back territory.

My head was crammed full, worries and fears shoved into every spare space of my mind. Even though I should've canceled on Alia and called Flynn to discuss all of this immediately, something about it made me pause. I refused to let Filippi's men tell him that I'd run home to Flynn. I was a woman, and I wasn't going to cower and let my husband handle this. So when I saw Alia waiting for me on the steps of The Met, I made sure my smile was extra bright and my laughter loud.

Alia's features had the cast of Asian descent including her long, straight black hair, but she was also tall. She'd been an amazing dancer at the burlesque club and then taken over the position of manager after Lacey had left.

"Wow, not a nanny in sight," Alia said after pulling back from a hug.

"I gave them both the day off. You okay braving a museum with these little devils?"

"Hey, as long as I can give them back to you when they start crying."

I grinned. "I respect the honesty."

"Where's Ash? You guys are two peas in a pod."

My heart contracted when I was reminded of my best friend and the secrets I was keeping from her. "She and Duncan left this morning for Dornoch."

"Private jet?"

"Commercial. First class. We kept the jet."

"Ah, yes, flying with three children is different from flying with one."

I grinned at her as we made our way to the entrance. It was busy despite it being a weekday. The Met was always crowded—people came from all over the world to see the exhibits.

"Carys isn't even a child. I swear, she's secretly a well-behaved twenty-year-old who can't speak yet," I said.

Alia and I donated a good amount to the museum and

then proceeded. I was always in awe every time I came to The Met. It wasn't just the architecture that floored me, but the exhibits, the art and culture. It was a mecca of beauty.

"Where to first?" I asked, leaning over the stroller to see how the boys were doing. Iain had fallen into a doze, but the other two were awake yet quiet. I wouldn't look a gift horse in the mouth.

"They have this tapestry exhibit on loan from the British Museum. You mind?"

"Nope. I'll follow you."

Alia smiled.

"How's Jake?" I asked.

"He's good."

"And you guys are doing well? I mean I know you're happy and married life is fun, but I meant the fact that you're not working right now because of the fire—"

"I'm actually really glad you brought that up," she said, shooting me a sidewise glance as she hit the elevator button. "Jake and I want to open up our own restaurant."

"That's great," I said, genuinely meaning it.

"Yeah, the thing is, this ideal spot became available, and we kind of jumped to sign the lease. And with the club being temporarily closed, it made the most sense to—"

"Jump ship?" I supplied in good humor.

She wrinkled her nose. "You mad?"

"No, of course not. I think it's great. You have to do what makes you happy. So the club is losing both of you?"

"Yeah."

The elevator doors chimed and then opened. We stepped inside, and then Alia hit the button.

"Oh, I'm such an idiot," I said with a wry grin. "The only reason you wanted to hang out with me was so that you could tell me you were leaving, and then I'd be the bearer of bad news."

"I really did want to see you," she protested. "But yeah, I

thought he'd take this news better from you. Especially if you were on top of him. Naked."

I let out a laugh as the elevator door opened. We stepped out and headed toward the tapestry exhibit. I asked Alia about the space, and she admitted it was in Brooklyn. I pretended to be shocked, but Brooklyn was actually pretty cool. From what I'd heard—not that I'd spent a great deal of time there. My life when I'd lived in New York had been pretty Manhattan-centric.

"So how was the opening?" Alia asked.

"Good. Extravagant. Campbell fashion."

"Sorry we couldn't be there," she said.

"If you'd been there who would've been running the club?"

Alia grinned. "Point. Hey," she said heading over to a gold-threaded tapestry. "Look at this one."

The drapery was at least ten feet high and twice as wide and didn't look like any of the others. For one thing, there was no depiction of an ancient scene, no story that was being told. No king triumphing or dying on a battlefield. The tapestry was yellowish gold with red fibers laced throughout. It was difficult to see what had actually been woven into the tapestry, so I moved the stroller back toward the middle of the room to take in the piece.

"There's a bunch of Italian words I'm not even going to try to say because I'll butcher it. But the tapestry is called *Falco*. Italy, 1363. That's Falcon in Italian, right?"

"I'd think so, yeah," I answered. I frowned as I saw what looked like the outline of a wing. "I'm not seeing much."

"The description says to look at it at an angle. You're not meant to stare at it straight on."

Alia and I moved to one side of the tapestry. It was a large bird of prey, what I assumed was a falcon, its wings outstretched, a sword dripping with blood grasped in its talons.

"Cool," Alia said. "Kinda gruesome."

"Gruesome," I repeated, something nagging at me. I pulled out my cell phone from one of the stroller pockets and unlocked it. Scrolling through my email, I found the flagged message from Flynn. I clicked on one of the pictures and zoomed in. I stared at it for a moment and then looked up at the tapestry and then back down at the photo.

"What are you looking at?"

"Nothing."

Alia glanced at me, brow furrowed in confusion. "Doesn't look like nothing."

"Am I allowed to take pictures in here?" I asked.

"Yeah, I think you can. I don't see a 'no camera' sign. Just make sure the flash is off."

I tried to get a good angle, but the glare prohibited me from a decent shot. Giving up, I walked to the description of the piece, thinking I'd just take a photo of it and research it in the library. I was old school that way. Maybe I'd try Google first, though.

Raising the phone again, I peered through the screen and tapped it into focus. My breath stopped. I read the words Alia didn't try to pronounce.

Compagnia Bianca del Falco. The White Company. A group of Italian mercenaries that went back to the medieval age, but that were still very much active today. The White Company had been hired by Arlington to assassinate Malcolm and Duncan. They'd only gotten one target.

I knew who was responsible for killing Arlington and Birmingham. The White Company had left their calling card in the form of a white ink tattoo of a falcon. The question begged: who had hired them?

Chapter 24

I needed a reason to leave The Met and Hawk came to my rescue. Granted, he came in the form of a temper tantrum, but I would take what I could. Shooting Alia an apologetic look, I headed for the exit. She was going to stay and enjoy the rest of the afternoon in the museum.

As soon as I got outside, Hawk settled down. I looked at him. "You have good timing, kiddo."

He smiled up at me. I was turning in the direction of The Rex when my cell phone rang. It was Jack.

"Please tell me you have something to report," I said.

"Hello, Barrett. Yes, I'm good. Thanks for asking," Jack replied dryly.

"Sorry. It's been a rough day."

"Can you come to my office? You can tell me about it."

"I have the kids with me."

"No nannies?" I heard the teasing in his voice.

"Why is that always a joke now?" I demanded.

"Because you've become an Upper East Side snob."

"Hey!"

"Kidding, kidding. So can you meet me here?"

"Yeah, I can. I'm headed back to The Rex to get a car. So it will be a little while."

"Take your time."

When I finally got back to The Rex, the boys needed changing, and they were tired of being in a stroller. I called Jack back to let him know that I was going to be delayed.

"I can swing by after work," he offered.

"I'd rather meet you at your office," I said.

He paused. "Flynn doesn't know what you asked me to do, does he?"

"No. And it's only gotten more complicated." I pinched the bridge of my nose. "Give me a minute to figure this out." It was stupid of me to think I could do all of this without Jen or Evie here.

My savior came in the form of Katherine, Glenna's granddaughter. Flynn and I were supposed to have dinner with her later that evening, but I called and begged her help.

"I have to run out for a little while. The boys are in their nursery, and they've been fed and changed," I said the moment she walked into the penthouse.

Katherine stared at me wide-eyed. "I don't know. There's three of them and one of me."

"You'll be fine," I promised. "And my phone is on ring."

I didn't think it was a good idea to explain to her just how terrifying Hawk could really be. But I had bigger issues at the moment, and time was getting away from me.

"Love your bangs!" I called to her as I grabbed my bag and rushed out.

A car was waiting for me in front of the hotel. I gave the driver the address to Jack's office and then settled back into the seat. My mind was a whirl. After I spoke to Jack, I would have to talk to Flynn and tell him what Alessandro Filippi was up to. Then I would need to inform Sasha.

Not to mention I had this White Company information looming. God, there seriously wasn't enough time in a day.

My phone rang. I expected it to be Flynn, but it was Ash. I silenced it even though she was probably just calling to tell me they'd landed and were back in Scotland. But I couldn't talk to her at the moment. My guard was down, and I knew I'd say something I'd regret. The easiest thing to do right now was to ignore her.

The car pulled to a stop. Jack's office was on the Upper East Side, about fifteen blocks from The Rex. On a good day, it took almost no time to get there. Today was a good day.

Climbing out of the car, I took the driver's offered hand. "Thank you."

"You're welcome, Mrs. Campbell." The man was new to our employ—I didn't recognize him.

"I'm sorry, I don't think I've asked your name," I said, craning my neck so I could study him. He looked like a seasoned man, burly and wide. Another Brad Shapiro type.

"Mason, ma'am. Pleased to meet you."

"Nice to meet you too, Mason." I headed into the office building, told the security officer on duty where I was going, and then pushed the elevator button. Jack was a senior partner in the firm, with his name on the door, and he'd earned it. He was one of the best lawyers in the city.

It was the end of the workday, but the office was still busy. Legal secretaries sat at their desks, shuffling papers and typing on laptops. Interns bustled down the halls, looking both frazzled and excited.

I greeted Jack's secretary who called him on the phone to let him know I was there. She moved to get up to escort me to his private office, but I waved her down. I knocked on Jack's door and gently pushed it open.

"Hey," he said with a grin. The guy was cute. He hugged me in brotherly affection and then gestured to the chair in front of his desk.

"You look good," I said, taking him in. Jack was average height and in his mid-thirties. At a time when people's bodies started changing due to metabolism and an overall lack of care, Jack had maintained his physique. The brown hair at his temples was threaded with gray and made him look distinguished.

"Thanks. So do you."

I rolled my eyes but smiled.

"Should we get right to it?" Jack asked, heading to his desk. He opened the bottom drawer and pulled out a file.

"Wow," I said when Jack put the thick stack in front of me. "You got a lot in just a few days."

"Most of it is childhood stuff, and I didn't know what you were looking for, so I just included it all."

"Your guy is good." I began to flip through the pages.

"Should be, he costs enough."

"But he's discreet. Discreet costs," I said, knowing I would easily hand over a small fortune for valuable information. You paid for things that mattered.

"What is it you're looking for, exactly?" Jack asked, leaning back in his chair.

"I don't know. Right now, I'm just hoping to get some information on him."

"Can I ask how you met the contender for the Italian mafia?"

I frowned and looked at him. "What do you mean 'contender'? Filippi told me he's the leader of the Italian mob."

"Not according to that information," Jack said, gesturing to the file. "Read the first page."

My eyes started at the top. "Filippi is Giovanni Marino's bastard? Wow."

"Yeah, from a Sicilian woman. So you can see why there would be some issue with Filippi taking over. The Italians won't take orders from a Sicilian boss—not unless he brings something to the table and proves himself."

I leaned back in the chair, finally understanding all the pieces.

"Barrett? What is it?" Jack asked.

"Who's in charge of the Italian mob now?"

"I don't know off-hand," he said dryly.

My cell phone rang, and I fished around in my bag to find it. "I need to get this," I said to Jack who nodded. "Hello?"

"Barrett, oh God, you have to get back here!" came Katherine's harassed voice.

"Why, what's the matter?" I demanded, my heart pounding in fear.

"Hawk—he—"

"Spit it out!"

"He drew on his brothers!"

I paused, registering what Katherine had said. "Are all my children still in the suite?"

"Yes."

"And no one's dying?"

"No one's dying."

My lips began to tremble. "Hawk drew—"

"Drew. On. His. Brothers!" Katherine repeated. "I don't even know how he found the red Sharpie! Flynn is going to kill me!"

"I'll be home soon," I promised. "You got this."

"But—"

I hung up on her and looked at Jack. He appeared dazed.

"You're not at all worried about your kids? Forget the kids! That poor girl!" Jack said with a laugh.

I chuckled. "I'm pretty certain Hawk is the spawn of the devil."

"Ah, a mother's love," Jack quipped. "Nothing like it."

"I have to go."

"Yeah, I figured."

Sweeping Filippi's file into my bag, I said, "So you'll look into who's actually in charge of the Italians?"

"I will."

"Good. Thanks. Now, are you going to introduce me to the woman who refuses to have you?"

Jack gave me a look. "On one condition. You be nice."

"I'm always nice," I lied, remembering how I'd treated Sasha's new love. Which only reminded me of something else I had to do.

"You've got to lie better than that, Barrett." He sighed. "When you meet Mellie, try not to scare the crap out of her. I'm having a hard enough time with her as it is."

Chapter 25

Hawk didn't just draw on his brothers. He drew on the white couch, the white walls, the floor, the curtains.

Katherine sat in a plush, comfortable chair, clutching a glass of scotch. "I'm so sorry," she said again.

"Don't be," I said in reply.

The boys were safely ensconced in the nursery and quiet. Iain and Noah were no worse for wear—they were just red.

I tried to hold in my laughter, but I couldn't. Katherine's trembling lip sent me over the edge until I doubled over onto the newly red-striped couch.

"It's not funny!" Katherine nearly bellowed. "You and Flynn have given me so many chances! And you set me up with a job and an apartment while I'm here, and how do I repay you? I let your son draw on your other children—and destroy this gorgeous suite!"

My gales of laughter echoed in the suite but didn't drown out the sound of the elevator doors chiming open. Flynn walked in, took in my hilarity, Katherine's pinched face, and then went right for the bar.

"What did I miss?" Flynn drawled.

Katherine took a hasty sip of her scotch.

I finally managed to rein it in. "Notice anything different?"

Raising his eyebrows, Flynn took me in first, his eyes scanning me from head to toe. When he deemed it wasn't me that had been altered, his gaze traveled around the room. I watched his face slacken in surprise.

"What the hell happened?" he asked.

Katherine trembled despite the fact that Flynn hadn't even raised his voice. It had come out in a dazed whisper.

"Hawk," was all I said.

His sigh was resigned.

"Don't look at Iain or Noah," Katherine blurted out.

Flynn closed his eyes like he was in pain. "The red?"

"Yep," I said. "The little bugger painted it red."

"I'm too young for a stroke," Flynn said. "Right?"

Katherine moaned. "Don't tell my grannie. I'll never hear the end of it."

I smiled at her but said to Flynn, "We haven't had dinner yet. I was thinking we could order room service? Catch up with Katherine."

"Something's actually come up," Flynn replied. "I'm sorry, Katherine. Can we have dinner another night?"

She jumped up from her seat, already heading for the elevator. "Sure. No problem!"

"Do you want my driver to take you home?" Flynn asked.

"No. I'll walk. Thanks!"

Katherine was gone before I could even say anything. I chuckled. "How is it she's still terrified of you?"

"Weren't you terrified of me when you first met me?" Flynn nearly purred.

I frowned. "Are you okay?"

"Fine," he clipped before finishing off his drink and then pouring another.

"You're not fine," I said. "Tell me what's going on."

"Where were you today?"

"At The Met with Alia," I said. "You knew that. Actually, there's something I wanted to tell you—"

"Before The Met. Where were you before The Met?"

"I took the boys to Central Park." I cocked my head to one side. "But you knew that already. Didn't you?"

His jaw tensed and his eyes went glacial.

"You're having me followed."

"No. Not followed."

I sighed. "You gave me a bodyguard and didn't tell me. Again."

"Lila got to you when she shouldn't have been able to. The bodyguard isn't even the point," he said.

"Well, yeah, actually it is." I glared. "Because the man is clearly spying on me."

"Not spying, protecting! So tell me, Barrett? Who is he?"

"He who?" I taunted.

"The man you're leaving me for!" he yelled.

My eyes widened in shock. "What?"

"Don't lie to me!" He gripped his glass of scotch as he stalked toward me, the fumes of liquor hitting me in the face. I finally realized that this wasn't his second drink. Probably his third. Or fourth. He'd been contained while Katherine was in the room.

"You met a man in the park. He kissed you. And then you went to see Jack Rhodes. You asked Jack to get you a divorce, right?"

I looked at him in disgust. "Do you even hear yourself right now?"

"Aye, I hate myself."

"And you hate me too, right?" I sneered.

"You've been lying to me, Barrett. Ever since Las Vegas."

I blinked, trying to clear the rage from my mind so that I could think. "My girls night out with Ash," I realized. "You were having me tailed then, too."

To his credit, Flynn didn't drop his eyes. He held firm, all but confirming my accusation.

I took the glass from his hand, downed the last of the scotch, and then chucked the crystal against a wall. A startled cry came from the nursery. My children were awake and they needed me, but at the moment, nothing penetrated the blind rage swirling in my belly.

"You still haven't forgiven me. After all this time. After all we've been through," I accused.

He remained stoically silent.

"I left my job for you. I had your children. I gave up everything," I said, resentful. "What more do you want from me?"

"Don't," he said harshly. "Don't for a moment blame me because you decided to have my children."

"Get out."

"No! You don't get to kick me out, Barrett. And you don't get to use our children as an excuse. Some things are unforgivable. I forgave you for Dolinsky."

"But you didn't forget," I said quietly.

"How can I forget when you wake up next to me in the middle of the night, trembling, and I know it's not because you had a nightmare?"

There was no shame I could hide from Flynn. Not even that I sometimes still dreamt of a man who had taken so much from me but had given me things too. Things I couldn't name. Things I couldn't share.

Grabbing my purse and phone, I headed for the elevator. My children were crying in the next room, but I couldn't be a mother to them. Not right now. And in that moment, I hated Flynn.

"Where are you going?" he demanded. "We're not done."

I looked at him, my gaze cold. "Yes, Flynn. We are."

∽

I hailed a cab when I was on the street. Climbing inside, I settled against the leather and closed my eyes.

"Where to, ma'am?" the man asked. His Staten Island accent was thick but somehow comforting.

"I don't know yet," I said, feeling weary. "Can you drive around for a while?"

If he thought my request odd, he didn't comment on it. He drove around for the better part of an hour while my phone rang every few minutes. It was Flynn, of course, but I wasn't in any place where I wanted to talk to him.

My heart ached. The things we had said to one another… my crying children…this would go down as one of the worst nights of my life.

Finally, I turned off my phone.

As the meter crept towards fifty dollars, I realized where I wanted to go. I gave the cabbie the address, and he cut off a truck to be able to swing a left. He pressed on his horn and yelled in a mixture of English and Italian. It only reminded me of Alessandro Filippi and the problems he'd caused—not just with Sasha, but also within my marriage.

Would Flynn ever trust me? Forgive me?

"So you're Italian?" I said to the cab driver, striving for conversation.

He looked at me in the rearview mirror, and I could hear the teasing in his tone when he asked, "What gave it away?"

Despite the heavy ball of despair in my stomach, I managed to laugh. "Can I ask you a politically incorrect question?"

"Sure."

"Why do the Italians not care for the Sicilians? And vice versa?"

"They're different," he said slowly.

"How? I'm genuinely curious."

"Sicily is an island and the Sicilian culture has a Mediterranean influence," he explained. "Italians—northern Italians

—usually known for their fair skin and hair—were conquered by the Anglos. You follow?"

"Yeah."

"They define themselves first as Sicilians, then Italians. They're just different," he finished.

There were nuances to every culture, every country. When Scotland was ruled by lairds, the Highlanders looked down on the Lowlanders. Even now, I knew Flynn had pride that his father's family hailed from an old Highland clan.

Flynn.

Just the thought of his name sent a wave of pain through my belly.

The cabbie pulled to a stop. "Thank you," I said. "You've been very helpful."

"You sure this is the right spot? This doesn't look like much of anything."

"Part of its charm." I gave him two hundred in cash. "Have a good rest of your night."

Chapter 26

Sasha's home didn't look like a home. He'd bought a warehouse in the Meatpacking District and then had it converted into the most amazing space I'd ever seen. There was a parking garage underground with an elevator. The only way to get to Sasha's private floor was to use the elevator and have a key.

I had a key, but I'd never used it. Until now.

The elevator doors opened, and I exited. The floor was private, with only one door that led to the apartment. There were three floors in its entirety, equipped with a private gym on the lowest level and the top floor was the master bedroom.

I hadn't even called to see if he was home. I doubted that he was, but I still did the courteous thing by knocking. No one answered. I knocked again. Just when I thought of using my key, the door opened.

Quinn—leggy, haughty Quinn—stood in the doorway. Her face was devoid of makeup, and her green eyes were wide with surprise.

"Barrett!"

"Hey, Quinn," I said, feeling my energy drain. "I'm sorry,

I didn't realize you were—that he—I'll go." I turned to leave, but her hand on my arm stopped me.

"Don't go. Come in."

"That's really okay."

"Please?"

Her voice was soft, vulnerable. It made my lip tremble. I let her tug me inside, this willowy girl whose grip was surprisingly strong.

I loved Sasha's place—the living room had a retractable roof with a skylight. It was currently pulled back to reveal the glass, and though I couldn't see stars due to the light pollution, it was still incredible, the architecture that existed.

"Would you like something to drink?" Quinn asked. I finally was able to notice what she was wearing—a pair of yoga pants and a gray sweatshirt with Navy written across it that hung off one of her shoulders. Her black hair was pulled back into a lopsided ponytail, and that's when I realized Quinn and I were more alike than I'd originally thought.

"Water, please," I said, even though I wanted a scotch.

Quinn moved around the living room like one who lived there, and I wondered if she did. She went to the bar in the corner, and instead of pouring me a glass of water, she reached for the bottle of Balvenie Triple Cask.

She set the glass down in front of me with a raise of an elegant eyebrow. I couldn't help the bubble of laughter that escaped. Quinn took a seat in one of the chairs angled toward the unlit fireplace.

"Thank you," I said, reaching for the scotch.

"Sure." She watched me carefully, as if she were afraid I would shatter like glass.

"I didn't mean to—I didn't know that you were—"

"Drink," she commanded in a surprisingly strong tone. It made me drink.

"Why aren't you drinking?" I asked.

"I might. Later. I'm sorry, Barrett. I don't know when Sasha will be back. There was a situation at the club."

I nodded absently. "I didn't come here for any reason other than friendship. I promise."

Quinn smiled, a genuine pull of her lips. It surprised me how approachable it made her look.

"I owe you an apology," she said, her smile drooping. "I behaved badly."

"I'm the one who behaved badly. I was protective, and it came across as possessive."

"No, you were just looking out for him. I respect that. I'm glad that he—"

"Can we please—"

"Start over?" we both said at the same time and then laughed.

"I'd like that," Quinn said, offering me an olive branch.

"Me too," I admitted.

We sat in silence for a moment, and then she asked, "Want to talk about it?"

"Oh, I… Yes, I do want to talk about it," I admitted. "But I don't know if I should."

As pissed as I was at Flynn, I couldn't bring myself to be disloyal to him.

"What would you do," I said hesitantly. "If the person you loved most in the world, accused you of something terrible but then didn't want to hear the truth? Didn't give you the chance to explain?"

Quinn tilted her head in thought. "Honestly?"

"Honestly."

She shrugged. "Punch them."

"Really?"

"I grew up with a brother. Sometimes a punch is what is needed—preferably to a sensitive area."

I blinked. "I like you."

Quinn and I sat in a strangely comfortable silence for a while. She got up at some point to make herself a cocktail and turn on the gas fireplace.

I wanted to call Flynn with every fiber of my being, but I held off. Something told me that we needed distance—he needed some time to sober up, and I needed some clarity. I could own my part in this disaster with Filippi. I was a great hypocrite, getting mad at Flynn for not letting me in on the Lila situation sooner, and then I'd hid Filippi from him. Not out of spite, more out of extreme forgetfulness. Plus, new disasters popped up every few minutes, and Filippi had been shoved to the back of my mind.

But there was a bigger issue. Flynn still hadn't forgiven me for Dolinsky.

Could I blame him?

"I'm sorry for intruding," I said, breaking the silence.

Quinn looked up from studying her cocktail. "Intruding? You didn't intrude."

"You sure?"

She nodded.

I paused thoughtfully. "You have questions you want to ask me. About what Sasha told you."

"I do," she agreed in her usual forthright manner.

"Go ahead."

"Really?"

"Yeah." I cocked my head to one side. "It's not going to be easy for either of us. You won't like hearing the answers, and it will be difficult for me to talk about it."

"Then maybe we shouldn't—"

"Not talking about it gives it power. Not talking about it is the same as burying it. So let's talk," I said frankly.

"Okay." She nodded. "Okay," she said again.

I could tell she was trying to get her bearings, so I gave her a minute. I finished my drink and then set the empty glass on the coffee table. Curling back up on the couch, I made myself comfortable.

"Are you in love with Sasha?" she asked.

"No."

"Were you ever in love with him?"

I paused. She held her breath while waiting for me to answer.

"No."

"But you had feelings for him."

"Yes," I admitted. "I did have some sort of feelings for him."

"But not love?"

"Not romantic love. Maybe romantic love. It's hard to sort out because I've never had to sort it out. I was in love with Flynn—*am* in love with Flynn," I added. It felt like it needed to be said. "There wasn't room to love anyone else."

"What about Dolinsky?"

It was like Quinn had punched me in the stomach. I was winded and unbalanced.

"Dolinsky... What do you know about Dolinsky?" I asked her.

She tapped the rim of her glass as she bit her lip. "I know that he was in charge before Sasha. I know that a lot of people weren't happy with the direction things were going. I know there was a coup." She took a deep breath. "I know you killed him."

"Sasha must really trust you if he told you that," I said, not at all surprised.

"He didn't tell me. I suspected."

"Oh?"

"He's told me enough. He's glossed over a lot, but I know the general ideas."

"The illegal stuff?" I guessed.

"Yeah. He told me he was responsible for Dolinsky's death. Something about his wording stuck with me. He didn't pull the trigger, but he was there when someone did. I thought about you and your relationship with Sasha. It was like a light going on. You helped him stage the coup, he helped you get back to your husband."

"Dolinsky was…terrifyingly charming," I said. Lulled by the fire and three fingers of scotch, I realized how easy it was to speak of things I would have otherwise guarded.

"Terrifyingly charming? What does that even mean?" she wondered.

"He wasn't just powerful. Flynn is powerful. Sasha is powerful. But Dolinsky… He was ruthless and evil. But not with me. With me, he was seductive. He lured me in. He had a way with words, he played the viola, and there were times that our eyes would meet and all I saw was sadness."

"Was it Stockholm syndrome?"

"Maybe. A little." I shrugged. "I didn't sympathize with him, not in the way someone who is kidnapped sympathizes with the kidnapper."

"Then what was it about him?" Quinn asked, enthralled.

"He introduced me to a world I never knew existed. His mansion was imperial Russia. Dolinsky was a modern-day czar, and he wanted to make me his queen."

I thought of the mink coat he'd given me. The mink coat I wore when I killed him. Flynn had taken that coat and burned it. And still the essence of Dolinsky remained in the ashes.

"I wasn't seduced by the money or the clothes or the jewelry. I was seduced because Dolinsky told me to embrace my own brutality. He told me never to be afraid of who I was becoming. He told me he saw me for who I was, who I could be. He thought I was as terrifying as he was, I just didn't know it yet. But he was wrong."

"He was?" Quinn asked, a note of something hopeful in her voice. I hated to disappoint her.

"He was wrong," I repeated. "Because at the height of his power, I brought him down. A woman brought him down. I took his power and killed him with it."

Chapter 27

Quinn's cell phone rang, disturbing the intimacy of the moment. She reached for the device that vibrated across the coffee table.

"Hello? Hey," she said with a glance at me. "Yeah, she's here. Hold on." She handed me her phone and then made a move to leave to give me privacy. I waved her down.

I put the phone to my ear. "Hey."

"I'm with your husband," Sasha said in way of greeting.

"You're at The Rex?"

"No, we're at *Krasnyy*."

Krasnyy was Sasha's Russian lounge.

"Who's with the kids?" I demanded.

Sasha asked the question. I heard a muffled answer, and then Sasha came back on the line. "Flynn says the nannies got back from the show."

"Fine. If that's all—"

"Barrett, what the hell is going on?" Sasha growled. "You're at my apartment, your phone is off, and Flynn is drunker than I've ever seen him. Not to mention he's miserable."

"He hasn't told you what happened?" I asked.

"No. He's sitting at my bar and broodingly staring into a glass of scotch. You need to talk to him."

"Not when he's like this."

Sasha cursed in a stream of Russian. "I'm giving you the phone. Talk to each other."

I briefly thought about hanging up, but that was a juvenile way of dealing with my hurt feelings.

"Barrett?" Flynn slurred.

"Flynn," my voice softened. "What are you doing, love?"

"Miss you." There was a smattering of static and then a mumbled, "Drive you away."

"You haven't. Put Sasha on the phone."

A moment later, Sasha came back on the line. "Yes?"

"I know this is asking a lot, but is there any way you can bring him home with you?"

"You don't want me to stick him with his driver and take him back to The Rex?" Sasha asked.

I ran a hand down my face. "I don't want our employees to see him like this."

"You both can stay in the guest room."

"You're the greatest there ever was," I said.

"Yeah, yeah, I've heard that before. Hold on, your husband is making a grab for the phone."

"I love you," Flynn yelled into my ear.

I winced. "Love you, too. I'll see you in a little while." I hung up before Flynn could further destroy my eardrum.

"Thanks." I tossed Quinn's phone to her.

"Sure."

"How much of that did you hear?" I demanded.

"Oh, you know—not a lot. There was a lot of noise."

I peered at her. "So everything."

"Yeah, everything." She shook her head and smiled ruefully. "Sasha tried to tell me, but I didn't believe him."

"What?"

"How you and Flynn are."

"What's that mean?" I demanded.

"You fight as much as you love."

"The stupid man," I said, feeling tears come to my eyes. "Will you finally tell me what your fight was about?"

"Flynn thinks I'm having an affair. I went to visit my best friend's brother who's a lawyer and Flynn assumed it was because I want a divorce."

Quinn's green eyes widened.

"Yep. This is my life."

"Why would he... How did he..."

"Another source of our problems." I briefly explained about the out-of-sight bodyguard, but didn't get into why I had one. One question would just spawn another.

Quinn shook her head in disbelief.

"I'm not, you know. Having an affair," I said to her.

"Well, of course you're not!" she insisted.

"You don't even know me."

"I know enough," she replied loftily.

"Thank you."

"You're welcome." She pointed to my empty glass. "Refill?"

I sighed. "Might as well."

The kids were fine, Jen assured me. They were asleep, and despite the fact that Iain and Noah had red streaks on their faces due to Hawk going Sharpie crazy, everyone was good.

As I hung up with the nanny, the apartment door opened. Flynn had his arm slung across Sasha's shoulders, but he drooped and would've stumbled if Sasha hadn't been there to prop him up. I rushed to Flynn's other side, and he immediately gave me some of his weight. The term "drunken lout" popped into my head.

"Jesus," I muttered. "How much did he have to drink?"

"He was already pretty drunk by the time he got to the bar," Sasha said. "My bartender cut him off after one drink. Campbell didn't like that too much."

"He's the reason your night with Quinn was ruined," I said in realization as we managed to lug Flynn into the guest room.

"Yep."

"You could've called me," I said as I maneuvered out from underneath Flynn's arm. He was still strangely silent, not having made a sound. Maybe he'd had so much scotch he was rendered momentarily silent. I turned on the bedside lamp so we didn't all tumble to the ground.

"I did call you," Sasha said. "You didn't answer your phone."

"Right. I turned it off."

We got Flynn to the bed and on his back. I took off his shoes and set them aside, but there was no way I was going to be able to undress him.

"You got this?" Sasha asked. "I can stay and help—"

"Nah, I'm good. Apologize again for me."

"I will."

"Will you guys be around tomorrow morning? There's some stuff we need to discuss."

"We'll be here."

Sasha ducked out of the room, and I was left with my snoring husband. Shaking my head, I brushed the dark locks off his forehead.

"What am I going to do with you, Flynn Campbell?" I asked. I didn't expect a reply, and I didn't get one. I tried to make him as comfortable as possible, but he was two hundred and fifty pounds of liquid scotch.

I kicked off my shoes, tried to find a spot on the bed, and fell asleep. I woke up a few hours later with Flynn's head on my chest, his arms wrapped around me. It was in that moment I realized what was going on with Flynn. What had happened with Dolinsky hadn't just happened to me—it had happened to Flynn, too. Every time I had a dream about Dolinsky, sexual or otherwise, it tore into Flynn's soul.

He accused me of having an affair because he could fight a living man. There was hope of winning me back from a living man—but not from a dead one.

Flynn sighed in his sleep and gripped me tighter. I ran my hand through his hair. The man drove me insane. But I loved him. Unconditionally. And he still didn't know it. I didn't know what else I could do to prove it to him.

I tried to extract myself from Flynn's heavy form, but he threw a leg over my body, pinning me to the bed. That wasn't going to work for my full bladder. I tried to shove him off me but that had no effect.

"Flynn," I said low in his ear, shaking him. He continued to sleep and my bladder was screaming. Drastic times. I put my fingers to his armpits and began to tickle. Just as I'd hoped, Flynn jerked and then rolled off me, trying to escape the tickling.

I jumped out of bed and ran for the bathroom connected to the guest room. When I returned, I saw two eyes tracking my movement.

"How are you feeling?" I whispered.

"I think I'm still a little drunk," came a raspy reply.

I climbed into bed and scooted closer to him. We were face to face, and even though there was only a bit of moonlight coming through the window, it was enough to see the anguish on his face.

"I want to be better. For you and for the boys." He paused. "Are you unhappy?"

"No."

"You sure?"

Despite the gravity of the situation, I smiled. "I'm sure."

"So you're not having an affair, and you don't want to divorce me?"

"Correct."

"Then who—"

I placed my fingertips to his lips. "I'll explain everything tomorrow."

He nodded, his eyes beginning to close. "I'm not good husband and father material," he murmured as he sank into the pillows.

There was no use arguing with him at the moment even though that statement couldn't be further from the truth. Flynn was loyal, protective, and he loved deeply. If that wasn't good husband and father material, then I didn't know what was.

Chapter 28

I woke up before everyone because I set an alarm. I wanted to apologize to Quinn and Sasha for ruining their night, and the best way I could see doing that was to cook breakfast. When I'd first started working for Flynn, he'd come to my prewar apartment once a week, and I'd give him a rundown of what I thought was going on in his club. I'd cook him lunch, and he'd eventually navigate away from work talk to grill me on personal business. Such simpler times, I thought wryly.

I enjoyed cooking, but there wasn't usually a need for me to do it. We had a housekeeper in Dornoch who cooked, and when I wasn't there, I was in a Rex Hotel. Room service with a push of a button.

I riffled through Sasha's massive steel refrigerator; it was a chef's dream. I pulled out eggs, bacon, and bread, and set them on the counter. I got the coffee brewing, hoping that might rouse some of the other occupants.

Sasha's living room was an open floor design with large windows. Morning rays filtered in, painting streaks of light on the wood floor. There was a spiral iron staircase that connected the three floors of the warehouse, very reminiscent of a fireman's pole. I saw a pair of long legs in yoga pants coming down the stairs and then the rest of Quinn. As she strolled across the living room to the kitchen, she covered her yawning mouth. She looked a little sleep dazed as she took a seat on one of the stools, resting her elbows on the counter.

"What's happening?" she asked.

"Cooking. You do know what cooking looks like, don't you?" I teased.

"How are you awake and coherent right now?"

I poured her a cup of coffee and set it down in front of her. "I have three children under the age of two. Enough said."

Quinn yawned again and then said, "You didn't have to make breakfast."

"I wanted to. You hungry?"

"I will be in a bit. I need a few more minutes to wake up."

"Is Sasha up yet?"

"Not officially," she said with a smile. "He kind of rolled over into my spot when I got up."

I chuckled. "I do that when Flynn gets out of bed."

"Is he okay?" she asked tentatively.

"He will be. What do you want for breakfast?" I asked, changing the subject. "Eggs? French toast?"

"French toast, please."

Just as I was setting Quinn's plate in front of her, Sasha came down the spiral staircase. He looked just as confused by what was going on in his kitchen as Quinn had been.

"Do either of you guys cook?" I wondered in amusement.

"Does boiling water count?" Quinn asked around a bite of French toast. Sasha snuck a piece of bacon off her plate and popped it into his mouth.

"Flynn's not up?" Sasha asked on his way to the coffee maker.

"Not yet."

"I'm up," came Flynn's reply. I looked to the doorway of

the guest room and took in Flynn's ashen face and tight expression.

I poured him a glass of orange juice and set it down on the counter before sliding two pieces of bread into the toaster. Flynn took a seat on the other side of Quinn, keeping his eyes downcast in embarrassment. We'd all been there—drinking too much and then being sorry for our behavior. But I'd never seen him lose control before.

"I'll grab you some painkillers," Sasha said with a teasing glint in his eye.

"Thanks," Flynn rasped.

Everyone was quiet after Sasha returned with Advil. I lightly buttered the toast and put it onto a plate for Flynn. Sasha didn't want any food, settling for coffee. I cooked myself some scrambled eggs.

"I'd like to apologize for last night," Flynn said. His eyes darted between the three of us, seeking forgiveness.

Quinn and Sasha were gracious in their acceptance of his apology. Flynn's gaze shot to mine, asking a silent question.

Instead of answering, I walked into the guest bedroom to get my shoulder bag. I returned to the kitchen, pulling out the file on Alessandro Filippi.

"I think it's time I brought everyone up to speed."

We moved to the living room and brought our cups of coffee. Quinn sat next to Sasha on the couch while I stood near Flynn who all but collapsed into a chair. And then I told them everything. From my first encounter with Filippi in Las Vegas ending with our time in Central Park when he finally explained his end game.

Quinn appeared composed as if everything I revealed didn't bother her. Her background must've prepared her for something like this. Sasha, however, was livid. Flynn might've been enraged, but at the moment, he still looked hungover.

"Someone wants to take down Flynn. Filippi says he knows who it is," I said.

"Yeah," Sasha growled. "He'll tell you, but he wants all the territory I took over after Marino died."

"So he has something to take back to the Italians and make a play for leader," I explained.

"No, I get it," Sasha voiced. "It's just bullshit."

"What happens if he doesn't get what he wants? Does he have the manpower and support to take it?" Flynn wondered. He reached for the file on the coffee table, hoping to find the answer in there.

"I don't know," I admitted. "I didn't get a chance to really read through that information." I placed a hand on Flynn's shoulder. "He threatened our children."

All traces of hangover vanished. Flynn suddenly morphed into the man I recognized. Calm, sure, lethal. "He did what?"

"Not outright, but it was blatant enough."

"I'll fucking kill him," Flynn stated.

"I'll help," Sasha added.

"Okay, before we do anything, first thing's first," I said, interrupting them before they could begin their masculine show. "We need to get the boys out of New York."

"Belfast," Flynn said. "We'll send the boys with Jen and Evie to Belfast."

"Who's in Belfast?" Quinn inquired.

"Flynn's uncle," I explained.

"And you trust him to see to your kids' safety?" she went on.

"James has ways," I said evasively, shooting Flynn a look.

When Quinn frowned, Flynn took pity on her and said, "My uncle might be a member of the IRA."

"What's his last name?" Quinn asked suddenly.

"Kilmartin," Flynn said. "James Kilmartin."

"Does he have a son named Brandon?"

"Yeah," I said in surprise. "How did you—"

"The Kilmartins are old friends of my father," Quinn said with a laugh. "Growing up, I had the biggest crush on Brandon."

I let out a surprised chuckle as did Flynn. "Small world," Flynn remarked.

"Yeah, small world," Sasha repeated with a glower.

Quinn patted his knee. "I don't have a crush on him anymore."

"That takes care of the boys," I said, feeling a smattering of relief. Though I hated the idea of sending them away, I didn't want them in New York where they could be used as pawns. I'd been through that before with Hawk. They'd be safe with James and his wife, Moira.

"Are you going to go with them?" Quinn wondered.

"No," Flynn answered before I could. "She'll stay. Filippi came to her, so I expect he won't want to deal with anyone else."

"Because he thinks she's weak," Sasha said.

"Because she's a woman?" Quinn wondered.

"Because I'm a mother," I said.

Quinn frowned. "But some of nature's fiercest animals are females protecting their young."

I grinned. "Exactly."

"The bastard won't know what's coming," Sasha said.

"They never do," I added.

Sasha finally smiled. "They never do."

"I don't know what's coming," Quinn said. "Would someone like to explain it to me?"

"I don't think we have a plan yet," I replied. "Filippi needs a tail."

"Aye," Flynn agreed. "And it can't be any of us. He'll recognize us."

"Duncan?" Sasha asked.

"Not Duncan." I addressed Flynn, "Lila is working with whoever is trying to bring you down."

"But Duncan tailing Filippi has nothing to do with Lila," Flynn said.

"So Duncan is supposed to tell his wife that he is needed back in New York to tail a mob boss trying to take you down?"

"That explanation works," Flynn said. "Are you sure you don't want Duncan around because of—"

"Not Duncan," I insisted. "Adding him into the mix will just make this explode."

Flynn and I had a stare off, but finally Flynn nodded. "Not Duncan. I'd call Ramsey, but he's kind of in the middle of his own thing."

His own thing being that he'd stolen Lord Birmingham's body so we could do our own investigation about how he'd died. That triggered what I'd seen at The Met.

"Speaking of Ramsey—I think I figured out who killed Arlington."

"Lila, Birmingham, Arlington…" Quinn stage whispered to Sasha. "Any of these names mean anything to you?"

Glancing out of the corner of my eye, I saw Sasha half nod, half shrug. A cell phone vibrated, and we all immediately checked to see if it was ours.

"Mine," Flynn said as he looked at the screen. "This is Campbell." He frowned and then began cursing up a firestorm. He hung up and gripped his cell phone so hard I was afraid he'd bend the device.

He looked at me. "It's Lila. She escaped."

Chapter 29

"Escaped? What do you mean 'escaped'?" I demanded.
"Who's Lila?" Sasha inquired.
Flynn glanced heavenward.
"You or me?" I asked Flynn.
"Take it away," Flynn offered. "Catch them up. I need to make a call." He stood and headed to the privacy of the guest bedroom. When the door shut, I looked between Quinn and Sasha.
"This is a swearing to secrecy sort of thing," I warned.
"I'm not being dramatic."
Quinn leaned forward, almost eagerly. Sasha nodded. I blew out a puff of air. "Jesus, I don't even know where to start."
"The beginning is usually a good idea," Sasha offered.
"Shut up," I said with a light tone. "Yeah, the beginning. Okay." I started with The Rex opening in Las Vegas. Quinn squirmed uncomfortably in her seat, and I knew she didn't like being reminded of her behavior. I moved quickly past all that and focused on Filippi, Duncan, and Lila. As I finished up, Flynn came out of the bedroom.

"Who did you call?" I asked him.

"James. Everything is cleared with him and Moira. I called Evie and Jen and told them to get the boys packed."

I'd taken the chair he vacated when he went to make calls. I gave it back to him, and then he effortlessly pulled me onto his lap. It was the most signifying touch we'd had all morning, and it made the tension in my heart ease. Flynn and I never had problems with physical intimacy. It was emotional intimacy that was the real beast.

"How did Lila escape?" I asked. "The guy you had with her was a professional, wasn't he?"

"Aye, a professional," Flynn said, his eyes meeting mine and then darting to other occupants of the room. "But Lila claimed she felt pain—contractions—and Angus rushed her to the hospital."

"How far along was she?" Quinn asked.

I looked to Flynn when I answered, "I don't know. Far enough along to have a baby bump."

"But I'm guessing she fabricated the contractions," Quinn said.

"It's a valid guess," Flynn said. "She slipped out and by the time Angus realized it…"

Sasha quizzed Flynn about Lila, and then Quinn joined in, throwing out her own questions. Their conversation hummed around me, but I quickly stopped listening. Not out of rudeness, but I was deep in thought, the semblance of a plan beginning to form.

"Barrett? Love," Flynn prodded.

"Sorry, what?" I asked as I adjusted my position on Flynn's lap.

"We were starting to brainstorm about how to deal with Filippi," Flynn said. He stole a hand across my back in a solicitous gesture, and I leaned into it, seeking the comfort of him and his body.

"I might have an idea," I said.

An hour later, with a plan hashed out, Flynn and I finally left. Instead of waiting for our driver to pick us up, we hailed a cab and were on our way back to The Rex. We were afforded no privacy, so we were silent. Flynn reached across the seat to grasp my hand.

There was still so much to say, but at the moment, I didn't care. There never seemed to be enough time lately. Unbuckling my seat belt, I scooted over the leather seat and tucked myself into the crook of his arm. He turned his head, brushing his lips against my hair, murmuring something in Gaelic.

I closed my eyes and breathed him in. We were both exhausted—and Flynn was still hungover. Though I hadn't poured the scotch down his throat, I felt responsible. When had Flynn and I stopped talking to one another, really talking to one another? We'd promised that our family would always come first, but maybe it was time to put our marriage first. Without a solid marriage, how could we ever hope to last?

We had started keeping secrets again. Maybe because the truth of Dolinsky had almost broken us. I didn't know why I'd hadn't told him about Filippi right away, but Flynn and I had always been a team. The moment we stopped being a team, we stopped being us.

"Actually, can you drop us at The Met?" I said to the cabbie while I was still nestled in Flynn's side.

The cabbie acted like he hadn't heard me, but even if he dropped us at The Rex, we could walk to The Met.

"I want to show you something," I said to Flynn. And maybe we'd get a few minutes alone to talk just the two of us.

The cab dropped us off in front of The Met, and as we climbed the steps, Flynn reached for my hand again. We were both tired and disheveled, Flynn in a wrinkled suit and my hair in need of a wash. We were far from the impeccable personas we portrayed when we were out in public, but it felt strangely liberating.

After we paid, I dragged Flynn toward the tapestry exhibit. We found the tapestry that had the falcon with outstretched wings. Seeing it again, knowing I'd put the pieces together, made me shiver.

"The white ink tattoos are exact replicas," Flynn said in stupefied amazement.

I nodded. "Yeah."

"I want to speak to the curator in charge of this exhibit."

"Pump them for information?"

"Or find a thread that leads us to who hired The White Company." His tone was bitter when he spoke of the Italian mercenaries who'd killed Malcolm and almost killed Duncan.

Despite the anger in the air, I chuckled. Flynn looked at me in confusion. "What?" he asked.

"You said 'thread' and we're in a tapestry exhibit." My chuckle turned into a laugh. I was wound so tightly. It was either laugh or cry.

Flynn's forehead smoothed out and he smiled. "It's good to hear you laugh, love." His grin faded. "We haven't done enough of that lately, have we?"

"No, we haven't," I agreed, getting myself under control.

He raked a hand through his messy hair, frustration evident. "There's so much I want to say to you and—"

"We don't have the time."

"Maybe we should make the time. Maybe that's been our problem all along." Taking my hand, he raised it to his lips. As his mouth left my knuckles, I unlatched my finger and skimmed it down his rough, whiskered cheek.

"I love you," I murmured. "I'm sorry if I ever made you doubt that."

"He owns a part of you I'll never have. Dolinsky," he clarified. "I'm jealous because I want all of you. And it's my fault you were with Dolinsky. It's my fault he has a part of you."

"He's dead, Flynn."

"And he's still hurting me. Bastard got what he wanted." He laughed bitterly. "He wanted to wreck me."

Even though we were in public, some things couldn't wait for privacy. So, I stepped close to him, placed my hands on his chest, and looked up at him.

"Who pulled the trigger?" I asked quietly.

Flynn's jaw softened. "You."

"Why?"

"For me."

I shook my head. "For *us*. Always for us. Whatever you doubt, whatever you think you see, whatever you think you know, remember that. Everything I do, I do for us."

"I never needed reassurance. Before you," he admitted, his face thoughtful.

"We need to get moving," I said gently. I would breathe easier and focus once I knew the kids were safe with James and Moira.

"When are you meeting Archer?" Flynn asked as we moved toward the exit.

"Not until eight," I said.

"It's fortuitous that he's in New York."

"Yeah. I'm glad I don't have to trek to DC."

"What are you going to offer him?"

"Nothing. Not yet."

Flynn arched a dark eyebrow. "Nothing?"

"I'm going to ask for what we need, tell him to trust me and that I'd make it worth it, but yeah, I'm not offering him anything."

"You think it's wise to have dinner with him at *Krasnyy*?"

"Filippi is having me watched. I can't have my relationship with Archer out in the open. Meeting with my FBI contact in a low-lit, sexy Russian lounge is a better idea than having him come to The Rex. Besides, if I can convince Filippi that I'm cheating on you with different men, that might work to our advantage."

"I don't like this," Flynn growled.

I rolled my eyes at him. "What else is new?"

Chapter 30

After we left The Met, we went back to the hotel, showered quickly, and then spent a few hours with the boys. Noah and Iain were still streaked with red due to Hawk's drawing skills, but no worse for wear. Hawk couldn't sit still, and I briefly sent up a silent prayer that he wouldn't somehow drive off Jen and Evie.

Now, I sat in the car on the tarmac as I watched our private plane depart with my babies on board. It wasn't just separation anxiety that had me upset. My heart squeezed in pain, threatening to choke me.

"Come here, hen," Flynn said, putting his arm around my shoulders and tugging me into him. I pressed my face to his chest and let out a shuddering breath. He held me tight against him while I let the tears fall. I wasn't usually a crier. But at that moment, I felt like a terrible mother, and the only way to deal with it was to let it out and soak the front of Flynn's shirt.

Flynn pressed a button, and the window separating us from the driver rolled down. "The Rex, please," Flynn said and then pressed the button again so we could have privacy. The car roared to life, and we began our drive back.

"Don't do this to yourself." Flynn's fingers grasped my neck. They were warm and strong, a solid comfort. "Don't feel guilty for doing what's best for them—for keeping them safe."

"Even if that means I'm not there with them?" I asked with a sigh.

"You're needed here, too," he said, his hand squeezing the back of my neck. "I need you." He turned my face to his and placed his mouth on mine. His tongue swept inside, carrying me away on a current of desire. All thoughts of my children and heartache were shoved to the back of my mind as Flynn's hands moved down my body, urging me onto his lap. I straddled him, cradling his angular jaw in my hands while looking into his eyes.

"It's nice to hear," I murmured.

"Don't I say it enough?" he growled. "If I don't, I'm an arse."

I smiled. "I need you, too."

The intensity of his gaze softened into tenderness. "Sometimes I think you don't."

I reached between us, palming the hardness of his erection.

He grinned. "Well, I know you'll *always* need that."

"You're good for more," I assured, climbing off him.

"Wait, where are you going?" he demanded, trying to haul me back onto him.

"I'm not dressed for a quick romp in the car," I said, looking at my jeans. I vowed to wear skirts for times like these.

"I want you," he said huskily. "Now."

I reached over and dragged the zipper of his fly down. Reaching into his trousers, I freed his erection. He was hard and ready.

"How much time before we're back at The Rex?" I asked Flynn.

"About ten minutes," he said.

I leaned over, squeezing his shaft. "Then I better be quick."

I stared into the bathroom mirror and swiped my eyelashes with another coat of mascara before closing the tube and setting it aside. My auburn hair was styled in big waves, diamond studs in my ears peeking out from the tresses. I looked ready for a night of clubbing—the dress I'd squeezed into was red but didn't clash with my hair. Though it was tight, the hemline was modest, hitting just an inch above the knee and the heart-shaped neckline showed off just a hint of creamy skin.

"You're wearing that to dinner with Don Archer?" Flynn asked in shock. He stood in the doorway, his gaze sweeping down my body.

"You know the kind of place we're going to. I can't wear jeans."

He came in and stood behind me. I gazed at our reflections in the mirror, watching his eyes heat. Apparently, the attention I'd given him in the Rolls had only inflamed his desire, but from the moment we'd returned to The Rex, we'd had to deal with other issues.

Ramsey had called to tell us that he'd anonymously returned Birmingham's body to a hospital, unable to glean how he'd died. We spent an hour discussing what I'd discovered at The Met and Ramsey's new focus was on The White Company. After hanging up with Ramsey, Flynn had called The Met, demanding an appointment with the curator of the tapestry exhibit. His request was taken seriously after promising a sizable donation.

Flynn settled his hands low on my hips and pressed himself against me. "We haven't finished what we started."

"That won't get finished until after I get home tonight," I said as I attempted to move away from him.

His hands tightened at my waist, preventing me from leaving. "Agreed. Doesn't mean I can't give you something to think about while you're at dinner."

Turning me around, he pinned me between his body and the bathroom counter. His hands glided up and down my arms, sending goosebumps dancing across my skin.

"Flynn," I began. "I'm going to be late."

"You had no problem operating on a short time frame earlier today," he said, reminding me of what I'd done to him in the Rolls.

"That was different," I protested.

"You're wasting time talking." He nipped at my lips before hoisting me up on the bathroom counter. Hiking up my dress, he tugged off my scrap of lace I called underwear.

"Spread your legs," he commanded.

I shivered with need, loving how he was looking at me. I obeyed.

Flynn's hands grasped my butt to yank me forward, so that I was sitting on the edge of the counter. He slid to his knees nuzzled my inner thighs, inching closer to my wet heat.

He inhaled deeply, closing his eyes, savoring me. I began to tremble even before his tongue snaked out to graze my skin.

I moaned in pleasure as he lingered and teased, his hands tight at my hips.

"You bastard," I growled. "You promised me fast."

He lifted his head, his eyes gleaming. "It will be. Now be quiet and let me love you."

My hand dropped back, and I pressed it to the counter to hold myself steady. He went back to lapping at me like a cat with a bowl of cream. Heat simmered low in my belly and spread, tiny sparks ready to burst into flame.

"No," I groaned when Flynn stopped.

"Trust me," he rasped. He stood, undid his belt and dropped his pants including his boxer briefs. He caressed his hard length a few times before guiding himself into my welcoming body.

I shuddered, gripped him tightly, and pressed forward so that he sheathed himself fully.

Withdrawing just a bit, he then slammed himself home. I was so primed it only took a few strokes before I was coming, clamping down hard on him.

"Again!"

"Bossy," he said with a grunt but gave it to me fully. Clasping his behind in my hands, I yanked him hard and fast, rubbing myself furiously against him, mindless of any pleasure except my own. I came again, my head lolling back as I rode out the storm of my release. After a few more thrusts, Flynn climaxed. His hold on me tightened and then went slack.

Our breathing was simultaneously harsh. When Flynn tried to move, I wrapped my legs around him, wanting him close for just another moment. He chuckled, the sound low and inviting.

I never wanted to leave this moment. I never wanted to leave him.

Chapter 31

Krasnyy was located in the heart of Soho. The name of the lounge was written in red on the exterior of the building. But otherwise there was no signage. You had to know what to look for if you wanted to find it.

The dim lighting from the sconces was warm and sensual. Cream plush couches filled the inviting room. The walls and arches of the doorways were made of Mediterranean white stone, giving the lounge a catacomb feel without it being sinister.

Sasha and Quinn sat at the bar, leaning toward each other while holding drinks. I strolled toward them, hating that I was interrupting their camaraderie. They each hugged me in greeting, and Sasha gestured to the bartender for another drink.

"Archer isn't here yet?" I asked.

"Not yet," Sasha confirmed.

Keeping the smile on my face, I placed my drink in front of my mouth when I asked, "Anything out of the ordinary?"

"Man alone in the corner," Quinn said with a bright smile on her face.

I surveyed the room, pretending to check out the crowd. My eyes purposefully skimmed over and dismissed him, but I got the general idea. Dark-haired, dark eyes, solitary.

"So he's now watching both of us," I said to Sasha. "Excellent."

Don Archer finally walked into the lounge. He was a distinguished man, still robust despite the fact that he spent most of his time behind a desk instead of in the field. His dark hair was liberally gray, and his face was prematurely lined from all the stress his job piled on him.

Stepping away from Sasha and Quinn, I headed for Archer who was examining the room. When he saw me, he smiled in recognition. After we exchanged polite greetings, I led him to a booth in the corner. He took the side of the booth facing the exit as I knew he would. I would've chosen the same seat—I hated having my back to Filippi's man.

"Interesting choice of meeting place," Archer said, gesturing to the decor.

"My friend owns the place," I explained. "You hungry?"

"I could eat."

I looked away from Archer and caught Sasha's eye and nodded. I turned my attention back to Archer.

We didn't discuss personal details. I had no idea if Archer was married or had kids. I didn't care. Just like he didn't care that I had children. We were engaged in a mutually beneficial relationship that was based on the exchange of information and favors. His colleagues didn't know about our association, but it was well known in his circle that you dealt with the lesser of two evils. Or in this case, the lesser of two criminals. Archer didn't approve of the SINS. But he knew we were good for our word. We'd stopped bringing illegal arms into the country, which had been a big win for Archer and those he reported to. Archer would rather continue our friendship than risk working with someone else.

Though we preferred to communicate by private email,

mostly about illegal tipoffs I gave him, what I needed from him now could only be handled in person.

"It's been a while since we've met like this," Archer said.

"It has," I agreed.

A cocktail server brought over a bottle of champagne, presented it to me, and then opened it. As she poured out two flutes of bubbly, the caviar arrived. Two servings were placed on the table, the champagne went into an ice bucket, and then the staff retreated.

"You're going all out," Archer said in amusement. "You must want something really bad."

"The caviar is going to do all the asking," I quipped. I took one of the shells that had a dollop of caviar in the center and scooped the black roe with a mother-of-pearl spoon.

"That was amazing," Archer said, setting aside his empty shell and reaching for his glass of champagne.

"The Russians know their caviar."

"And the French know their champagne," he added, taking a sip. "So, should we get to it?"

I nodded. "I need a hacker."

He blinked. "I like how you don't mince words, Barrett. Why do you need a hacker?"

I held his gaze. "I can't tell you."

"I knew the caviar was an expensive ploy. Is it SINS business?"

I shook my head. "It's personal business. Family."

"Barrett—"

"I need help," I said quietly. "And I know it's a lot to ask of you, but if you help me with this, I promise you it will be worth it."

Archer's eyes gleamed in interest. "Go on."

"I can't tell you any more. You either trust my word or you don't." I leaned forward ever so slightly. "So? Will you help me?"

At the end of a two-hour meal, sated on Russian delicacies and lulled by French champagne, Don Archer finally agreed to help. The next morning at eleven a.m. I stood at the clock in the main terminal of Grand Central Station.

My phone rang, and I answered it. "No, I don't have him yet," I said automatically.

"Have who?" came Ash's voice.

Fuck. I'd been dodging her calls. "Uh, Flynn hired a new employee, and I'm picking him up at Grand Central." Not an outright lie, but still a lie.

"How's it back in Dornoch?" I asked, quickly changing the subject.

"Things are good," she said. "The gallery is busy, and Carys is a crazy fast crawler now. She's gotten really good at getting away from me."

I let out a laugh. "Yeah, I know how that is. How's Duncan?" I forced myself to ask.

"He went to visit Ramsey in London yesterday, so I've got the house to myself."

"Nice," I choked out.

"You okay?" she asked. "You sound funny."

"Yeah, no, I'm good. Just distracted. Can I give you a buzz later?"

"Sure. Give the boys a kiss for me."

"I will."

I hung up, pushing down the wave of guilt. I focused on the busy terminal, my eyes scanning for a man who could be a hacker. My gaze seemed to land on every pale, skinny guy who passed by. It might've been a preconceived cliché, but I couldn't help it. Archer had only given me a name and the time of his train arrival. Dex Hollingsworth was supposed to find me.

"Barrett Campbell?" I turned. And blinked. The man standing in front of me wasn't pale or skinny. He grinned, cute dimples flashing in his cheeks, his dirty blond hair peeking out from a Red Sox cap. And he was hot.

"Dex Hollingsworth?"

"That's me," he said, holding out his hand.

I shook his hand. "You're not what I expected."

He chuckled. "Let me guess. Pale, skinny, and dorky?"

"With glasses," I added.

"I wear contacts." He adjusted the backpack on his shoulders and reached down to grab his duffel bag. "Where are we headed?"

"This way," I said, leading him toward the exit where my driver was waiting. "How was the train from DC?"

"Fine," he said with an amused smile.

"How did you come to work for Archer?" I inquired, pushing the door open and holding it for Dex.

He chuckled. "He didn't give me much of a choice."

After we were on our way toward The Rex, and the partition was closed, I asked Dex, "So you hacked into the FBI database, found stuff you shouldn't have, and Archer recruited you to use your powers for good instead of evil?"

Dex stretched out his long legs and lifted the brim of his hat. "Pretty much. So Archer was pretty vague on what I'd be doing."

"Ah, yeah, that's because he doesn't know. I didn't tell him."

"You asked for a hacker, didn't tell him what it was for, and he just came through for you? That's some real clout."

"Yeah," I said because it was true. I wasn't about to tell Dex the intricacies of my relationship with Archer. Dex didn't really look like he cared; he was getting paid a small fortune.

"Archer said you're the best and you're discreet."

"I am and I am," Dex promised with an arrogant grin.

"You were a jock in high school, weren't you?" I asked, smiling ruefully as I took him all in. The body, the hat, the cockiness. I was going to have a good laugh when Flynn and Dex met.

Dex nodded. "How did you guess?"

Chapter 32

We got back to The Rex, and I took Dex to the hotel room he'd be staying in. He whistled, setting down his backpack and dropping his duffel on the queen-sized bed.

"Nice digs," he said.

"Glad you think so. Feel free to order whatever you want from room service and the minibar."

"Thanks."

I went to the desk and set down the two files. "Everything you need to start with is in these files. Alessandro Filippi and Lila St. James."

"What is it you want me to find?" he asked, reaching for the files, curiosity and eagerness on his face.

"I don't know," I said. "Anything that looks suspicious or links them. Lila St. James has disappeared from Las Vegas. I was hoping you could find out where she went."

"Who are these people?" Dex asked.

I paused, closing my mouth.

"I'm going to find out. You know that, right? It might be easier if you gave me a brief rundown."

"Brief, yeah, not the word I was going to use, but okay." I sighed and then presented a clinical explanation of Lila and

Filippi. To Dex's credit, he didn't bat an eye. He seemed more in shock over the luxury of his hotel suite than anything else.

"I'll find something," he vowed.

"What if there's nothing to find?"

"There's always something to find. You just have to know how and where to dig. Trust me, I've got a good shovel," he teased.

I let out a relieved breath. I believed him. After giving him my cell phone number and Flynn's, I left, wanting him to work his magic as soon as possible.

The penthouse suite was quiet; Flynn had gone to meet with the curator who'd been in charge of the tapestry exhibit at The Met. We were supposed to go together, but the curator only had a brief block of open time before she was heading out of the country. Flynn and I had compromised—he would talk with her and glean any information he could about The White Company, and I would pick up Dex from Grand Central.

I was contemplating calling Moira so I could check in on the boys when the elevator doors opened, and Flynn strode in. Energy radiated off him, the scowl on his face intense.

"What?" I demanded. "What the hell happened now?"

"You ever feel like we're just being reactive?" he wondered, some of his scowl diminishing.

"It's hard to be proactive when we don't have all the information," I pointed out.

"Lord Chatsworth, dead, white ink tattoo. I got the call from Ramsey as I was coming out of The Met. Family is saying it was a heart attack."

"Fuckedy, fuck, fuck," I said.

"My sentiments exactly," Flynn said bleakly.

"The White Company strikes again. What the hell are we going to do about this? This is no longer random, right?"

"Not random," he agreed. "But we still don't have the connection."

"We can't keep waiting for answers, Flynn. Too many fires. Not enough extinguishers."

His blue eyes gleamed. "The curator was very helpful."

"She was?"

"Aye. She told me who loaned the tapestry for the exhibit."

"Well?" I demanded. "Who?"

"Giovanni Marino, Jr."

My eyes widened. "You mean—"

"Aye. Alessandro Filippi is trying to take out his own brother."

"And if we told Marino that—as a show of good faith—maybe he'll tell us how to deal with The White Company?"

"That was my thought."

My cell phone rang, momentarily cutting off our conversation. It was Dex.

"Come on," I said after I hung up. I grabbed Flynn's hand and tugged him toward the elevator. "Dex found something."

"Already?" Flynn asked. "That's impressive."

"Just hold onto that feeling," I told him.

He frowned. "Why?"

Dex opened the door to his suite, and I watched Flynn measure him up. And down. Dex still wore his Red Sox baseball hat, but it was on backwards. He'd taken off his shoes and had obviously made himself comfortable.

"Hey, you must be Barrett's husband. Dex Hollingsworth, nice to meet you." He held out his hand to Flynn. Flynn took it and shook it slowly.

"Nice to meet you," Flynn said gruffly.

Dex cocked his head to one side. "You're Scottish, yeah?"

"Aye," Flynn said.

"Cool. I studied for a semester at St. Andrews. I loved it."

Just like that, Flynn's countenance softened. Nothing

melted my Scotsman's heart faster than when he found others who loved his country.

We stepped into the suite and closed the door.

"Lila is in New York," Dex said. "I found the flight log with her as a passenger. Four days ago, she got onto a plane in L.A. and flew to New York."

"L.A.? She was in Vegas," I said.

"She rented a car."

"Under her own name?" Flynn asked.

"No. Under Alessandro Filippi."

"So now we have confirmation that Lila and Filippi are working together," I said.

"Aye," Flynn said. "But something still doesn't add up. Filippi told you he wasn't after me. Which means—"

"There's a third party involved. Hidden."

Dex waited until Flynn and I were finished before saying, "When Lila got to New York, she went underground. She's lying low, but she's still in the city."

"Can you put her on the 'no fly' list?" I asked.

"Already did it," he assured me. "If she tries to fly somewhere else, I'll know about it. I'm going to do some digging on Alessandro Filippi. Maybe she's tucked away in his apartment."

"That would be too easy," Flynn replied. "But sure, let's hope for it, anyway."

We left Dex and headed back to the privacy of our suite. I collapsed onto the couch, yearning for a drink despite the fact that the sun hadn't even set yet.

"We're on borrowed time," I said quietly.

"What can Filippi do?" Flynn wondered, sitting next to me and stealing a hand across my back. "Realistically? The only leverage he has is the knowledge that someone wants to take me out."

I snorted. "So what else is new, right?"

Flynn chuckled, pulling me into his side. "The boys are safe. You're here with me. We'll figure out the rest."

"We're being watched," I told him. "Filippi had a guy at Sasha's lounge when I met with Archer."

"Aren't you sick of being reactive?"

"You know I am."

"We are Campbells," he said softly, though his tone was steel.

"And what does that mean, Flynn?" I asked.

"We're fighters."

"Don't you get tired of fighting?"

"Fight or die, love. When you have something someone else wants, there's always a chance they'll try to take it from you. The trick is not to let them."

I snuggled into his chest and closed my eyes. His fingers scratched the back of my head as he continued to speak, his brogue another comforting caress. "It's all right if you're tired. I can fight for the both of us."

"Do you know what I love most about you," I whispered.

"What's that, hen?"

I lifted my head so I could stare into his cobalt blue eyes. Reaching out, I stroked my hand across his stubbly jaw. He'd started to grow his beard again.

"I love that you find your way back to me. You somehow always find a way to work things out."

He smiled thoughtfully. "You're home. I need you to know that. I know I don't say it enough, or prove it enough—"

"You do," I assured him. "I know I'm loved. I know you love me."

"It's not enough," he said. "I hate that my jealousy and insecurities can sometimes get the best of me. I hate that about myself."

"Don't," I said. "Don't hate anything about yourself. Even when I'm spitting mad at you, I never ever think about leaving. I take you, Flynn Campbell, flaws and all."

He smiled just before placing his lips on mine. "Thank you," he whispered. "For always choosing me—even when I'm at my worst."

"I choose your worst over anyone else's best."

Flynn stood up and held out his hand to me. I placed my palm in his, and then he swept me up into his arms, carrying me toward the bedroom.

Life could go to hell in a moment. It usually did. I wasn't going to tell Flynn we didn't have time.

Flynn placed me in the center of the bed and then lowered himself on top of me. We stared at each other, our hands beginning to roam.

"I love you," he said.

I grinned wickedly. "Prove it."

Chapter 33

"Demure or sexy?" I asked Flynn as I stood in the closet, riffling through my clothes.

Flynn loomed in the doorway of the walk-in, his gaze sliding up and down my body. "If you wear that, you'll be sexy."

I was currently wearing nothing but a pair of lace panties and heels. "Not helpful," I said.

"Demurely sexy," he suggested.

"Are you sure I have to go to this thing with you? I wasn't a fan of the guy's father. I doubt I'll like him much. And I'm going to have to keep my mouth shut."

"Such a hardship, I know," Flynn teased. He was already dressed in an impeccable three-piece gray suit. "Marino is bringing his wife, so you have to be there."

Dinner with the leader of the Italian mafia in New York. Just another day, I thought snidely. Though Flynn and I had spent the afternoon in bed together, I wasn't lulled into a state of acceptance.

"You know how these things go," Flynn went on.

"Aye," I quipped, pulling out a long-sleeved black dress with a modest neckline. The dress was tight, but there was no skin on display. It was the kind of dress that allowed for earrings but no other jewelry.

"Very nice," he said, though with Flynn's brogue it sounded like 'verra nice.'

"Thank you. I was thinking of wearing the sapphires you bought me for my birthday last year."

He nodded. "I'll get them out of the vault."

I headed to the bathroom to finish getting ready. I pulled my auburn tresses back into a low bun and pinned it. I slicked my lips with red lipstick and added some mascara to my lashes. Flynn returned and handed me my earrings.

"Ready?" I asked with a labored sigh, turning away from the mirror.

"You're beautiful."

I smiled. "Thank you."

Grabbing my clutch on our way out, I straightened my spine, resolving that I could play the role of chattel for the evening.

"So, where is this Italian family-run restaurant we're going to?" I wondered after we'd gotten into the Rolls. "Staten Island?"

Flynn laughed. "Get it all out now, love."

"I'm done," I assured him.

He took my hand and brought it to his lips. "We're going to Mulberry and Broome."

"Mulberry and Broome," I repeated. My eyes slid to his. "We're going to Little Italy? There aren't any good restaurants left in Little Italy!"

"Woman, your snobbery is going to be the death of me."

"I'm not eating chicken parm," I stated.

Twenty minutes later, the car pulled to a stop outside of a restaurant. The outdoor cafe was bustling with customers, and I saw waiters, middle-aged and older men, catering to them.

Flynn exited first and then helped me out of the car. He put his hand to my waist, and we strode toward the entrance.

The hostess at the front of the restaurant told us there was a wait until Flynn gave his name.

She smiled in understanding. "Of course, Mr. Campbell. Please follow me."

The restaurant was just as busy inside as it was in the café. We passed the kitchen which I had to admit was emitting some delicious aromas. Someone, probably the chef, yelled in Italian. The hostess led us to the back where we were showed to a private room with a booth. I knew instinctively this was where Giovanni Marino, Jr. held private council.

"I'll tell Mr. Marino you're here," the hostess said. She closed the door and Flynn and I were alone. Marino wanted us to have to wait for him. This was a machination meant to put us in our place.

I fit myself into Flynn's side, reached up to angle his head down so I could whisper in his ear. "Camera."

Flynn angled his head and nipped at my ear. "I saw."

If anyone looked at the camera feed, all they'd see were two people who looked like they were about to have sex in a booth. Flynn pulled back but kept his arm around me while we continued to wait for Marino to make his appearance.

He made us wait twenty minutes.

The door opened and Giovanni Marino, Jr. sauntered in. Whereas Filippi had the stamp of his Sicilian genes, Marino resembled his late father completely. Bulbous nose and fair coloring.

"Campbell," he stated, holding out his hand. "Sorry to keep you waiting."

A lazy grin appeared on Flynn's face as he clasped the other man's hand. "You should be. I'm starving!"

Marino's laughter was booming, and then he turned his attention to me, his gaze turning appreciative. "A pleasure to meet you, Mrs. Campbell."

"Barrett," I corrected as his mouth grazed my knuckles.

"Barrett," he repeated, his hand dropping mine.

"Is your wife joining us?" Flynn asked.

"Ysabel is at home with our daughter. Gisella got the flu," he explained.

I didn't know if it was a lie or not, but I took the comment seriously. "I'm sorry to hear that. I was looking forward to meeting your wife."

"Another time," Marino promised.

"Perhaps I should leave you two men to discuss the situation," I said, attempting not to sound like I wanted to bow out. I looked at Flynn and widened my eyes, trying to appear doelike and demure. It nearly killed me to do it.

It was Marino who replied, "Yes, that might be best."

He might as well have patted me on the head and dismissed me like a child. I smiled and feigned that I didn't want to run him through with a fork.

With one look at Flynn, I nodded and then headed out of the door, closing it softly behind me. Half of me was grateful that I had a reprieve, the other part of me was angry that I didn't get to sit in and listen to the "big, bad men" talk.

The Rolls was still parked outside the front of the restaurant. The driver nimbly hopped out of the front seat and came around to open the door for me. "You're back sooner than I expected."

"Change of plans," I explained easily. I climbed into the car, wondering what I was going to do to pass the time until Flynn was done.

"Home?" the driver asked once he was back in the front seat.

"I guess." The car started. "Wait, no. Take me to *Krasnyy*, please."

I didn't want to go back to The Rex to sit and wait for news. I'd have a cocktail and eat some dinner. I sent Sasha a text asking if he was around, and then I thought to text Quinn. She answered that she was already there with her best friend, and just like that I had the promise of a girls' night out.

Krasnyy wasn't yet busy. It was a lounge that catered to the late-night crowd, and I knew in a few hours, it would be packed with people. I found Quinn sitting at the bar, looking regal and completely done up. Her black hair cascaded down her back, and she wore a strapless black dress that highlighted her creamy Irish skin. A woman sat next to her, and though she was also dressed to go out, she looked more girl next door than vamp.

"Barrett!" Quinn greeted, throwing an arm around my shoulder. "Meet my best friend from Boston. Shannon, Barrett, Barrett, Shannon."

"Nice to meet you," the blonde said with a genuine smile.

"Glad to meet you," I said.

"Let's get a table," Quinn suggested.

"You guys go ahead. I'll grab a drink and then meet you over there."

After I got my vodka gimlet, I headed toward the back of the lounge and found Quinn and Shannon at the corner booth. I slid in next to Quinn and set my drink down.

"Where's Sasha?" I asked. "Or did you ban him from hanging out with you guys?"

"He had other plans tonight," Quinn said. "Don't know what, didn't ask."

Yeah, I knew how that went. I turned to Shannon. "You're visiting from Boston?"

She smiled and shook her head, her sleek blond ponytail swinging. "No. I moved to New York about six months ago."

"Oh," I said in confusion. "But Quinn said Boston, so I assumed—"

"We grew up together," Quinn jumped in to explain. "Shannon and I have known each other since we were five."

Conversation began to flow. I could tell they'd already been here for a few cocktails because Quinn was looser than I'd ever seen her. She smiled easily and her laugh was genuine. I knew what it was like to have a friend who you had real history with. I felt a pang of guilt when I thought of Ash.

"Where's Flynn tonight?" Quinn asked when Shannon was in the bathroom.

I knew Flynn and Sasha had spoken of the dinner Flynn was having with Marino, but I didn't know if Sasha had told Quinn.

"Business dinner," I said.

"I know about Marino."

I let out a breath of air. "Good. Marino's wife stayed home at the last moment, so I bowed out."

"Probably better," she said. "The last thing you'd want is to be sitting there while men discussed women like horses or whores."

"It's like you know me," I teased. I glanced at my phone that was resting in my lap. It had been silent. No texts or calls from Flynn, so I knew he was still with Marino. I was getting antsy.

"I'm back," Shannon said. "What did I miss?"

"A guy at the bar staring at Barrett," Quinn quipped.

"What?" I asked distractedly.

"Never mind," Quinn said with a laugh.

My phone buzzed, but it wasn't Flynn. It was Brad Shapiro, head of security at The Rex. A sense of dread turned my stomach. Brad never called me.

The lounge had grown busier and louder, and I knew I wouldn't be able to hear a thing. "Excuse me, guys, I need to take this."

Phone and clutch in my hands, I scooted out of the booth and headed for the exit, answering the call. "Hold on, Brad."

Once I was outside, I went around the corner away from the lounge, tucking myself between a wall and a metal fire escape.

"Hey," I said, my heart beginning to pound. "Can you hear me?"

"Yeah," Brad said. "I tried calling Flynn but his phone is off. You need to get back to The Rex."

"Why?"

"Lila St. James."

The name whipped through my ears, and my vision narrowed in rage. "She's there?"

"She's here," Brad said, his tone bleak. "And she's dead."

Chapter 34

Five days ago, Lila St. James was found dead in a Rex Hotel suite.

Four days ago, the news that Flynn's pregnant mistress was found dead hit the tabloids.

Three days ago, Duncan had come clean to Ash, telling her it was his baby Lila carried.

Two days ago, Ash stopped taking my calls.

Yesterday, Duncan showed up in New York, looking distraught, lost, and miserable.

Today.

Today, Flynn was arrested for the murder of Lila St. James. I watched as the cops cuffed him. The paparazzi that had been camped out on the sidewalk just outside The Rex Hotel ever since the news of Lila's death broke flashed their cameras. I blocked them out. I blocked everything out except for Flynn's blue gaze that never left mine.

He mouthed something at me before ducking his head to be put into the squad car.

"What did he say?" I asked Duncan who stood at my side.

"'*Tha gràdh agam ort,*'" Duncan said. "'I love you. Gaelic."

"We should go back inside," I said.

"Probably," he agreed. We turned back to find sanctuary in The Rex, but not before I faced the paparazzi. I didn't say a word, but my smile was wide and a touch devilish. The cameras snapped like crazy, and hopefully that would confuse the hell out of the media for the time being.

Before Duncan and I even made it to the private elevator, I had my cell phone out and I was calling Allen Masterson. He was one of the best criminal defense lawyers in the country. He was good at intimidation and had worked his magic when Fred Winters had detained me.

I snorted in ironic, black humor. By all accounts, I should've gone down for Dolinsky's death. I *had* killed him. It had been the truth. And now, Flynn might go down for a murder he didn't commit.

The elevator doors opened into the penthouse suite as I hung up with Masterson. There was nothing more I could do at the moment. I had Dex Hollingsworth hacking into the NYPD database for the autopsy report.

"Does Flynn have an alibi for the night Lila died?" Duncan asked me, taking a seat in a chair.

I curled up onto the couch, exhaustion and adrenaline warring within me. "Yes."

That night, Flynn had been with me for a few hours, but I'd left him with Marino. When Flynn returned to The Rex at dawn the next day, he'd come in the back way, his white dress shirt splattered with blood. I hadn't asked questions, but Flynn had told me that they'd found Filippi. I didn't know if Filippi was dead or alive, but knowing Flynn, knowing his protective streak, he would want Filippi dead—even if that meant never finding out who wanted to take down his empire.

Flynn would find a way. We always found a way.

"I'm going to have to release a statement to the press," I said, putting a hand to my head.

"Is that a good idea?" Duncan asked.

I glared at him. "You want to talk to me about good ideas?"

"Barrett—"

"My best friend isn't talking to me. And I don't even blame her!" I snapped, my emotions finally spiraling out of control. I'd tried to keep them locked up, but it was too much. There was nowhere for them to go except *out*.

Duncan's face was bleak, but he didn't even try to deflect my anger or the insults I hurled at him. Ash wasn't speaking to me; she wasn't even in a place where she could hear my sincerest apology about keeping Duncan's infidelity from her. I'd left countless messages, telling her that when she was ready, I'd be here. Even if that meant she yelled and screamed and called me bad words. She was Ash and I was Barrett, and we'd get through this.

I hoped.

"I'm sorry," Duncan said, his voice low and raspy.

"Is she still in Dornoch?" I asked.

"No. She took Carys and went to Switzerland. Apparently, her parents have a house there."

Not so much a house as a ski lodge. Ash had taken me there one winter break in college. That sweet memory was a painful reminder that I might have destroyed a long-time friendship.

"Will she come back?" Duncan asked.

"I don't know," I said truthfully. "The people closest to her lied to her, kept her in the dark. Would you forgive that?"

Duncan didn't answer. He didn't have to.

My cell phone rang, and my heart leapt with hope that it was Allen Masterson and there was news about Flynn. But it wasn't him; it was Dex.

"Hey," I said into the phone.

"Hey, can you come down to my room? I think I found something."

"Be right there," I said, hanging up. I looked at Duncan. "Dex has some info."

Duncan shot up from his chair, and we left the suite. Dex was staying a few floors below, and when we got to his door, I knocked. When he didn't answer right away, I knocked again and called out his name. He finally answered, eyes bloodshot. There was a palpable nervous energy about him.

As Duncan and I stepped into the room, I noticed the two dozen or so empty Red Bull cans. "Please tell me you've slept."

He shook his head, the ends of his blond hair looking electrified. "I never sleep when I'm on a job. I'll stay awake and then crash later." Dex's eyes darted to Duncan.

"Right," I said. "Sorry. Duncan, Dex, Dex, Duncan."

"You're the baby daddy," Dex said, causing Duncan to wince.

Though Duncan was reeling from Ash walking out on him, I could only imagine how he felt about the death of his unborn child. Though he'd had no real relationship with the mother, it still must've been devastating. A child was a child, right?

"I've got Lila's autopsy report," Dex said, taking a seat at the desk chair and pressing a few buttons on his high-tech laptop.

"She was sixteen weeks pregnant," Dex went on. "They did a blood test on the fetus. Lila's blood type was O, the baby's blood type was O."

I frowned, not knowing where Dex was going with this. Looking over at Duncan, I saw that he was just as confused as I was.

"Okay. Mom and baby both are type O," I repeated.

Dex nodded, suddenly looking very excited. He stared at Duncan. "I did a little digging into your medical files."

"Mine? Why?" Duncan asked.

"Because I was curious. Know what I found?"

We shook our heads.

"Your blood type is AB. That's the rarest blood type, *and* it means you aren't the father. You can't be. It's impossible."

My mind began to whirl.

"The father is A, B, or O. It's the only way for the kid to be O," Dex went on.

Duncan looked shocked, and I wondered if I could have pushed him over with a finger. My mind started working again.

"Duncan's not the father," I repeated. "So you think—"

"My theory? There were no signs of struggle. No bruises, no strangled windpipe from asphyxiation. I think she knew the person who killed her. My theory? The father of Lila's baby killed her. We find the father, we find the killer."

Chapter 35

"I'm not the father," Duncan said in a daze.

I passed him a bottle of scotch. "Drink."

He obeyed. We were back in the penthouse suite, leaving Dex to work his magic. He was a technological mole, burrowing and digging for useful kernels of information.

It was early afternoon, and I'd been awake for hours. I hadn't slept well since the news of Lila's death. I wouldn't sleep deeply until Flynn was released. And that might not be for a long, long while. I shoved that thought away immediately.

Allen Masterson had called, telling me that they wouldn't set bail for Flynn. I was hardly surprised. Charged with murder, Flynn was a flight risk. I wasn't ashamed to admit that I'd have encouraged it. We could've left the U.S., taken the boys, disappeared to some remote island with pale blue water and white sand. Left all this crap behind.

"I should call Ash," Duncan said, startling me from my thoughts.

"And tell her what?" I sniped. "The baby wasn't yours, but you still screwed a woman who wasn't your wife."

"Enough," Duncan rumbled. "You have no right to

judge me."

"Like hell I don't!" I shouted across the living room.

"After what you've done?" he wondered. "Dolinsky?"

"That's none of your business!"

"No?" he taunted. "Do you know how many nights I stayed up with Flynn, watching him drink himself into a stupor because he couldn't stomach the idea of his wife with another man?"

"If you think what I did with Dolinsky is at all like what you did with Lila, then you're an eejit, and I'm ashamed to call you family. A hot piece of ass paraded herself in front of you, and because you were drunk, you thought with your dick."

Duncan's anger deflated. "You're right. What happened with Dolinsky was not—"

"Enough. Enough about Dolinsky. I can't keep hearing about him. I didn't let him ruin my marriage, and I refuse to let him ruin my relationship with you."

Duncan nodded, and then he took another swig of whisky. "I just wish I could remember that night."

"What night?"

"The night I met Lila."

"You don't remember?"

He shrugged. "Bits and pieces. Drinking, of course. Gambling. Lila hitting on Flynn and then me. My memories of that night come to me in snapshots. Like little blips between black spots.

"I don't remember getting up to the hotel room. And the next thing I knew, I was awake in the morning, naked, with Lila next to me."

"How much did you drink?" I asked.

"Don't remember. Enough to get me to blackout."

"Which has to be what? At least half a bottle of scotch?"

"Aye."

"And Flynn? Was he keeping up with you?"

"For a time," Duncan said. "He left me alone to go do something, and then Lila somehow convinced me to leave the casino with her."

I was quiet a moment. "You sure you were drunk?"

"Aye. Drunk as a skunk."

"What did you feel like in the morning?" I asked. "When you woke up next to Lila?"

"Disgusted, appalled—"

"Physically," I interjected. "What did you feel like physically?"

"Hungover," Duncan said automatically.

"Yeah?" I prodded. "And was this hangover different from your other hangovers?"

Duncan blinked and then cursed boisterously.

Something unfurled in my belly. Relief maybe. Duncan wasn't an adulterous prat after all.

"That bitch drugged me!" Duncan yelled, looking like he was about to hurl the bottle of scotch at the wall.

"Do not throw that," I stated, making a grab for the bottle. "That's Balvenie Triple Cask."

Duncan relinquished the bottle but not before taking a deep drink. I did the same.

"Think Ash will believe me?" Duncan asked.

"I think we're going to need some solid proof before we tell her," I said. Ash was at the height of her anger and hurt—there was no hearing anything through those emotions.

"How do you suppose we get proof?" Duncan asked bleakly. "The only person that could admit the truth is dead."

A few hours later, Duncan was gone, the bottle of scotch with him. I'd drunk just enough that I was drowsy. I fell asleep on the couch, too tired to even make it to the bed. I dreamed of Flynn, our house in Dornoch, our boys.

A ringing jarred me awake. Sasha's name flashed across the screen.

"Hello," I answered, my voice raspy with scotch and sleep. The sun had set while I slept, but my nap felt like mere minutes. Tiredness tugged at my spine, my body sinking into the sofa.

"Meet me for a drink," he commanded.

"I'm exhausted."

"Please, Barrett," he said, his voice low, pleading.

I sighed. "Where?"

"That bar where you met Winters while I sat in the corner pretending not to eavesdrop."

I knew why he'd chosen that place. It was a dive, it was dark, and the bartender never asked questions.

"See you in twenty," I said.

"Ten," he said. "I'm already on the Upper East Side."

I threw on a fresh shirt, stuck my hair under a Mets baseball hat, and grabbed a pair of sunglasses. Even though I'd slip out the back, I didn't want to give the media any chance to recognize me.

I arrived at the dive bar before Sasha and tucked myself into a corner table. It was just past seven, still happy hour, but the bar was fairly deserted, and I was grateful for the loud, scratchy speaker system playing some '80s metal song I'd never heard.

Sasha walked in, found me immediately, and nearly ran to the table. He took the chair next to mine and scooted closer to my side, so we were both facing the entrance.

"I'm sorry," he said quietly. "I know you've got a wealth of your own shit to deal with right now—how is Campbell?"

"I don't know," I said truthfully, a lump forming in my throat. "They won't set bail. I think I'm going to have to contact Archer, ask him to pull a few strings."

Sasha nodded absently. "He can't go to trial. He can't use his alibi."

I peered at him in understanding. "You know about his alibi?"

"Yes. I was with him. And Marino."

"And you were…" I prodded.

"Let's just say it involved Filippi and a host of illegal activities that would land us all in hot water. But Flynn's not a snitch."

"No, he isn't."

"We'll find a way to get him out of this mess."

"I have Dex digging around for Lila's killer, but until we know more, we just have to wait. I hate that Flynn is…"

Sasha's hand covered mine. "How are the paparazzi?"

"Still camped out, waiting for me to make a statement. Which I refuse." I quickly caught him up on what we learned about Duncan not being the father but still not any closer to knowing who was.

"Have you heard from Quinn?" Sasha asked, changing the subject.

I closed my eyes in thought. "She called me a few days ago, after the tabloids broke the story. But no. I haven't heard from her recently. Why?"

"She left for Boston yesterday," he said slowly. "To see her father."

"She didn't call you or text?"

"She called and left a really strange voicemail."

"Strange? How so?" I asked.

"She called me Sasha and reminded me to feed the dog."

"You don't have a dog."

"I don't have a dog," he agreed. "And Quinn never calls me Sasha."

"What does she call you?" I wondered.

Even in the dim bar, I could see the slight dusting of color on his high cheekbones. "I'd rather not say," he said. He ran a hand through his blond hair. "I don't think she made it to Boston, Barrett. I think something happened to her."

Chapter 36

"I'm sorry, Barrett," Don Archer said, his voice crackling through the speaker. "But my hands are tied."

"Why?" I demanded. "How can *you* not have jurisdiction to get Flynn released? He didn't do it, Don!"

Archer sighed. I didn't know if he believed me or not, but the sigh was telling—I wasn't going to find help from Archer and the FBI.

"If I get him out, everyone will know we have...an understanding. I can't have that, Barrett. Our relationship works because it's unknown. I get him out, people start asking questions."

I'd visited Flynn just that morning. Dressed in orange, wrists shackled, he still managed to look lazily arrogant, as if he couldn't be bothered with all this trivial bullshit, like it was only a matter of time before he was free. But I knew Flynn better than anyone, and I'd seen the worry in his eyes. He was afraid he was going to go down for a murder he didn't commit, left to rot in prison.

I had to get him out.

Looking around the quiet penthouse suite, I knew my life couldn't be about raising the boys alone, telling them their father was wrongly convicted. The boys needed their father. I needed Flynn. And I'd do anything to free him.

"Who has the power?" I asked softly.

"Barrett," Archer warned.

"Who has the power to get my husband released?" I demanded.

He gave me a name.

"Who is he?" I asked.

"The most powerful man in Argentina," Archer said. "He knows the judge."

"What will he want as payment?"

Archer went silent.

"I see," I murmured.

"Don't do it," he advised.

"I have to. I can't wait and hope. I won't let Flynn go down for a crime he didn't commit."

He sighed. "I'll email you everything you need to know. That's the best I can do."

"Thank you."

"I'm sorry I can't do more. Truly."

Without replying, I hung up. Despair consumed me, but I knew what I had to do. If there was a choice between buying Flynn's freedom or letting him die in prison, then I knew the answer. I just hoped saving him didn't break us.

"What happened to your eye?" I asked.

Duncan winced. "I ran into Jack's fist." He looked at my packed suitcase near the elevator doors. "Where are you going?"

"Tell me more about what happened with you and Jack," I asked instead of answering.

"He showed up at my suite door, didn't say a word, and then decked me. Guess Ash told him what I did."

I shook my head. "Doubt it. But Ash went to Switzerland. She only goes to Switzerland when something is wrong, and she has to work it out."

"I have to go to her," he said. "Letting her walk out was a mistake."

"She needs time," I reminded him.

"Time for what? I'm not the father of Lila's baby. I didn't even sleep with Lila—"

"We don't have solid confirmation of that yet."

He glared at me. "Ash isn't answering my calls—and I've left her tons of voicemails. I have to go to her and make her listen to me."

"You want another black eye?" I demanded.

"This is my marriage. Don't tell me how to fix it."

I sighed. "Marino called," I said, changing the conversation. "He says the leader of The White Company is willing to talk with us. Two days from now. In Naples."

"Is that why you're packed?"

I shook my head and then rolled my eyes. "He wants to speak to a man. Marino informed him that Flynn is unavailable. It has to be you, Duncan. You're co-leader of the SINS. You're a Buchanan."

"Damn. I really wanted to go to Ash and Carys." His wounded eyes hardened. "But Ash will still be pissed at me in a few days, right? That'll keep."

"There's the dark humor I know and love," I teased.

"So if you're not the one going to Naples, why are you packed? Where are you going?"

"Don't worry about it."

"Barrett," he began.

"I don't have time for this," I said quietly.

Sasha was still concerned about Quinn, Dex was strung out on Red Bull trying to find Lila's killer, Ash wasn't speaking to anyone about anything, Flynn was in jail, and the last thing

I needed was Duncan asking questions about what I was going to do to free Flynn.

"Do you trust me?" I asked.

He groaned. "I hate it when women ask that. No good comes from a question like that."

"What would you do if it were you? And Ash was in trouble?"

"Aye," he said. "I understand."

"Good."

His eyes pinned me. "But will Flynn?"

"Guess we'll see."

"Are you going alone?"

I nodded.

"Why?" he demanded. "When Flynn finds out—"

"I'll handle Flynn," I said. "Because God willing, this will get him released, and then he and I can have one of our infamous rows." I shook my head and looked at the ceiling so tears didn't fall from my eyes.

"I never thought I'd want the day where Flynn and I fought," I said.

"It's better than the alternative, aye?" he asked dismally.

A cold numbness had spread through me the moment I stepped foot on the private plane. I was in an insulated bubble, focused, detached, cool. I got a call from Sasha when I was thirty-thousand feet in the air. Not even the news that Quinn was officially missing penetrated it.

"I've called her father," Sasha said.

"Good," I said.

"I tried calling Duncan, but he didn't answer. I could really use his help."

Duncan was called The Tracker for a reason. He was able

to find anyone and anything. "He's on his way to Naples," I explained. "To meet with The White Company."

Sasha cursed violently in Russian.

"I'll call Brandon Kilmartin."

"How is he going to be of any help?" Sasha growled.

"He's a friend of Quinn's. And he's Flynn's cousin. And," I emphasized, "he's got skills we can use."

Sasha made a noise but said nothing.

"Pride," I reminded him. "This is Quinn we're talking about."

"You're right." He sighed. "Where are you?"

"Taking care of some of my own stuff," I said evasively.

The only person who knew my true whereabouts was Brad Shapiro. He hadn't tried to talk me out of it. He even volunteered to tag along. As much as I wanted a familiar face with me, it would be more signifying if I went alone.

"We'll get her back, Sasha. I promise."

I hung up and shoved all of that to the back of my mind. I picked up my iPad, opened the document Archer had sent me, and began to read about the most dangerous crime lord in Argentina.

Chapter 37

Mateo Sanchez was fucking loaded. And not loaded like Flynn and I were loaded but *loaded*. The guy's yacht had a helipad. I knew next to nothing about yachts aside from the fact that they floated. But even I knew this was no ordinary yacht.

It was wealth epitomized. And it was gorgeous.

I waited for Sanchez on the second-tier private deck. Standing at the railing, I gazed out at the expanse of the ocean. I dragged in a breath full of sea and sun. I closed my eyes and briefly pretended this was a vacation and nothing more.

I felt him before I heard him.

I turned.

Mateo Sanchez stood ten feet away from me, hands in the pockets of his white linen pants, the air teasing the dark hair gracing his forehead. His white linen shirt was open at the neck to reveal tan skin and a smattering of hair the same dark shade of brown on his head. Though I couldn't see his eyes because a pair of sunglasses shielded them, I knew Sanchez was looking his fill.

A slight smile played about his lips. "Welcome aboard, Mrs. Campbell." His words were tinged with a slight Spanish accent and I knew, even if he hadn't had the power to his name, women still would've wanted him.

"Call me Barrett," I said automatically.

He strode toward me and held out his hand. I placed my palm in his, and he brought it to his lips and briefly kissed my knuckles.

"Barrett," he repeated with a nod. "Call me Mateo."

I held in the urge to laugh. The most dangerous man in Argentina and I were on a first name basis.

"Mateo," I murmured.

His hand holding mine tightened ever so slightly. "Have you eaten? I have lunch prepared. And then after, I thought I could give you a tour."

"Lunch sounds wonderful," I said truthfully. I was famished, not having eaten much since I'd left New York only twenty-four hours ago.

"Come," he said, a hand going to the small of my back as he led me inside. Though the full-length glass sides of the room let in sunlight, the interior was cool. A table with white linen and china had been set, a bottle of champagne chilling in the ice bucket nearby.

Mateo helped me with my chair and then moved to his seat across from me. I took off my sunglasses and set them aside. I looked around, marveling at the beauty and craftsmanship of the yacht, smiling and shaking my head.

"What is it?" Mateo asked, pulling my attention back to him. He'd taken off his sunglasses, his dark eyes curious and pinned on me.

"I was just thinking, that if I had a view like this, in a place like this, I'd never leave."

Mateo smiled, showing genuine amusement. "It is difficult," he agreed. "To pull myself away. The ocean is so peaceful."

Though I hadn't seen anyone, servant or guest, since I'd arrived by helicopter, I wasn't surprised when a man dressed in white chinos and polo entered the opulent room to pour our champagne.

"Please serve the lobsters," Mateo said, not taking his eyes off my face.

The servant bowed slightly and then departed.

"I hope lobster is acceptable," Mateo said pleasantly.

"Ah, I'm allergic to shellfish."

Mateo blinked.

I smiled. "I'm just teasing. Lobster sounds wonderful."

He chuckled, playing with the stem of his champagne flute while he shrewdly observed me. "Your husband must enjoy your sense of humor."

I inclined my head and eyed him, letting him know that I *knew* what he was doing. "Most men enjoy my sense of humor."

"I'm sure," Mateo murmured.

I'd spent most of the flight from New York reading all about Mateo Sanchez. Though there were photos of him, they weren't as forthcoming as seeing the man in person. In the photos he was shielded, either by sunglasses or terrible lighting.

I knew he was in his late thirties, the youngest of three children, his father's forgotten son. From an early age, Mateo wanted power and wealth. By his mid-twenties he'd achieved both.

He also had a daughter. A three-year-old named Sofia. Sofia's mother wasn't in the picture from what I could conclude.

The servant returned and placed two plates in front of us. The lobsters had already been taken out of their shells, so all I had to do was pick up a fork and knife. I took a dainty bite and chewed slowly.

"How is it?" Mateo asked, not yet having sampled his own meal.

"Cooked to perfection," I said honestly. I raised my flute of champagne and took a small sip.

"A diplomatic answer," Mateo said as he watched me.

"It's delicious," I rushed to assure him, throwing him a teasing smile. "My stomach has been upset the last few days. Nothing seems to calm it."

"You're worried about your husband," Mateo said, not taking offense that I nearly insulted him.

"I am," I admitted. "But let's talk about that after lunch."

"I think we should talk about it now," Mateo said, finally taking a bite of his food. "But you need something to eat."

"You wouldn't, by any chance, have a mango aboard, would you?" I asked.

He chuckled. "I do. Mango it is."

Mateo didn't press an invisible button or make a call, so no servant appeared. But I had no doubt one had been waiting in the wings, listening intently for any sign that Mateo needed something.

Mateo set his knife and fork down. "I'll wait until you have your food."

"Please," I said. "Eat. Before it gets cold."

He inclined his head. "If you insist." Mateo resumed eating.

I sipped at my champagne, the bubbles settling my stomach.

"Tell me about your husband," Mateo said.

"Don't you already know about Flynn?" I asked pointedly.

"I do."

"Then you know why I'm here."

Mateo leaned back in his chair and surveyed me. "I do. I'm guessing you know what I require in form of payment?"

I quirked my lips. "Shall I straddle you now? Or wait until you finish your lobster?"

Mateo's eyes darkened with lust.

"I know about you, Mateo," I said softly, reaching for the

clip holding my hair hostage. Auburn waves spilled down my back and over my shoulders.

Mateo's eyes dipped to the swell of my breasts. I was wearing a simple dress, white and A-line, but it hugged all the right places without being overt.

"I know how you made your fortune and your power. I know that women love you." I cocked my head to one side, wondering if Mateo realized that he had leaned forward, eager for my next words.

I licked my lips. His eyes dropped to my mouth, but I waited until his gaze returned to my eyes before I began speaking again.

"You've had girls in their twenties. Stupid girls, pretty girls, naïve girls. But have you ever had a woman, Mateo? Have you ever had a woman who knows what she wants? A woman in her twenties is vastly different from a woman in her thirties. And you know it.

"You're a worldly man. Powerful. Rich. Don't you get tired of having women telling you what you want to hear because they want things from you? I want something from you. I do. I admit it. Freely. And I'll give you a night with me in exchange for it."

"Willingly?" he asked huskily.

"Willingly," I repeated.

Mateo set his napkin on the table before rising. He came to stand next to me and reached a hand down to help me up. His palms splayed my hips before hauling me toward him.

I was average in height and even with the short heels I wore, I was no match for Mateo's height. Tall men didn't scare me, though.

I placed my hands on Mateo's chest, feeling the strength, the power. I looked up and smiled.

"You want me," I said to him.

"Yes."

"You'll make the call and get Flynn released from prison."

"Yes."

"Your word is your honor," I said.

He smiled slightly. "Yes."

"So is mine," I assured him. My hand went to the back of his neck; my fingers sank into his dark hair.

"What do you want more?" I whispered as his mouth came closer. "Me? Or a business proposition?"

Chapter 38

"Let's go out onto the deck for a little more privacy," Mateo suggested after we'd finished our lunch. When we were on the private deck, sitting underneath an overhanging awning out of the sun, he asked, "How are you feeling?"

"A lot better. Thank you."

My stomach and nerves had settled. I'd had every intention of spending the night with him to ensure that Flynn was released from jail. But there was another way, a better way.

"How would you like to expand your product's distribution?" I asked.

He smirked. "What a diplomatic word."

I shrugged. "It is a product. We don't have to get into morality and philosophy. You have a product you want to sell, and I have a way to distribute it."

"Go on."

"You get it to Scotland. Dornoch, specifically. We have a Scotch distillery. We'll pack it in the boxes sent to the U.S. and we'll distribute it."

"I get my product to the U.S. just fine. Why do I need you?" he inquired.

"You don't. But you want more of your product leaving

Argentina, more channels of distribution, then why wouldn't you expand? At the moment, you don't have trouble with red tape or the American government, but you know how quickly they shift alliances. They go where the money is."

"The American government is full of vipers pretending to be garden snakes," Mateo said, his voice bathed in truth and irony.

"Yes," I said immediately.

I didn't claim to be a good person. But there wasn't anything I wouldn't do for my family. Did I really want to get into the drug business? No. Was it an opportunity I'd take? Yes.

"Three years," Mateo said. "In exchange for getting your husband out of prison, I want a three-year deal, and I'll give you twenty percent of the profits."

My eyes narrowed. "One year—and you keep all the profits."

"You think drug money is dirty? Is that why you don't want it?"

"I think it's a business I don't want to be in long term. And I'd rather not feel like I'm indebted to you. Just a mutually, beneficial arrangement."

I knew how Flynn felt about drugs. To him, any sort of drug was distasteful, but I was going to use whatever bargaining chip I had.

"Two years," Mateo offered. "And fifteen percent of the profits."

"One year. And we distribute in England, too."

"Done."

We shook on it, and then Mateo dropped my hand. "We should celebrate our new business arrangement."

I chuckled and shook my head. "I'm not sleeping with you."

He threw back his head and laughed. "Can't blame a man for trying, can you?"

"Nope. I would've been offended if you hadn't."

∽

Three hours later, all the details of our arrangement were ironed out. Before Mateo escorted me to his waiting helicopter, he made the call for Flynn's release.

"It's been a real pleasure," Mateo said, holding out his hand to help me into the cockpit.

"It has, hasn't it?" I agreed with a smile.

"Until next time, Barrett."

The helicopter lifted off, and soon Mateo was nothing more than a speck below. I settled back into my seat, not bothering to make polite conversation with the pilot as he flew us to Buenos Aires.

By the time I got back to the capital of Argentina, it was evening. I could've stayed the night in the hotel suite I'd booked, but I wanted to get back to New York as soon as possible. There was a lot to discuss with Flynn. I was more than prepared for his anger, but I'd weather it—as long as I could do it with my arms around him.

When Mateo's pilot had come for me earlier that day, he'd made sure I had no personal weapons on my body. In a show of good faith, I'd left everything, including my cell phone. There had been no need for it.

I had at least twenty missed calls. The most recent was from Flynn, and before I did anything else, I called him back.

"Barrett," he breathed. "Hen, what the hell did you do?"

I sank down to the floor, my legs giving out at the sound of his voice. I leaned back against the bed and closed my eyes.

"Are you safe?" I demanded. "Where are you?"

"Aye, I'm safe. I'm at The Rex. Where the hell are you?"

I paused and then, "Buenos Aires."

"By yourself?"

"Yes."

"Where the fuck is Duncan?"

"Naples."

"What—"

"Let me talk!"

"Fine," he growled. "Sorry."

"First of all," I said, "Are you—are you okay?"

"Aye, love," his voice softened. "I'm fine. I just miss you. And the boys. God, I feel like I haven't seen them in years."

"I'm getting on the plane tonight."

"So you'll be back in New York when?"

"It's an eleven-hour flight. I'll be there early tomorrow morning."

"I won't sleep until you're back with me."

I let out a laugh that turned into a sob. "Welcome to my world."

"Just tell me, love. What did you do?"

"You really want to know now?"

"Aye."

"I made a deal with Mateo Sanchez for your release."

"Who's Mateo Sanchez?"

"The most powerful man in Argentina."

"Barrett—"

"It's not what you think."

His sigh was relieved.

"You're not going to like the alternative," I warned him.

"Believe me, if it means another man didn't get to sample your charms, then I'll jump for joy."

"Sample my charms?" I teased. "What are you? A character from a romance novel?"

"Barrett," he growled. "Come home."

"I'm on my way."

Chapter 39

I got on the plane and to distract myself from takeoff, I listened to the voicemails. One from Alia telling me the date of the restaurant she was opening with her husband, Jake. Another from the contractor letting me know The Rex Burlesque club repairs were completed. One from Sasha threatening to murder Brandon with his own two hands but only after they found Quinn. Duncan had arrived in Naples. Moira sent a video of the boys, and my heart leapt into my throat. On and on, but nothing from Dex or Ash.

I was worried about Quinn. I didn't know much about her upbringing except that her father had made a lot of money doing business with criminals and was probably one himself. Quinn had been sheltered; she'd had nice clothes, expensive cars, whatever she wanted. I just hoped wherever she was, whoever she was with, had only kidnapped her to get our attention, to let us know they weren't playing around. But they had yet to make contact, so we had no way of knowing their intention.

"Hold on, Quinn," I whispered.

Twelve hours later, I landed in New York. The excitement of being reunited with Flynn had adrenaline pumping through me. Even though it was a few hours before dawn, I was wide-awake.

As I got into the car that would take me back to The Rex, my phone rang.

"Flynn was arrested?" came Ash's shrill voice.

I immediately held the cell away from my ear and grimaced. "It's too early in the morning for this. Or late at night, depending on your viewpoint."

"Don't be glib," she snapped. "You couldn't call and tell me your husband was arrested?"

"You weren't answering my phone calls," I answered calmly. "I wasn't going to leave that piece of information in a voicemail. Furthermore, do you really think I would've stooped to that level to get you to talk to me?"

"I would've come," she said, her voice soft. "Stood by you."

"He's out now."

"I heard. Duncan," she explained. "Left a voicemail."

"What else did he tell you in the voicemail?"

"Only that."

It wasn't my place to tell her, I knew that, but she did have the right to know. And I doubted she would give Duncan the opportunity to explain. That left me.

"He didn't do it," I said.

"Flynn? I know he didn't kill Lila."

"No. Duncan. He didn't sleep with her—that wasn't his child."

She paused. "How do you know?"

"Genetically impossible." I told her what we'd found in the autopsy.

"Still doesn't prove he didn't fuck that whore," she said in anger.

"Ash, come on."

"No, you come on! How would you feel in my situation? Everyone lied!"

"Jack punched Duncan in the eye."

"That makes me feel a little better," she said. "But even if that's not his child, he still slept with her."

"No, he didn't," I insisted. "He blacked out, Ash. The night he met Lila. Don't you think that's weird? How much scotch does it take for your husband to black out?"

She didn't reply and I went on, "Someone drugged Duncan and made it look like he slept with Lila."

"Why?"

"For the same reason someone had Flynn arrested for Lila's murder. Someone is out to get Flynn."

"So why didn't this person drug Flynn and have him wake up next to Lila?" she demanded.

"I don't know," I said. "Maybe Lila tried to get Flynn to pay attention to her but he wouldn't. Maybe someone is going after those close to Flynn to make him suffer. I don't have the answers, Ash, but I do know Duncan—and his story about that night is true. I'd bet my life on it."

"It's not enough for me," she said quietly.

"I know. But I'm working on getting you proof."

"Okay," she said tiredly.

"But you have to answer when I call."

"Okay."

"I miss you."

"I miss you, too," she said. Her voice had begun to thaw, but that didn't mean her anger had. I wasn't going to push my luck.

"So how the hell did Flynn get out on bail if he was charged for murder?" she demanded.

I sighed. "Yeah, about that… So I was in Buenos Aires…"

Flynn met me in the lobby and we ran to each other like two lovers in a sappy romantic comedy. He lifted me in the air, and my legs wrapped around his waist. I kissed him like an ocean and a war had separated us for years.

"Barrett," he breathed when my mouth finally left his only to pepper kisses across his face. "Barrett, love," he tried again. "Let's go upstairs before we give the employees a show."

I grinned as he set me down on the floor. Grabbing my hand, he tugged me toward the elevator. Once we were in private, he pinned me against the elevator wall, his hands framing my face.

"You're safe," he growled.

"Yes." My hands plowed into his hair as I tried to get him to kiss me again. The doors opened, and he hauled me into the suite.

"You scared the shite out of me," he stated, his eyes dark and dangerous.

"I did what I had to do." I began backing away even as Flynn stalked toward me.

"And what was that?" Flynn demanded as he whipped his gray sweater up over his head and tossed it aside.

"I made a deal with Mateo Sanchez."

Flynn continued to come for me, his intense stare making me shiver in anticipation. Though Flynn appeared mad, I never worried that he'd hurt me.

"What kind of deal?" he whispered when he was standing directly in front of me. His bare chest brushed my shirt and my nipples pebbled. He reached up to cup my breasts, and he groaned when he realized I wasn't wearing a bra.

"You want to talk about the deal now?" I demanded.

His grin was wolfish. He tore my T-shirt in half and then dropped to his knees. Placing his mouth on my bare belly, he bathed me in light kisses. My hands went to his hair, and I closed my eyes, reveling in the moment. Right now, nothing else mattered except this. So much of our time together was made up of separations and reunions.

Flynn's hands tugged at my jeans, and then he was pulling

me down to the floor. Our mouths collided, our bodies fused together. We crashed and obliterated. When he slammed inside of me, I no longer felt empty and adrift. We stared into each other's eyes, refusing to break our connection. His hands held my hips as he rolled us so that I was atop him.

"Ride me," he gritted out. His fingers slid between our joined bodies and I ignited, going up in flames. He speared up into me, calling out my name, cursing in Gaelic, praying to a God neither of us believed in.

I leaned over and pressed my cheek to his chest. Flynn's fingers trailed up and down my spine for a moment and then stopped.

"You're crying, love," he murmured.

"I know," I said into his heated skin.

His hands came around to tug gently on my hair, forcing me to look at him. "Why, hen?"

My lips wobbled. "I didn't know if you'd ever—if we'd ever—"

"Shhh." His thumbs brushed away the tears on my cheeks. "I'm here now. I'm not going anywhere."

Chapter 40

While I took a shower, Flynn ordered food. By the time I got out of the bathroom and into comfortable pajamas, weak winter light shone through the windows. We sat down on the couch, and I snuggled into him. We were silent, but every now and again Flynn would kiss my hair.

He finally broke the quiet when he asked, "So tell me what happened with Sanchez."

I started at the beginning. I told him about our deal—in exchange for getting Flynn out of jail, we'd smuggle cocaine into England and the U.S. for a year.

He looked like he was about to argue, but I stopped him before he could start.

"There was another form of payment he would've gladly accepted, but I thought it would result in multiple deaths."

Flynn didn't find me funny; he clenched his jaw and a muscle in his cheek started to twitch. "How are we supposed to go about this?" he wondered.

"Sanchez will get the product to Dornoch. We will package it in bottles of scotch and have them shipped here."

"Bottles of scotch?" he murmured thoughtfully.

I smiled. "From our very own scotch distillery."

"Use a legal drug to hide the illegal one. Brilliant," Flynn allowed. "Just one problem. We don't have a scotch distillery."

"Not yet," I agreed. "But we will."

"And it's just for a year, aye? No longer?"

"No longer. I don't like being under someone else's thumb." He seemed to respect that.

Flynn shook his head. "You're unbelievable, you know that?"

"You," I said with a smile.

The elevator doors opened, and an attendant wheeled in our food. As if on cue, my stomach growled. I ate the entire stack of pancakes and then fell into a sugar coma.

"How are you feeling?" Flynn asked, polishing off the last bite of his eggs.

"Full and sleepy," I said, my eyes drifting closed.

"Let's go to sleep," he suggested, tugging me up from the couch.

"You didn't sleep?"

He shrugged. "You were on a plane, and I hadn't seen you in days. I wanted to go to bed with you, so I waited."

My hand caressed his jaw. "Romantic idiot," I teased.

He chuckled and led me to the bedroom. I sank into the bed and tried to cover myself with the comforter, but I was exhausted.

Flynn settled in next to me and dragged the quilt up over us. There was still so much I had to tell him. I gave him the bare bones about Quinn missing and having Brandon helping Sasha in the search. Nothing would be solved at the moment, so I left the rest until later. Lack of sleep and the gamut of emotions I'd felt the last couple of days finally took their toll. With Flynn at my back, his hand resting on the bare skin of my belly, I fell asleep.

I woke up a few hours later in the same position, but Flynn wasn't next to me. It was full-on day, and the sun was trying to peek through the drawn curtains but only a shaft of light managed to get through. I slowly climbed out of bed and went in search of him.

He sat on the couch, his head in his hands, body taut. He wore a pair of flannel pajama bottoms but no shirt. I watched the muscles of his back tense and release.

His rugged beauty momentarily stunned me. I never got tired of looking at him, watching him. He moved with assurance and confidence, but Flynn was a beast in human form. He was king of the jungle.

"What time is it?" I asked.

"Just past two," he said, voice strained and tight.

"Been up long?"

He shook his head. "Come here, love."

Worry skittered down my spine. Flynn had something to tell me, and I knew it wasn't good. I sat down on the couch next to him, dread curling in my belly, drifting up my throat.

Flynn paused.

"Just tell me," I whispered.

He put a hand on my thigh, maybe to anchor me, maybe to prepare me for what he was about to say. "Quinn's been found."

"Oh God," I whispered. "Is she—"

"Fine. She's fine. Sasha and Brandon found her on a boat at the docks. She was drugged, but no worse for wear."

My hand flew to my speeding heart. "Scare the crap out of me, why don't you?"

He licked his lips. "There's more, hen."

I stared at him and waited.

"The boat…there was an explosion. And Sasha…"

My blood turned to ice. "Sasha what?" I grasped Flynn's arms, my nails digging into his skin. "Sasha what!"

Chapter 41

"It was a trap," Brandon explained.

"And Quinn was the bait," Flynn finished.

Brandon nodded and ran a hand through his hair. "Should've seen it. Should've known."

"It was Filippi," Flynn added. "He had insurance policies in place in case of..."

Their voices turned to buzzing in my ears, like annoying little insects. I stared at the white floor of the hospital, trying to get my breathing under control. After Flynn had told me the news that Sasha was in the burn unit, unconscious, sedated and hovering near death, I'd thrown on clothes, and here we were. If Sasha lived, there would be severe damage and scarring. If he didn't—

My mind refused to go there.

"Love," Flynn said. His arm hooked around my shoulders, and he pressed my face into his chest. "Let's go visit Quinn."

"I'll stay here," Brandon said. "Don't want to overwhelm her."

Quinn was in a room down the hall, kept under observation until the drugs were out of her system. She was sitting up in bed, staring out the window. She looked lost and alone.

Fragile. Broken. I hated seeing her that way. Where was the woman who'd been ballsy enough to call me out on my relationship with Sasha? Sasha would need *that* woman to help him heal. If…

"Quinn," I said quietly.

When she didn't look like she'd heard me, I said her name again, a little louder. She turned glassy green eyes to me. She saw me without seeing me.

I touched Flynn's arm, and he nodded in understanding. He went over to Quinn, wrapped his arms around her, and murmured something in Gaelic. I could tell she didn't comprehend what he was saying, but she closed her eyes, and a shudder went through her. Flynn released her, and with one final look at me, he left.

Pulling up the chair next to her bed, I took a seat. I grasped one of her hands in mine and held on, not saying anything. There were no words for a situation like this. Quinn had been drugged and used as bait to draw out the man she loved. And now the man she loved was fighting for his life.

"What if he dies?" she asked, shattering the quiet.

I took a deep breath. "Then he dies."

She flinched. "I love him so much."

"I know." I paused before asking, "What happens if he lives?"

She cocked her head to one side. "What do you mean?"

"He'll be scarred."

"I don't care about any of that," she snapped, finally showing me some of her fire.

"I don't just mean on the inside."

Her gaze dropped to her lap.

"He'll be in pain. It will take a long time to recover. This might be something neither of you can overcome."

"Fuck you," she yelled. "Fuck you and your bullshit! I love him! And I'll be there for him—every step of the way."

Her anger didn't faze me; I took it as a good sign. "He'll

need more than that. He'll need you to be strong for him. He'll need you to be stronger than *him* because he'll want to give up."

"You don't know." She glared defiantly. "You don't know at all how he's going to be."

"If he lives, he's going to wish he died."

She blanched, her creamy complexion turning ashen. "How can you—"

"He's a warrior. He'll hate that he's become a burden. Do you think he'll be okay with you playing nurse? He'll hate your cheerleader attitude. He's going to be surly and grumpy. He's not going to be the Sasha you know. He'll probably never be the Sasha you know ever again."

"Are you talking to me, or are you talking to yourself?" she demanded, some of her ire lessening when she realized I was the only one willing to speak the truth. No kid gloves for her.

"I'd die for him," I said. "Like I'd die for Flynn or Ash or Duncan. He's family. I'll stand by him through all of this. But he won't need my assurance the way he's going to need it from you."

She took a deep breath and nodded. "Okay." She bit her lip. "It's weird."

"What is?"

"Hospitals. They have places for people to pray, but they don't have places for people to get drunk."

I dropped her hand and stood up so I could embrace her. "Damn. You're exactly what he needs to get through this."

If he lives neither of us said. But that's what we were thinking.

I left Quinn and went in search of Flynn. I found him in the corner of the waiting room, cell phone to his ear. A smile bloomed bright and beautiful when he saw me and then he let out a laugh.

"Aye, I'll tell her. All right. Bye." He hung up and looked at me.

"What's got you grinning?" I demanded.

"Our children."

"What did they do? Burn down Moira and James's house?" I quipped and then blanched when I realized what I'd said.

"Ah, love…" He shook his head. "The last of the red Sharpie has finally faded."

"Excellent."

"I thought so."

"But…" I prompted.

"It seems Hawk was getting jealous of all the attention the twins were getting from both Moira and James so he bit things."

I raised my eyebrows. "Things?"

"And people," Flynn added. "And animals."

"Give me a list," I said, feeling a gurgle of laughter threatening to come out of my mouth.

"Table legs, chair legs, his brothers, James's arm, the dog's tail."

"Oh, no…" I began, no longer able to contain my mirth.

"Aye," Flynn stated. "Seamus nipped Hawk back."

"Is he seriously hurt?" I wondered.

Flynn shook his head. "Surprised more like. Maybe that will curb the random biting."

"Moira and James's wedding anniversary is coming up, isn't it?"

"Aye. Why?"

"I was thinking they deserve a good vacation after we take back our devil children."

Chapter 42

I blinked blearily as I stumbled out of the bedroom the next morning. Flynn was long gone, no doubt briefing Brad and making phone calls.

"You look like crap," Ash said from the confines of the couch as she flipped through a magazine.

"Why are you here?" I muttered, heading toward the kitchen, needing coffee.

"You're kidding, right?" She looked me up and down. "You forgot pants."

I looked down. I was wearing a thong and a short T-shirt. Apparently, I needed coffee and bottoms.

"So you came," I stated, heading back toward the bedroom.

"Flynn called me. Gave me the rundown. How's Quinn? Sasha?"

I'd spent most of yesterday at the hospital with Quinn, waiting for news on Sasha. "Quinn's okay—physically, anyway. Not a lot of change where Sasha is concerned," I said, finding a pair of loose sweatpants in the bottom drawer of the dresser.

"Prognosis?" Ash asked from the doorway of the bedroom.

I shrugged and she let out a sigh.

"Thanks for being here," I said to her.

"Of course," she said. "Listen. I had a lot of time to think on the flight over here. Whatever happens with Duncan, I want that separate from you and me. You're my best friend in the entire world. You're like a sister to me."

"Be pissed at me all you want," I said, inhaling a shaky breath. "But forgive me in the end, okay? I can't handle the idea that you—that we won't—"

Ash ran toward me and enveloped me in her arms. "I'm here, aren't I? I know my priorities."

I closed my eyes briefly and nodded against her shoulder before pulling back. "Where's Carys?"

"With Jack. So I'm flying solo. I'm all yours."

We headed out of the bedroom, and Ash resumed her seat on the couch while I made coffee. I bumbled, dropping coffee grounds, spilling water.

"What's wrong with you?" Ash asked, coming to my aid, waving me to sit down in a chair. "You seem tired. Tired and scattered. Is it Sasha?"

"Yeah. I didn't sleep well last night." I tried not to think of my dear friend in the ICU with guards by the door. We weren't taking any chances that someone could come back and finish the job they'd started.

"Is it too early to start drinking?" I asked only half joking.

She let out a huff of air. "I wish I could. I'm pregnant. Duncan doesn't know—and you can't tell him."

"Are *you* going to tell him?" I wondered.

"In a bit. When I'm ready to…forgive him."

"He didn't do it, though. Sleep with Lila."

"It's never been about the infidelity. The supposed infidelity," she said slowly. "It's the lying part, the secrecy part I'm having trouble with."

I nodded in understanding. "Ash?"

"Yeah?"

I smiled softly. "Congratulations."

"Flynn?" I called out, entering the suite.

No answer.

The bouquet of white orchids rested on the coffee table. Smiling, I went to the arrangement. There was a card. Flynn never left cards with his flowers.

The elevator doors opened and Flynn strolled in. "Hen," he greeted, coming to me and placing a quick kiss on my lips. "Beautiful flowers. Who are they from?"

I cleared my throat. "Sanchez." I handed him the note, the handwriting written in gold ink.

Flynn snorted. "You're a crime lord whisperer, you know that?" He shook his head in amazement. "The man's in love with you."

"Hardly. He's just impressed that I spoke my mind."

"Keep telling yourself that." He leaned over to pick up the vase.

"What are you doing with those?" I demanded.

"Throwing them away."

"Are you crazy? Give them back to me!"

"You're accepting flowers from another man?" His shocked face peeked out from behind the orchids, staring me down in hopes of making me cave.

"They're gorgeous," I remarked. "And it would be stupid to throw them away just because they came from a drug kingpin. Really, Flynn. Sometimes you're way too emotional."

"Me? Emotional?" He set the flowers down on the coffee table. "Are you trying to start a fight?"

I cocked my head to one side. "I don't know. How will it end?"

"With you getting your way, no doubt." All his anger evaporated; his smile was winsome. "Guess it's my own bloody fault for having a wife that's stunning, intelligent, and funny."

"Those are my only good qualities?" I teased. I went to him and brushed my lips against his.

"You're dynamite in bed—and I'm sure Sanchez is fantasizing about you."

"Let him. You get the real deal." I sailed past him toward the kitchen, wanting to grab a snack. "You hungry?"

"No," Flynn said. "Don't eat too much. We have dinner plans in a few hours."

"With?" I asked as I opened the refrigerator.

"Michael O'Malley."

I turned my head to look at him over my shoulder. "Who?"

"Quinn's father," Flynn explained.

"Is Quinn joining us?"

"No."

"Christ," I muttered. "He wants Filippi, doesn't he?"

"Aye."

"But Marino isn't going to give up Filippi, is he?"

"Doubt it."

"Will O'Malley start a war?"

"Over his daughter getting kidnapped and held as bait? Damn fucking right."

I put a piece of bread in the toaster. "Ash is in town."

"When did she get here?"

"This morning, I think."

"Has she forgiven Duncan?"

"Nope."

"What aren't you telling me?" he inquired.

"What makes you think I'm hiding something from you?"

"Because your best friend shows up after days of ignoring all of our phone calls."

"She came because you called her and told her about

Sasha. She's put all her shit aside—at least with me. She and I are good. She's still freezing out Duncan."

Flynn pinched the bridge of his nose. "This is getting ridiculous."

"You think?"

Chapter 43

Flynn pressed a button on the iPad, and then Duncan's bruised face filled the screen. "What the hell happened to you?" Flynn demanded.

"This," Duncan said, pointing to his left eye, "was courtesy of my brother-in-law."

"And the rest?" I asked.

Duncan grimaced. "The White Company."

"Why?" Flynn growled.

"Blood payment," Duncan explained. "Mercenaries with a bloody strange code of honor. In exchange for information, they wanted to make sure I really wanted it."

"Anything broken?" I asked before Flynn could pepper him with questions.

"Nose, a few ribs." He shrugged and then winced. "They dumped me back at my hotel room in Naples. I've been steadily drinking for the past two hours, so if I start to fade out…"

"Tell me what happened," Flynn said.

"First tell me if you have any internal bleeding!" I demanded.

Duncan grinned. "Nope. All good."

I scooted closer to Flynn on the couch and rested my hand on his leg. We were dressed for dinner and didn't have a lot of time before we met Michael O'Malley in the restaurant downstairs.

Duncan took a long pull of the bottle he was drinking from and then said, "They're skilled fuckers. I'll tell you that much. We ever need a job done… I told them who I was. The leader knew since they were hired to kill me and Da." Duncan paused and then swallowed. "Anyway. I explained what was going on with you and how you would've come yourself, but you were behind bars, aye? They accepted me in your stead. I asked them who was behind the House of Lord murders and how it was getting done.

"The leader, Antonio—who was older than I expected, said that if I wanted the knowledge, I had to pay and money was no good. So I paid their fee, and they divulged everything."

He paused again, took another swig. I could see that his eyes were bleary, even in the dim lighting of his hotel room.

"They use this neurotoxin. I'll remember the name of it tomorrow when I'm sober. This neurotoxin—they get it from some fish. It goes in the bloodstream, stops the diaphragm, and the victim dies of respiratory failure. There's no antidote, it's more potent than cyanide, and it doesn't show up on a tox screen."

"It's genius," I murmured.

Duncan nodded.

"But why leave a tattoo?" Flynn wondered.

"It's the same as leaving a business card," Duncan explained. "For those that knew what to look for."

Flynn appeared thoughtful. "Did Antonio tell you who paid them?"

"Aye. But here's the thing. They don't take just any case that comes their way. They're selective."

"So it's not just about money," I stated.

"Exactly."

"I hate to rush you, Duncan, but we've got dinner plans—"

"Jane Elliot," Duncan blurted out. "Jane Elliot hired them."

"Please tell me you don't mean Jane Elliot, Ramsey's fiancée?" Flynn remarked.

"Sorry," Duncan muttered. "One and the same Jane Elliot. She wanted all the men who were part of the secret government agency that her father belonged to killed. She blames them for letting her father take the fall."

"Jane Elliot hired Italian mercenaries to take out the men who indirectly killed her father," I said, leaning back on the couch.

"And she kept it from us." Flynn's jaw clenched. Duncan began to sway even as he continued to drink. "For fuck's sake," Flynn muttered. "Duncan, put down the bottle and go to sleep."

"And sleep on your back," I commanded, not wanting his broken rib to puncture his lung.

Duncan reached toward the screen, and then he disappeared, the iPad going dark. "He'll be okay," I said, trying to reassure Flynn. "Buchanans are a tough lot."

"Aye," Flynn agreed, a glint of humor in his eyes. "Jane Elliot…couldn't be more Buchanan than if she'd been born to one."

My mind reeled. I liked Jane. The young woman had remarkable courage and backbone. I didn't think anyone was more surprised than her when she fell in love with Ramsey. Then again, Ramsey was a charming man. We'd hoped her love for Ramsey would buy her loyalty and protect the SINS.

"You all right?" Flynn asked, taking my hand when we stepped out of the elevator. Flynn and I put the Jane discussion on hold since we were on our way to meet with Michael O'Malley at the bar and restaurant, and we didn't want to be late.

"Stunned stupid," I admitted.

"Aye. Me too." Flynn flashed a grin and brought my hand to his lips. "Did I tell you how beautiful you look?"

I wore a simple wrap black dress and diamond studs. I'd left my hair down and free. I was presentable but hardly a knockout at the moment.

"Thanks, love."

He tugged me into his side as we walked through the lobby, heading for the restaurant. We gave the host a wave and then went to our usual table, a booth in the corner. O'Malley hadn't arrived yet, so Flynn ordered a scotch, and I ordered a sparkling water.

"Not drinking?" Flynn asked.

"Pacing myself," I answered.

Michael O'Malley arrived at the table. Quinn's father was tall and lean, with the same shade of green eyes as his daughter. But instead of dark raven hair like Quinn, O'Malley was blond.

O'Malley robustly shook Flynn's hand before his gaze slid to me. "You must be Barrett," O'Malley said, nearly pushing Flynn out of the way to give me a hug. "My daughter speaks very highly of you."

"I'm so glad," I said. I gave the older man a genuine smile. "I really like Quinn."

Once we were seated, O'Malley said to Flynn, "I hope you won't be offended if I order Irish whiskey."

Flynn chuckled. "By all means."

"What are you having?" O'Malley asked me.

"Sparkling water."

"You can't toast with water."

"You're right," I said dryly, shooting Flynn a look. "I'll have an Irish whiskey, too."

Chapter 44

The waiter came and O'Malley ordered us two glasses of Bushmills. When the server disappeared, O'Malley turned his attention back to us, more specifically, Flynn. "I want the bastard who took Quinn."

Flynn didn't take his eyes off O'Malley when he replied, "And I'd like nothing more than to give him to you."

O'Malley heard the sincerity in Flynn's voice, and though some of the tension left his body, it didn't disappear from his clenched jaw. "But?"

"But he belongs to Giovanni Marino first. You'll have to sit and discuss with him what will have to be done."

The waiter returned and dropped off our drinks. He looked like he was about to disappear again when Flynn said, "Let's order."

When we were alone again, we got back to discussing the situation.

"I don't like Marino," Flynn stated. "I don't trust him. I don't trust his word. Still, I know what my word is worth, and I'm not willing to put that on the line. If it got out that I—"

O'Malley waved his hand. "I understand your position.

But perhaps you and I could come to our own arrangement. After all, we're practically family."

Flynn smiled. "How do you figure?"

"My daughter is in love with the Russian. The Russian considers your wife family. Your wife is married to you. Ergo…"

"Ah," Flynn said. "To be clear, I consider the Russian my family."

"The Russian who is currently fighting for his life in the burn unit," O'Malley spat. "Whatever deal you think you have with Marino, I wouldn't put it past him to have made an alliance with his brother, called for peace, and turned against you."

A muscle in Flynn's cheek began to tick. Discreetly, I put my hand on his thigh. He took my hand and gave it a squeeze but didn't let go.

"You know that Filippi and Marino are brothers?" I asked.

"I know a lot more than you think," O'Malley said.

"How?" I wanted to know.

"I have my sources," he evaded with a shrug. "Marino can't be trusted. Just like his father."

I was thrown back into my memories of the night Marino was killed on the docks. Flynn had been shot; Sasha had saved him. He'd been my family even back then, before anything had been solidified.

"They came after my daughter to get to Sasha. Filippi wanted insurance—but how do you think he made that happen? He had help, Flynn. And I'd bet you anything Marino aided him, all the while pretending to be your ally. Why? Because even if Filippi and Marino go to war with each other, one thing remains true: they want the territory the Russians took from the Italians."

"You find a way to prove that to me—solid evidence—then I'm with you. We go to war," Flynn stated.

O'Malley nodded. "More than fair."

Our appetizers arrived just as my phone vibrated. I checked the screen. Quinn was calling me. "It's your daughter," I said to O'Malley, holding up the phone, about to answer it.

"Don't tell her I'm here," he stated.

Nodding, I pressed a button. "Quinn?"

"He's awake!" she blurted out. "Sasha's awake!"

O'Malley came with us to the hospital. Though Quinn was surprised to see her father, she didn't seem to question why he was there. Brandon hadn't left Quinn's side and even now, he stood sentry.

"What happened?" I asked, running to her, my heels clacking on the white floor.

"Brandon and I were sitting in the waiting room," she explained. "The doctor came out and said that they've been slowly weaning him off the sedation drugs and that Sasha woke up."

"Have you seen him?"

She shook her head. "They said I can see him tomorrow. Visiting hours."

I took her hand and squeezed it. "Go home, Quinn. You need to sleep in a bed tonight."

"I doubt I'll be able to sleep," she said. The tiredness of her face belied her words.

"I'll take you home," Brandon said. "No arguments."

"I'll join you," O'Malley said.

Quinn and Brandon turned in the direction of the exit and began walking away. O'Malley paused to look at us, his bright green gaze darting to Flynn and holding it there. Ever so slightly, Flynn inclined his head.

We watched them leave, and then I went to the nurses' station. When the nurse on duty gave me the runaround about waiting to see Sasha until tomorrow, Flynn swooped in, dropped his name, and told her he wanted to speak to the doctor.

The woman blanched at the unyielding, formidable command. Flynn always got his way, and the nurse realized that when she paged Dr. Bridgefield and he came immediately. I instantly felt bad for the man. He looked like he'd been catching a few minutes of sleep and Flynn's edict disturbed him.

"As I told Ms. O'Malley," Dr. Bridgefield began. "Visiting hours are tomorrow. He's resting now. He's in a lot of pain and even though he woke up for a bit, we've put him back under sedation. We want to keep him comfortable."

I hadn't seen Sasha since he had been brought to the hospital. I had no idea how he looked, but I needed to see for myself. Even if he was asleep and didn't know I was there, I wanted to see him. For my own benefit.

"Five minutes," I said, widening my eyes and pleading with him.

Dr. Bridgefield hesitated but a moment before he relented. "Five minutes. And then you come back tomorrow like everyone else."

Chapter 45

The right side of his face was burned, the blond hair on his head was sheared close to the scalp. I couldn't tell what had been cut and what had been burned away from the fire. Splotches of red and black covered him, his body raw and gruesome.

And the smell...

Dear God, the smell.

It took all of my willpower not to vomit into my medical mask. Dr. Bridgefield had tried to warn me while I was putting on sterile scrubs, gloves, and mask. In the burn unit, infections could spread easily. Every protocol needed to be followed.

Still, no amount of warning could've prepared me for this. Not only was Sasha unrecognizable, but also his injuries were substantial. If he survived, he would have months, maybe years of healing. Painful years. Ugly years. Lost years.

I was alone with him, and I took a seat by his bedside. I wanted to hold his hand, but they hadn't been spared. I gently touched my pinky to a swatch of skin that wasn't charred. He stirred, ever so slightly.

My heart broke for him—and for Quinn. This would change them. This would change all of us. But I believed

Sasha was strong enough to heal. Maybe he would never be who he used to be. Maybe his sense of humor would be gone. No way to know at the moment.

I lifted my eyes to see that Sasha's were open. Ice blue slits rested on me. I smiled, forgetting I was wearing a surgical mask.

His blue gaze was unwavering. He attempted to whisper, but it sounded like a wounded dying animal. I could only imagine the pain.

"Don't talk," I said quietly. "Just rest."

The stubborn Russian refused to listen to me and kept trying to say something. I shifted closer, leaning my head toward his mouth, hoping to hear him.

"*Milost'*," Sasha murmured.

I knew a few Russian words, mostly curse words. I shook my head. "I don't understand—"

"Mercy," he breathed.

My eyes flew to his; there was no hint of agony in his gaze, only emptiness. I could pretend to misunderstand, to blame it on the drugs, but I knew the truth.

It would've been easier if he had died in the explosion. For him, anyway. He was a warrior—a broken warrior.

"You sure?" I asked.

"*Da*," he whispered. "Help me go."

"Quinn?"

"Better…off…without me. Like this."

We stared at each other, communicating without words, not needing them. Finally, I nodded. I pulled my pinky away and stood. Sasha's eyes drifted shut, and he fell back asleep, the pain meds fed into his IV knocking him out.

I left the room, briefly nodded at the two Russian men who stood guard outside Sasha's door, and then briskly walked toward the end of the hallway toward a trashcan.

"Barrett?" Flynn asked, rising from his chair.

I didn't answer him as I tore at my surgical mask. It fluttered to the ground as I stuck my head in the trashcan and vomited. Standing up, I wiped my mouth with the collar of the scrub shirt. I wanted to get out of the hospital. The smell of scorched flesh lingered in my nose. It was so strong I tasted it at the back of my throat.

My stomach was in knots, my heart was heavy, but there was no question about what I was going to do.

"Love?"

I looked at Flynn who watched me with an intense gaze. I wondered if he knew, if what Sasha had asked me was written all over my face.

"Let's go home, love," he said gently, taking my hand.

I stared out the living room window and watched the snow fall. I'd gone to bed a few hours ago, only to toss and turn, and when I did doze, I dreamed of fire and death.

Pulling my legs up to my chest, I rested my chin on my knees and wondered if it was worth getting decked out in winter clothes to go for a walk.

"Hen?"

I turned my head to see Flynn standing in the living room, his hair mussed from sleep. Though it was the middle of the night, he seemed strangely awake.

"Did I wake you?" I asked.

He shrugged and then walked over to me. He wove his fingers through my hair as he leaned down to brush his lips across my forehead.

"Sasha?" he asked knowingly.

I nodded and turned to look back out the window.

"He's strong."

I paused and then, "Let's say he lives. Let's say he heals. He's never going to be the same person again."

Flynn's hand moved underneath my hair to hold my neck,

but he was silent, letting me talk. I wasn't ready to tell Flynn what Sasha asked of me. I didn't know if I would. This was my burden to bear.

Could I live with myself if I helped Sasha end his life? Could I live with myself if I didn't?

"What is it, love?" Flynn asked. "I know there's something you're not telling me."

I looked up at him. My eyes pleaded with him not to ask me. I hated keeping secrets from Flynn, but this wasn't about him. It was about Sasha and me, and for whatever reason, Sasha wanted me to carry this out. Maybe he didn't trust Quinn to do it; maybe he didn't want to put the burden on her, make her live with the knowledge that she killed—even in the name of mercy.

But Sasha and I...

Of course he'd ask me to do this.

"Take me to bed," I said to Flynn, leaning in to his touch.

"Aye," Flynn rasped. "I'll take you to bed and make you forget what has you worried." Our coupling was sweet, full of anguish, and I fell into a deep sleep around dawn.

The next day, Duncan was back in New York. I didn't know how he had been let on an airplane, looking the way he did. Ash refused to see him. She was holed up in Jack's apartment with Carys, and she wouldn't let Duncan inside.

I was fed up, sick to death of their stupid, childish fighting. Ash was no longer being rational—and she was keeping Duncan's daughter away from him. She claimed it was because Duncan looked terrifying with a swollen black eye and bruises all along his face and neck.

"I don't have the patience for this shit," I snarled at Flynn after hanging up the phone with Ash.

He looked up from the paper he was reading, humor lit in his eyes. "Why do you get in the middle?"

"They put me in the middle!" I yelled.

Shrugging, he went back to reading the paper. I snatched it out of his hands and threw it to the ground.

"What do you want me to do about it, love?" he asked calmly. "As you pointed out we have other things to worry about. Like Ramsey, like the distillery and Sanchez, like who actually killed Lila."

And the fact that one of my closest friends wanted me to help him end his life. But of course I didn't add that.

"Did you tell Ramsey it was Jane who hired The White Company?" I asked, wanting, needing to discuss something else to keep my mind off Sasha.

"Aye." He blinked blue eyes at me. "To say he flew into a rage is a drastic understatement. But in his defense, he's not upset that she did it, only that she didn't clue him in."

"Why didn't she clue him in—clue any of us in? It's not like any of us were unhappy when we got the news about Arlington."

"Because it wasn't just Arlington," Flynn reminded me. "There were two others. Jane had a vendetta, and she didn't trust Ramsey with the truth of it."

Secrets, lies, more secrets. We were buried beneath them, trapped.

Doomed.

Chapter 46

I lasted two hours at Alia and Jake's restaurant opening. Though I was happy for them, believed they'd make the tiny brick-walled restaurant in the heart of Greenpoint a complete and utter success, I could no longer pretend to be happy.

I knew what I had to do.

Tears had been lurking behind my eyes all day. I hadn't been able to force myself to go to the hospital or talk to Quinn. I didn't know if she'd seen Sasha; I didn't know if he was awake. All I knew was that every moment he was still on this earth, he didn't want to be. That weighed heavily on me. And I couldn't drink it away—or numb it—because the truth didn't die, no matter how hard you tried to kill it.

"You all right, love?" Flynn asked, wrapping an arm around my shoulders.

"Upset stomach," I lied.

"Let's go home," he suggested.

I shook my head. "You stay. This is important."

"You sure?"

"Yeah."

"Take the driver."

"No, I'll just grab a cab."

He leaned down to kiss me. "I'll slip out of here in about an hour."

I kissed him again, taking a moment to savor the feel of his lips on mine. "See you soon." I headed toward the front of the restaurant to the waiting hostess. I was just shrugging into my black coat when Alia spotted me in the corner. She sauntered toward me, high heels clacking on the polished wood floor. Her dark eyes glittered in the dim lighting, her long black hair sleek and shiny.

"Where are you going?" she asked.

"Home," I said. "I'm not feeling well."

"Headache?" she pressed.

"Stomach."

She raised her eyebrows. "Not from our food, I hope."

I grinned. "No. Your chef is very talented."

"Have some champagne." Alia thrust her flute at me. "It settles the stomach."

"I'd love to. But I really just… I need to go. Please don't be mad."

"I'm not."

"Promise?"

She grinned. "You showed up, didn't you?"

"Ah, that was a not-so-subtle dig at Lacey."

"What? You mean she couldn't fly all the way from New Zealand just for this?" She shook her head. "She did send me a video message apology."

I looked around the restaurant, catching Flynn's eye and smiling. "You did it, Alia. You and Jake. You said you wanted to, and you made it happen. I'm so happy for you."

Alia leaned down and embraced me. "Thank you."

I hugged her back before pulling away. "I promise we'll celebrate, just the two of us, hard core."

She snorted. "I'll believe that when it actually happens."

I chuckled. "It might be late, but I promise. And you know I don't break my promises."

"That's true," she agreed. "You are a lady of your word."

With one last hug, I departed, heading out into the dark, cold night. I hailed a cab and gave the cabbie an address. I settled back against the seat, my heart thudding in my ears. It took twenty minutes to get back into the city, the taxi turning down a dark, nearly abandoned street. Halfway down the block, the cabbie stopped.

I looked out the window at the deserted street. There were no lights except for street lamps. It was quiet, and no one was about.

"You sure this is the place?" the cabbie asked, looking at me in his rearview mirror.

"Yes." I handed him a fifty. "Keep the change."

"You want me to wait?" he asked.

I shook my head and then climbed out. I lingered until the cabbie put the car in gear and drove away. When I was sure I was alone on the derelict street, I walked around the corner and found the two metal doors on the sidewalk. Crouching down, I knocked three times and moved to the pavement.

A few seconds passed, and then the metal doors opened to reveal a set of stairs. I carefully navigated my way down them and came to stand on a cement floor.

The doors slammed shut, sealing me inside. It was dark, and I pressed my hand to a wall as I continued walking. Lights flickered on, low, but enough that I could finally see my way. The hallway opened up into a square room. A man sat in a folding chair, dressed in a dark suit; he was money, he was power.

He was the head of the Chinese mafia with connections to the black market. He had gotten me the same untraceable neurotoxin The White Company used.

He rose when I came to stand in front of him. The man was trim and lean. Handsome. He didn't say anything and neither did I.

Opening my clutch, I stuck my hand in the slit of the

lining and fished out the wad of cash. I handed it to him and waited for him to count it. When he finished, he inclined his head and reached into his breast pocket to pull out a capped syringe.

I took it and put it under the lining of my clutch before zipping it closed.

"Hungry?" he asked, startling the quiet. "My family restaurant makes the best Peking duck in the city."

I smiled. "Another time. I have somewhere to be."

Chapter 47

I managed to get into Sasha's hospital room, sight unseen, dressed in scrubs that had been easy to procure. The guards were not around and I wondered if Sasha had had anything to do with that.

Gray walls, florescent lighting. No wonder so many people died in hospitals—the decor was downright depressing.

I took a seat next to his bedside; machines beeped, monitors I didn't understand showing his stats. "Hey," I whispered.

His eyes opened. Blue. Bright. Filled with anguish. And hope.

"Are you sure this is what you want?"

He closed his eyes, like he was bracing himself. Fortitude. Finally, he nodded.

"Why not Quinn? Why isn't she doing this?"

"Not strong enough," he rasped, struggling to speak.

"Don't feel guilty," I said, my voice steel. "For asking me to do this for you. I'd go to hell with you. I'd fight by your side, every step of the way."

He blinked and I noticed the sheen, but I continued to talk. "I wish I was having another child," I said. "Boy or girl, I'd have named it Sasha."

"Barrett," he whispered.

I got up and leaned over to kiss a swatch of skin on his forehead. "You've been… If it weren't for you…"

His hand reached out, searching for mine. I took it, held on to it, making sure my tears didn't fall. My emotions didn't matter. Not now. I could crumble later.

"Take care of Quinn."

"I will."

"Happy."

"She will be," I assured him. "Promise."

He cracked a smile. I brought his hand to my lips and kissed his hand. "I love you. Be at peace."

He closed his eyes, signaling he was ready. I dropped his hand and went for the syringe in my pocket.

"I don't want you to stay," he said. "After you do it…leave."

"I don't want you to be alone," I whispered.

"Born that way. Die that way."

I glared at him.

"Someone could see you," he said quietly. "Don't want trouble for you. I sent my guards away. You have to leave before they come back. We don't have a lot of time." His eyes went flinty. "Let's do this, Barrett."

I got up and moved on wooden legs to stand by his IV. I uncapped the syringe and looked at it a moment.

"No regrets," he said. "I don't have any."

My eyes flew to his. "Really?"

He shook his head, a rueful pull of his lips appearing on his scorched, terrifying face. "Can't regret your own mortality."

I shot the syringe into his IV line, my hand shaking ever so slightly. "You can curse it though."

"*Da*," he agreed.

When I was finished, I put the cap back on and stuck it in

my pocket. I looked at him and then leaned over to brush my lips against his.

"Well, I guess I do have one regret," he said, his eyes drifting shut.

"Yeah? What's that?"

"Never got to sleep with you."

I laughed and headed for the door, wanting that to be the last moment of me he remembered.

Heart heavy, tears finally spilling over onto my cheeks, I made it out of the hospital. I gulped a breath of cold air, choking on it. I shoved my hands into my coat pockets, burrowing into the collar, wanting to climb under the covers and never get up.

"Barrett."

I whirled to find Flynn waiting for me. "What are you doing here?"

He cocked his head to the side. "Me? What about you? I thought you weren't feeling well."

"I'm not feeling well," I murmured, my gaze dropping from his. I couldn't do this with him now. I didn't have the strength to lie to him, to protect him from the knowledge of what I'd just done, of what Sasha had asked me to do.

"So you came to the hospital for a stomachache?"

"Flynn, I…"

"Yes?" He waited.

In three strides I was in his arms, clutching his solid frame and shaking like an alcoholic without a drink. Flynn's arms came around me and his lips brushed my hair.

"You're a good liar, Barrett." When I stiffened, he clarified, "I mean that as a compliment. But you're also my wife, the mother of my children, and I know you."

His arms tightened around me, refusing to let me go, not that I wanted to go anywhere.

"You left a good friend's restaurant opening all in the name of not feeling well. Very out of character. If you'd truly been feeling ill, you would've held it in, sipped on club soda, done anything to stay. Because your friends mean the world to you. And then I started to think about what could drag you away from a celebration. Only a friend in need."

He gently threaded his fingers through my hair, forcing me to look up at him. He stared down at me, eyes clear. The cold air swirled around us. The snow had already turned to brown slush. Nothing like a New York winter to remind me it wasn't home. I missed Dornoch. I missed my children.

I'd learned to live with my choices, my losses. But Sasha… What I'd had to do for him… I didn't know if I'd ever make peace with that.

"What did you do, Barrett?" Flynn asked quietly.

"I—"

"Wait," he said. "Let's go back to The Rex and then you can tell me."

Reluctantly, I nodded. Flynn took my hand and led me away from the hospital toward the street. Flynn raised his free hand to flag down a cab.

"Where's the car?" I asked.

"I wanted to come here alone," he explained. My phone rang, and I fished around in my coat pocket, wondering if it was a call from the hospital, letting me know that Sasha had passed on. But it wasn't the hospital—or even Quinn. It was Dex.

"Hey," I said, trying not to sound short or exhausted.

"Hey," he said, sounding like he was bouncing off the walls. A diet of Gummy Bears and Red Bull probably had turned him into a superhero.

"Bad time?" he asked.

If only he knew…

"No," I assured him. "What's up?"

"I think I found something," he said, voice all but

humming with excitement. "I think I found Lila's boyfriend. A few months ago she was seen with a guy. Andrew. Andrew Schaefer."

Chapter 48

I came to with Flynn's arms wrapped around me, blue eyes trained on my face. "Hen," he said, voice thick with worry. "What just happened? Your hand went slack in mine, and you went down."

"Phone call," I murmured, closing my eyes briefly.

"You dropped your phone," he explained. "It shattered."

Dex. Phone call. Andrew. This was all about Andrew.

"Help me up?" I asked, putting a hand to Flynn's chest. He stayed close, a hand on my back. "What happened?"

"Dex," I said. "News about Lila." My head swam, my stomach churned. I gulped in air as I leaned into Flynn's side.

"Easy," he said when I pulled away and tried to stand upright. I was wobbly, shaky. Dumfounded. "What's the news about Lila?"

"She was dating Andrew," I whispered, my eyes flying to Flynn's.

His mouth gaped. "Your brother?"

I nodded. Flynn's mouth continued to hang open. He was completely gobsmacked, and it would've been completely funny…under different circumstances.

"I can't—cab," he clipped, holding his hand up again.

I looked around for my phone, finding it a few feet away. Picking it up, I pressed the power button. Surprisingly, the shattered screen lit up and turned on. And began to ring immediately. Because the screen was broken, I couldn't see who was calling. Thinking it was Dex, I answered it and said, "Dex, I'll be back—"

"Not Dex," came Ash's angry voice.

A cab stopped at the curb, and Flynn opened the side door for me. I made my way toward the car, pinching the bridge of my nose.

"Ash," I began, sliding into the cab. "Now isn't a good time."

"You told Duncan I was pregnant!"

Flynn scooted in next to me, shut the door, and then gave the driver The Rex address.

"I did not tell Duncan you were pregnant," I said, my eyes darting to Flynn. "I told Flynn who told Duncan." Ash's sputter of indignation was loud in my ear.

"Look," I snapped. "I've had a rough day. And this bullshit going on between you and Duncan is childish and pointless. You love him, he loves you. He didn't fuck Lila or knock her up. So forgive him, let him move back in, and get over it!"

I pressed the end button—or what I thought was the end button. The phone went dark, and I shoved it in my pocket.

Flynn didn't say anything; he didn't need to. He wrapped his arm around me and pulled me into his side. I cuddled up next to him. I didn't know what to feel, what to think. There was so much going on in my head.

As soon as we got back to The Rex, we headed straight for Dex's suite. I knocked on the door and he answered immediately, looking jubilant and frazzled.

"How long since he's slept?" Flynn whispered.

"My bet? Four days."

We sat on the edge of the bed while Dex took up residence

in the desk chair. He scrolled through pictures of Andrew and Lila holding hands and standing on the sidewalk kissing.

"Wait," I said to Dex. "Can you go back to that last photo?"

Dex hit the arrow. My brother's face was turned to the camera, a content smile on his lips as Lila kissed his cheek. They looked happy. And in love. My gaze went to the corner of the picture, my mouth opening in surprise. Even though half the sign was missing, cut off by the end of the frame, I knew it.

"That's Paddy's," I said. "The Irish bar in my hometown. Good find, Dex."

He looked momentarily confused by my lack of reaction. Then again, he hadn't been there when I'd fainted. I got up from the bed. "Promise me you'll sleep tonight," I said.

"I will. One more thing," Dex said as Flynn and I started to move to the door. "Your brother… He's the father of Lila's baby."

Nausea swam through my throat, but I choked it down. Flynn's arm wrapped around my shoulder.

Dex hastened to reassure me. "Even though my theory— we don't know for sure that he's the one who—"

"I know," I cut him off. "Let's go. Dex, thank you for everything."

Dex gave a halfhearted salute before falling onto the bed, face first. Dramatic, maybe, but I understood what it felt like to run on fumes for days.

Flynn waited until we were in the elevator before he asked, "What are you thinking?"

"What if this has never been about you," I asked.

He frowned. "What do you mean?"

"What if in trying to take you down, Andrew was really going after me?"

The elevator doors opened, and we stepped into the penthouse. I kicked off my shoes and shrugged out of my coat, leaving them where they fell. Immediately, I went for the iPad resting on the coffee table.

"You think this is Andrew's crazy vendetta to bring you down all because of some nasty feelings from his childhood?"

"Pretty much," I said, taking a seat on the couch. iPad in hand, I opened a new browser window and searched for Paddy's. "Think about it. Andrew and Filippi work together, right? Filippi wants to take out Sasha because he took over Italian territory." I momentarily swallowed a lump of emotion when I thought of my friend.

"But Sasha is also one of my closest friends." I looked up at Flynn who nodded for me to go on. "Take out Sasha, hurt me. Lila was supposed to seduce you. Drive a wedge in our marriage and that would've hurt me."

"But it didn't go according to plan," Flynn said. "Lila appeared to go after Duncan."

"Yes. They planted the seed that Lila was carrying Duncan's baby."

"All that did was hurt Ash and Duncan," Flynn pointed out.

"On the surface maybe. Ash is my best and oldest friend. Her hurting hurt me."

Flynn shook his head. "Still seems like a stretch to me."

I shrugged. "Think what you want. But I know my brother. He's an angry man who was once an angry child who never felt like he got what he deserved. This is personal. And we keep fucking up his plan."

"So what are we going to do?" Flynn asked, a slight smile curving his lips.

"May I borrow your phone?" I asked him.

He reached into his pocket and then handed it to me. I dialed the number to Paddy's Irish Pub.

"Paddy's," a gruff voice answered. I could hear music and laughter in the background, and I was instantly nostalgic for my hometown. Memories of my deceased parents came at me, and I shut them down, refusing to think about them.

"Please tell me you finally put in a new jukebox," I teased. I could picture Paddy on the other end of the phone. Irish through and through. Burly with an easy smile and ruddy face.

"Is this who I think it is?" Paddy demanded, fond affection in his voice.

"Who do you think it is?"

"I'll be damned," he muttered. "Miss you, girl. When are you coming home for a visit?"

"Sooner than you think. Hey, by any chance, have you seen my brother around?"

"Yeah, actually, I have."

"Thought so. Anyway, Paddy, do me a favor. If you see Andrew, don't tell him I asked. I want to surprise him when I come for a visit."

"You got it. Listen, I gotta get back to these clowns. They're drinking me out of house and whiskey. See you soon, yeah?"

"Yeah."

I hung up with Paddy and grinned at Flynn.

"What's that look for?" Flynn wondered.

"Paddy can't keep his mouth shut."

"But you told him not to say anything if he saw Andrew." Understanding dawned. "You want Andrew to know you're coming."

"I want the bastard to know I'm coming. And I want him to underestimate me, which he will. That's always been his weakness."

Chapter 49

I sat in the large tub, the water almost too hot for my skin. I made it hotter, wanting it to burn me. Flynn had given me a moment to myself, but he was back now, sitting quietly in the steamy bathroom.

"I'm worried about you," Flynn said quietly. "This thing with your brother… If he did kill Lila…you can't go charging in there."

"Why not?"

"Aside from the fact that Andrew is probably unhinged—"

"Not probably," I interjected. "Definitely. Definitely unhinged. Only an insane person would take years of animosity and turn it into a revenge project."

"I can't let you—"

"Careful," I mock warned, but Flynn didn't smile.

"I'm serious. Things have a way of getting out of control and I don't want—I just—"

"Yeah, I know." I shook my head in wry amusement. "I haven't thought about Andrew in years."

"Really? Not even a passing thought?"

I shrugged. "Not really." It was the truth. When Andrew had lost money in Flynn's New York casino and all but bartered me in lieu of his debt, I'd realized that Andrew didn't—couldn't—love me the way a brother was supposed to. So, I'd severed ties and never looked back.

There was no mourning our lack of relationship because there was nothing to mourn. I had Jack, Ash's brother. He was more than enough brother for me.

If Andrew was responsible for killing his pregnant girlfriend, then that was an entirely different brand of evil. It took a cold bastard to do something that terrible.

I stood up, water sluicing down my body. Flynn's intense eyes followed the curves of my body, resting on my flat belly. Well, flat-ish, belly. I'd had three children. Nothing ever went back to the way it was.

He grabbed a towel and stood. After putting it around me, he pulled me against him. He was shirtless, wearing nothing but his boxers. I breathed in the scent of his skin and closed my eyes. I wanted his strength. I wanted his acceptance when I told him what I'd done.

When Flynn made a move to step away, I held on, forcing him to keep holding me. His hand wrapped around the back of my neck. He gave it a gentle squeeze, and I looked up at him.

"Whatever you've done, whatever is weighing on you, just tell me," he said quietly.

He lifted me into his arms and carried me to the bedroom. He placed me in the middle of the bed and then crawled up next to me, propping his head on his bent arm.

I looked at the wall when I finally had the courage to tell Flynn what I'd done. I waited for the onslaught, the anger, the horror. But it never came.

"Look at me." Flynn's voice was low.

I did as commanded. His expression was soft, compassionate. Suddenly, I was in his arms, and I was crying for the loss of a dear friend.

"You're the bravest person I know," Flynn whispered,

kissing away the tears on my face. I snuggled into his embrace and closed my eyes.

"Sleep, love, it will be better in the morning."

It wasn't better in the morning. It was worse. My actions from the night before came rushing back at me, leveling me emotionally. I was open, raw, unable to think clearly—even after a cup of coffee.

Flynn was already gone from the suite, and I hated that we never seemed to wake up with one another. We were always busy, running from one crisis to the next. Even when we were with the boys, we never just spent a Saturday hanging out in our pajamas, watching cartoons, and eating Cap'n Crunch. Maybe that would've been my life if I'd married someone else, had kids with someone else.

But I didn't have a normal life. I could never hope for average. Maybe it was stupid to yearn for it. But average people didn't have mob bosses as their best friends or a crazy brother hell-bent on revenge.

My cell phone rang. I couldn't see who was calling, but I answered it anyway. "Hello?"

"Barrett," Mateo Sanchez greeted, his tongue rolling around the r's in my name.

"Mateo."

"Did you get my flowers?"

I looked at the orchids on the coffee table. "Yes, they're lovely. I meant to call and thank you, but things have been... hectic...since I've been back."

"Not a problem," he said smoothly. "I was calling to discuss the progress of the distillery."

Ramsey had left London and gone home to Dornoch. He was currently throwing himself into the construction of the distillery. Anything to take his mind off Jane. As far as I knew, their relationship was over. I still hadn't spoken to either of them about it.

"Things are coming along," I said, getting back to the matter at hand.

"Is your husband still reluctant to be in business with me?"

I laughed. "Reluctant? No. Upset that another man is sending me flowers? Yes."

Mateo chuckled.

"You did it on purpose," I accused, ensuring that my voice was nothing but teasing.

"Maybe."

"I threw them away."

"No, you didn't," he said. "Because they don't mean anything to you. They're just flowers to you."

"You speak with such confidence that you know me," I quipped.

"I do know you. You're a woman who would do anything for her husband and her family. That kind of loyalty…it's unusual."

"Why did you really call, Mateo?" I asked. Tired. Not in the mood for more games or subterfuge.

He paused for a moment and then, "Goodbye, Barrett."

Depression sank into my bones. Everything looked gray, felt gray, tasted gray. I didn't even have the energy to cry, so I sat on the couch, staring at the TV that wasn't on.

The elevator doors opened, but I didn't bother to turn my head to see who it was.

"You fucking bitch."

I flinched like I'd been punched. My head whipped to the woman looming tall, angry, a force to be reckoned with. What I imagined I used to look like before all this became too much.

"Quinn, I…"

What was I supposed to say? That I was sorry? That I hurt, too?

"Sasha is writhing around in pain, no thanks to you," she seethed.

I blinked. "He's what?"

"In pain. Because of you."

"But I—he's supposed to be…" I couldn't say it, hope flaring in my heart.

"Dead?" she snapped. "Because he made a choice and didn't involve me? Instead, he involved you."

"Would you have done it?" I asked, finally shaking off some of the apathy. "If he'd told you what he wanted, would you have helped him?"

She fell silent, but her green eyes continued to spark with anger.

I lowered my voice. "He didn't want that on you, Quinn. He didn't want you to carry around that burden forever."

"But he had no problem asking you to do it?" she asked in disgust. And something else. Hurt. She was hurt.

"Is it because he asked me and not you or because I'm another woman?"

"You're not *another* woman. You're the *other* woman. And I think—I think you'll always be the other woman."

"He wanted to protect you."

"I don't need protection. I'm not a child."

I looked at her for a long moment and then nodded. "You're right. So, do you want to know what your father's really doing in New York?"

Chapter 50

I stalked down the white hallway of the hospital, anger making my steps fast and had me balling my fists at my sides. I arrived outside of Sasha's hospital room, guarded by Big Russian and Bigger Russian.

When I went to open the door to Sasha's private room, they blocked my entrance. I tilted my head back and glared at them.

"Move."

"He does not want visitors," Big Russian said with a clipped accent.

"Get out of my way," I snapped. "Or I'll have your balls."

Bigger Russian spoke in Russian, and the only word I recognized was *Dolinsky*. Big Russian sighed with a look at me, but he moved out of the way.

I entered the room, shut the door, and glared at the occupant in the bed.

"Don't look at me that way," Sasha said, his voice tight with pain. "This is your fault."

"My fault? How do you figure that?"

"You really need me to spell it out for you? Whatever you

gave me last night didn't kill me, it only made me sick to my stomach and then I crapped my pants."

"I had assurances—"

"Well, they were bullshit assurances!" Sasha yelled with surprising energy.

I suddenly started to giggle. Giggles turned to guffaws and guffaws turned to boisterous laughter. I held my sides; they ached from the strain. I looked at Sasha who was watching me with knowing blue eyes.

"I'm so glad you're not dead," I blurted out, emotion gurgling up inside me.

"Should've just asked you to put a bullet in my skull," he remarked gloomily. "At least then I'd know it would've worked."

"You weren't always this dark, you know."

"Sorry. I'll try to be a 'glass is half full' kind of guy. Forget the fact that I look like a horror movie extra—I'm not vain—the pain, Barrett. The months and months of recovery."

"Doesn't make you a coward," I said softly, taking a seat by his bed but not touching him. Though I was in scrubs, I didn't want to risk giving him an infection.

"Feels that way," he admitted. "I guess there's one good thing about all this."

"What?"

His ice blue eyes went cold. "I no longer have the cigarette burns courtesy of my bastard father."

My stomach lurched. "Sasha—"

"No. I won't talk about it."

"Okay." I sighed. That piece of Sasha's history would eat away at me. "Quinn's pissed at you."

"Yeah."

"You have to stop sheltering her."

"She doesn't deserve this."

"She's a grown up. Let her make her own choices."

"I don't want to talk about Quinn."

"Fine," I said. "You want me to tell you a joke? A burned guy walks into a bar…"

He smiled, but it looked like a grimace of pain. "So why didn't I die?" he asked. "I'm being serious, here."

"I don't know," I replied honestly.

"Did you tell Flynn our plan?"

"No. Why?"

"Because your husband always seems to be one step ahead of you."

"You think Flynn knew I was planning to—and that he somehow, what? Tampered with the drug I was given?"

"You have any better theories?"

"No. I don't."

He closed his eyes.

"Should I go?"

"Not yet," he said, eyes still closed. "Talk to me about something else."

"You've heard of Mateo Sanchez, right? The guy sent me flowers."

I left the hospital an hour later, lighter but pensive. Sasha had a good mind—he saw pieces to the puzzle when I'd missed them. I didn't doubt for a second that Flynn had gotten involved. It explained his reaction when I told him what I'd done—or thought I'd done—for Sasha. And it explained why he'd been waiting for me outside the hospital.

I was in no great hurry to confront him about it; there was no anger on my end. I should've been mad, but I wasn't. Sasha was alive. In pain and in great need, but alive, and I wouldn't be sad about him still being here. With me. Whatever he needed, I'd give it to him. The next many months, maybe even a year, were going to be difficult for him. But I'd make him laugh and I wouldn't coddle him.

He had Quinn for that. Unless he broke up with her, pushed her away because he thought that was best for her. I hoped Quinn stuck to her guns and proved to him she wanted to be with him. But that was between them.

I walked into the lobby of The Rex and immediately went to the elevators. I wasn't going to the penthouse—frankly, I was sick of being cooped up in there, waiting for Andrew to make his next move, waiting for some other bomb to detonate. Instead, I went to the glass lounge on the roof. If anyone thought I looked strange in the pair of scrubs I was wearing, they didn't let on.

At this time of day, the lounge wasn't yet open, so there was no hostess at the stand, not even any servers setting up for the evening. I went behind the bar and poured myself a glass of sparkling water and then took it to one of the large leather couches that faced the skyline.

I heard Flynn's soft footsteps approach, and then he was sitting next to me, his arm brushing mine.

"Why?" I asked, clutching the glass of sparkling water.

He didn't even pretend not to know what I was talking about. "Because if Sasha died, there would've been another upheaval with the Russians. I couldn't allow that."

"For the SINS, you mean."

Sasha and the Russians funneled legitimate money to our cause for a free Scotland. If Sasha was no longer in charge that alliance might change. I hadn't even considered it.

"Aye, for the SINS," Flynn said softly. "But also for you. This would've broken you. Losing a friend, being the one to help him end his life."

"You're not mad that I didn't confide in you?"

Flynn's arm snaked around me and pulled me into his side. I burrowed into him, breathing him in, wondering what I did to deserve such a man who understood me, even before I understood myself.

"Are you mad that I interfered?" Flynn asked.

"Point taken, love." I leaned back and smiled at him. "So you let me pay the head of the Chinese mafia ten thousand dollars for a diuretic?"

"Fifteen," Flynn said with a grin. "I gave Li Chan five grand to go through with the con."

Chapter 51

"We're never going to find a manager," Flynn muttered, tossing the last applicant's resume into the garbage.

"Who would have thought that good help was so hard to come by," I teased.

"I don't have time for this. How much money do you think it would take to get Lacey back here for a few weeks?"

I smirked. "More money than we have."

"She's that happy with the surfer?" Flynn asked.

"Way to be subtle," I said with a laugh. "Tell Brad to call her himself."

"She won't return his calls."

"She doesn't return my calls half the time," I quipped. "She's having fun. Let her."

He ran a hand across his face and then looked around the newly reconstructed club. It was ready for reopening, but we didn't have management in place to ensure everything went smoothly. We couldn't worry about that too—not while we were dealing with all this other stuff.

"Why don't we promote from within?" I asked. "How about Katherine?"

"Katherine? Katherine who's afraid of her own shadow?" Flynn asked dubiously.

"She's not afraid of her own shadow."

"You're right. She's just afraid of me."

"That is true," I agreed. "Look, we don't have anyone else lined up, and she's part of the SINS family. What do we have to lose?"

He sighed. "You make a good point. All right. Let's give her a shot."

"If this works out, Glenna is going to kill me," I muttered, pulling out my new phone so I could call Katherine. "Katherine might never go back to Dornoch."

Flynn shook his head. "I can't wait to go back to Dornoch. And to our distillery that is a cocaine front."

"Just for a year," I said. "Then Sanchez will become a distant memory."

He raised an eyebrow in disbelief and shook his head. I snorted in humor while dialing Katherine.

A man answered, causing me to falter. Katherine didn't have a boyfriend. Did she?

"Hi," I greeted. "Is Katherine available? This is Barrett."

"Barrett," the man repeated slowly. "No, Katherine isn't available at the moment. She's…indisposed."

The hairs on the back of my neck stood up. "Andrew?"

"I hear you've been looking for me."

"What have you done with Katherine? Where is she?" I demanded.

"I haven't done anything to her." He paused. "Yet."

Anger, volatile, hot, dangerous. I shoved it away and forced myself to sound cool and unaffected when I asked, "What is it you really want, Andrew?"

"How about a trade?" he suggested. "You for her."

"Me for her," I repeated, looking at Flynn whose blue eyes had darkened with rage. He nodded imperceptibly. "Put her on the phone."

"I had a feeling you wouldn't believe me," Andrew said.

I heard shuffling and a moment later, a bone-melting scream. Protective anger surged through me, but I forced myself to remain calm, even after I heard Katherine's whimper of my name.

"Where are you?" I asked coldly.

"You know where I am. And I think it goes without saying, but I'll say it anyway. Come alone or I'll kill the girl and make you watch." He hung up, and I set the cell aside before I decided to throw it against a wall of the club.

I was almost one hundred percent sure that Andrew had killed Lila, his pregnant girlfriend. Which meant he'd killed his own child. I couldn't let Katherine take the brunt of Andrew's anger. Who knew what the madman would do to someone I cared about? He was capable of anything.

After an hour meeting with Duncan and Brad, we had a vague outline of a plan. It wasn't solid and things could go wrong. But we didn't have time to form anything better. None of us knew what we were walking into. Duncan was still recovering from his broken ribs, but we needed him. Like a true Scottish warrior, he assured me he could do this.

Flynn didn't want me to go even though he knew I had to. Andrew wouldn't deal with anyone else. He wouldn't accept anyone else, and I wasn't going to let Katherine die.

We piled into a black SUV with Brad behind the wheel. The drive was silent and tense; there was nothing to say. Flynn and I sat in the farthest back seat. I leaned into him, his arm around me, his lips in my hair.

My childhood home was three hours outside of the city. It was late afternoon by the time we made it Upstate. The temperature had dropped, and the roads were slick. Brad turned the car down a forested road and parked.

"Be vigilant," I said to him and Duncan.

"Aye, lass," Duncan said. "You as well."

The two men climbed out of the car, and I watched them find their way to the tree line while they waited for Flynn. It had begun to snow on our drive up, and it made them look like blurry black dots. We only had a few more hours of daylight.

"Be careful," Flynn said.

"I will."

"Why don't I believe you?"

I would've laughed, but it wasn't funny. Maybe I was reckless, maybe I was stupid, maybe I was willing to do anything for family.

Katherine was innocent. Could I really live with myself if I let her suffer at my brother's hands?

Life was a series of choices, and there was nothing black and white about any of it.

I turned to face him. "Promise me something."

"Anything."

"Do not put yourself in jeopardy. Let Duncan and Brad handle it. I couldn't bare it if you… Just please. No risks."

"I want the same promise from you," he commanded. "Don't trust anything Andrew says. Watch his body. The body always gives away a tell."

I nodded. "You better go."

Flynn grabbed me by the collar of my coat and hauled me to him. His lips covered mine, desperate and needy. My hands went to his face as I tore my mouth from his.

"Stop it," I commanded, breathless. "This isn't the end for us."

"I know."

"Then kiss me like you'll see me later for dinner."

A small smile broke out on his face. He leaned in and gave me a quick peck on the lips. "See you soon, love."

He got out of the car, and a few minutes later, he joined

Duncan and Brad. They melted into the wilderness, and I sent up a prayer, a thought, a hope, that they'd get through this unscathed.

I didn't include myself in that. Though I'd told Flynn I'd be careful, and I would, I wouldn't be able to live with myself if I didn't do everything possible to get Katherine away from Andrew. She was bait to him, nothing more.

Andrew was enjoying his own sick game. Let him. Let him choke on the pieces.

He might have already killed her. That was also a strong possibility—and the idea of it had me sick to my stomach.

I got into the driver's side of the car and slowly maneuvered it up the snowy road. Fifteen minutes later, my childhood home came into view. It was a two-story wood structure with its own private driveway. One hundred-year-old trees surrounded the house, and I remembered that sometimes during violent rainstorms, branches would scratch against the windows. On nights like those, I'd leave my bedroom and fall asleep on the couch. My parents would find me in the morning, and Mom always made me pancakes.

My life had been happy, easy. And then they'd died, leaving me with Andrew, a resentful, callous caregiver—a man who wanted to destroy me. It only reinforced what I'd already learned; family wasn't family just because of shared blood.

I slid out of the car before all my courage deserted me. It was cold and the sky was white; heavy snow was imminent. I tromped up the steps of the front porch and knocked on the door. It opened, revealing an armed man with facial hair and dead eyes.

I looked up at him and stated, "Take me to my brother."

He didn't answer, but he did step aside. I entered the foyer of my childhood home. It no longer looked the same. Andrew must've redecorated it. Or maybe it had been Lila. Had my brother been planning on raising his child here?

The front door shut, and it sounded ominous and final—

like the lid of a coffin closing. I shook off that morbid thought and removed my coat. I wore a skintight black turtleneck dress and leather boots that stopped just below my knee. My hair was twisted up in a bun and held with a hairpin.

"I'll have to search you." His eyes drifted down my body. I hoped he hadn't violated Katherine.

"That won't be necessary, John."

Chapter 52

I should've known it would come to this.

All roads led here, but four years ago, when I met Flynn Campbell, I had no way of knowing this was how it was going to play out.

"Barrett," the brown-haired man greeted, his smile wide and insincere. "So good to see you."

"Where is she?" I demanded, forcing myself to remain calm when all I wanted to do was unleash the beast, unleash the monster and let blood spray.

"She's here," he said with a negligent shrug. "And still in one piece." Andrew chuckled. "For now."

"Who are you? What have you become?"

He raised an eyebrow. "I could ask you the same question. Wife to a known criminal. Mother to his children." He sneered in disgust. "I'm ashamed of you."

"Me?" I laughed, the sound shrill, empty, cold. "I can still look in the mirror. What about you?"

"I finally have what I want," he said. "You. Here."

"I didn't come for you," I lied. "I came for her."

Cocking his head to one side, he studied me like an animal

in a zoo. "I never understood that about you. Your intense, unwavering loyalty."

"You never understood a lot of things about me."

He rolled his eyes, looking bored. "Should we get on with this?"

"You let her go. Now. You have what you want. You got me here. Let her go," I repeated.

He studied me for a moment. "Are you afraid?"

"To die?" I asked. "No."

"Most people would be afraid."

I smiled, showing a lot of teeth. "I'm not most people."

"No, I guess you're not," Andrew said. "Let's go sit in the library." He looked at the giant standing next to me. "Bring up the girl."

I followed Andrew to the second floor, down the hallway to the last door. The room had once been my father's office. It had a view of the front of the property, and I always wondered how Dad never seemed to get distracted.

It no longer looked like the room I remembered. I took a seat on a new black leather couch. A fire crackled in the hearth, but I hardly noticed the warmth. It was chilly in the room.

My brother used to be a man of extreme and volatile temper. I hardly recognized him now. His brown eyes were watchful, careful.

He took a seat in the matching leather chair, looking comfortable and assured.

"Why didn't you have me searched?" I asked.

"Where would you be hiding a weapon?" he inquired.

"I could have a gun strapped to my leg."

"Maybe," he agreed. "But we both know you wouldn't do anything to jeopardize the girl."

"How long?" I demanded.

Andrew cocked his head to one side. "How long what?"

"How long have you been planning this?"

"From the moment Campbell took you in form of payment. I had plans to take him down. I was going to. You weren't supposed to fall in love with him. You weren't supposed to marry him."

"And that's when you decided to take me down with him?" I asked in genuine curiosity. I could hardly follow Andrew's thought process—because it wasn't logical—he wasn't being rational.

"You were supposed to stand by me," he said, anger suddenly appearing on his face.

"Let's not pretend you ever gave a shit about me," I said, bitter and accusatory. "You hated having to take care of me after Mom and Dad."

"Your mother was a fucking slut," he said.

Andrew was a grown adult, had been for years, and yet, he still blamed my mother for the demise of his parents' marriage. The truth was, my father and Andrew's mother had been done a long time before my mother even appeared on the scene.

I just grinned.

"You're just like her," Andrew spat. "Another fucking slut, spreading her legs for a man who bought her."

Andrew's coldness was a veneer, and not a good one. Over the years, his anger and resentment had turned into something else, hardened into insanity.

"Tell me about Lila," I said, changing the subject.

"A means to an end," he said with a shrug.

"I saw photos of the two of you," I persisted. "You both looked happy."

"That was before," he grumbled. "Before the plan all went to shit. She was supposed to seduce Campbell, but she couldn't even do that."

"So you concocted for her to get Duncan into bed?"

"Neither one of them took what she was offering. So we set it up to look like something happened."

"She was carrying your baby," I said softly.

"I wasn't sure it was mine. Lila was a dancer in Las Vegas."

"It was."

He scoffed. "How do you know?"

"Autopsy. Blood type."

Andrew paled and then resolutely shook his head. "I don't believe you."

"Believe what you want." I shrugged like I didn't care because I didn't. "Tell me about Filippi. I'm curious about your partnership."

"He wanted the Italians. I wanted Campbell destroyed. He came to me. Thought we could work together."

Two men who wanted what others had.

"Thou shalt not covet," I mocked.

There was a knock on the library door and then it opened. The armed man, John, hauled Katherine into the room. Her brown hair hung loose, her lip was bloody, and she looked like a rag doll a moment away from having its stuffing busting out.

I feigned disinterest even though it took all of my willpower not to surge to my feet and go to her. I looked back at Andrew who was watching me closely.

"Well, are you a man of your word?" I demanded. "Are you going to let her go?"

"Why would I do that?" Andrew inquired. "I now have you both. I think you'll both make excellent bartering chips."

I laughed, making sure it was apathetic. "Flynn won't give you shit."

Andrew looked like he was considering my words. "I guess it doesn't really matter, does it? I wanted to destroy Campbell. If I kill you, the mother of his children, that'll bring him to his knees."

My heart tripped, but I forced myself to remain cool. "Sure. You could kill me. But then what's stopping Flynn from killing you? He'll come after you with a vengeance. And it won't be fast, either. He'll make it hurt. He'll draw it out. He'll make you cry and beg and still he won't end it. You think you've won, Andrew, but you haven't. You asked me if I was afraid to die. I'm not." I gazed at him unflinchingly. "Are you?"

Chapter 53

Andrew smiled. It wasn't the reaction I was expecting. "Take the girl back to the basement," Andrew commanded his man.

John hauled Katherine toward the door. She finally lifted her face, and I could see her eyes. There was no fear in her gaze. She was shaking, but I realized it was in anger. Katherine wanted to fight.

But it was stupid to fight a man who had a gun.

If Andrew separated us, it would be harder to get out of there. Together, we stood a chance.

"So how were you going to do this?" I asked Andrew as I went to the liquor cart in the corner. "Were you going to have your man do it? Bullet to the head? What? Are you going to kill us both at the same time?" I poured myself a drink and waited for his answer.

"I'm going to make Campbell watch," Andrew clipped, his eyes dark with insanity.

I snorted and took a drink. "To do that, you need Flynn. You don't have Flynn."

"How do you know I don't have Flynn?"

My gaze snapped to his.

His smile was evil. "Like he'd leave you to do this alone. I know he's close. So enjoy the scotch, Barrett. Because it will be the last one you ever have." Andrew looked at his man. "Take them both to the basement."

Andrew wanted theater? I'd give him theater.

I threw my glass of scotch into the fireplace. Flames erupted from the open hearth, causing just enough of a distraction for Katherine to slip out of the giant's grip and dash out of the library. The man growled and ran after her.

Andrew's face had slackened in shock and before it had a chance to wear off, I moved. I went for the liquor cart. Wanting to add to the mayhem, I picked up two bottles of liquor and threw them into the fireplace. Glass shattered and alcohol burned; the flames whooshed out of the fireplace, engulfing the edge of the carpet.

"You fucking cunt!" Andrew screamed, holding up an arm to shield his face from the sudden heat.

I was steps from the window and took advantage of the commotion. I made it to the window and flipped the latch before gripping the sill. It wouldn't budge. I'd forgotten that some of the windows in the house were warped from years of humid summers and wet winters. Even if I'd gotten the window open, the old tree next to the house was no longer there. Probably cut down.

Andrew looked at me, a deadly smirk across his face when he realized I was trapped.

"I can't wait to tell Campbell that you burned to death," Andrew stated. "Horrible way to die." He looked around the room one last time and then went for the door. He shut it behind him. I heard the snick of the lock. The sound of something scraping across the wood floor and thumping against the door told me that Andrew wasn't taking any chances with my escape.

Smoke continued to fill the room, and the heat from the flames licked at my skin. Sweat dotted my brow and panic made my hands clammy. I looked around the room, wondering what I could use to break the window. The desk chair was heavy wood. No way I could lift it. My eyes landed on an iron fireplace poker in the corner near the source of the fire.

Holding my breath, I ran for it. I wrapped my hand around it before realizing it was hot to the touch. I yanked my throbbing hand back. Tears leaked out of the corners of my eyes. I couldn't touch the iron; I needed a buffer. My dress was too thick to rip. I yanked up my dress and tugged down my underwear and hastily swathed the handle of the iron poker.

I coughed as smoke billowed from the fireplace. My eyes watered, and my head swam as I moved toward the window. Gripping the iron poker, I tried to maneuver it under the sill, but I couldn't get any leverage.

With renewed force and frenzy, I attacked the glass. Small cracks began to form in the corners.

The blazing heat was behind me, and I knew I was nearly out of time. I refused to die in a fire. I refused to give Andrew the satisfaction.

With one last burst of energy, I launched the poker at the window. I felt the cold air seeping through the hole in the glass. I prodded the small opening, and soon I had a big enough space to crawl through. I dropped the iron poker onto the floor, and before I could think too much about it, I managed to slither through the window. Shards dug into my knees and hands, but there wasn't anything I could do about it. There was a thin lip of an edge where I was able to perch haphazardly. There was a rain gutter on one side, but it wasn't sturdy enough for me to shimmy down.

I was on the second floor of an old-style farmhouse. It was at least ten feet from the ground. I still felt heat at my back—I dared a look behind me and saw that the fire had engulfed the entire room.

Scooting toward the rain gutter, I turned my body so that I was sitting at an angle on the ledge. With one hand on the rain gutter and the other on the shelf, I tried to distribute my weight. I'd have to dangle and drop. I was wearing relatively flat boots, so hopefully I wouldn't break an ankle.

There was another *whoosh* of air and the shattering of glass. The flames must've found the last of the liquor. Tendrils of fire snaked out the window to lick across my hand still on the windowsill. Without thought, I let go, letting the rain gutter take all of my weight. It groaned in protest and I felt it loosen.

And then I was falling.

Falling…

Chapter 54

There was no pain. Just cold numbness. Wet. I felt something on my cheeks. Tears? No, that wasn't right. Snowflakes, maybe. I stuck out my tongue and caught a few.

There was a buzzing in my ears. Annoying. Insect like. I wanted to sleep. Sleep forever.

"Barrett! Barrett! Come on, hen, wake up. Wake up for me."

"No," I grumbled.

"Love, open your eyes."

The tone of voice was commanding. Insistent.

I opened my eyes and stared into dark blue ones. A smile of relief brushed Flynn's mouth. Behind his head, I saw flames coming from the roof of my childhood home. I was too dazed to care.

"What hurts?" he asked.

"Not sure anything does," I said stupidly.

"Don't move. I don't know how you fell, what you hit, but you need an ambulance."

I heard a click and then a barrel of a gun was pressed against Flynn's temple. "I don't think she'll need an ambulance," came Andrew's low voice. "Stand."

Flynn put up his hands, showing he wasn't even trying to go for his own weapon. He stood, his face blank, his eyes still on me.

"John, search him," Andrew commanded.

"Just a pistol," John said after patting Flynn down and removing the weapon.

Flynn moved out of my sight line. Andrew loomed over me, shaking his head. "You thought you won."

Snow was seeping through my dress, but I was no longer numb with cold. I was hot, so hot. I didn't feel anything except heat.

"If you're going to kill me," I said, "then let me sit up. I'm not going to let you put me down like a beaten dog."

"Barrett, don't," Flynn said.

John punched Flynn. The crunch of his knuckles hitting my husband's flesh made me sick to my stomach.

"Help me sit up," I said to Andrew, reaching out my left hand for his. It took effort.

He appeared to debate for a moment before grasping my fingers and hoisting me up. My spine felt like it had absorbed the fire from the house and was burning through my bones, liquefying me from the inside out.

"Any last words, sister?" Andrew mocked.

With the last of my energy, I yanked the hairpin from my hair and stabbed him in the Adam's apple. His eyes widened in surprise.

"Fuck you, Andrew," I spat right before I passed out.

Sirens. Flashes of blue eyes. Moving lips but no sounds. Hot then cold. Cold then hot.

Something in my arm. Needle. Burning. Medicine. Nothing.

Nothing for a long, long time.

Beeping. Loud.

Soft voices.

"Her injuries were extensive," said the doctor.

"Will she walk again?" asked a woman.

Ash.

"We won't know that for a while yet. She has a severe concussion. She shattered her leg and from what I can tell, when she fell, she landed on her pelvis. Spleen and liver were damaged. We were able to repair the liver, but we had to take out the spleen."

I couldn't feel anything. I must've been heavily medicated.

"The good news is your wife is breathing on her own. That's a very good sign."

I finally opened my eyes. Everything looked harsh and white with the sun streaming through the open blinds. I squinted in pain.

"Blinds," I rasped.

No one heard me, so I tried again. "Blinds," I said a little louder. "Too damn bright."

Three heads swiveled toward me. Ash was the first to move, and she did my bidding by closing the blinds.

Flynn stood with his hands in his pockets, looking bleak and lost.

The doctor came to my bedside and smiled. "Mrs. Campbell, how are you feeling?"

I ran my tongue across my dry lips. "Is that a serious question?"

He chuckled and then pulled out a penlight. He shined it into one of my eyes and then the other. Satisfied, he nodded and then clicked off the penlight and stuck it back in his white doctor coat.

My right leg was in a cast, all the way up to the thigh. My hands were scraped but exposed.

"Barrett?" Flynn called.

"Hmm?"

"Did you hear what Dr. Carson just said?"

"No," I said. "Sorry. I was...taking stock."

Dr. Carson nodded. "Understandable." He gave me a brief rundown of my injuries and prognosis. I pretended to listen even though I'd already overheard everything I needed to know.

"How long have I been here?" I wondered, looking at Flynn and not the doctor.

"Three days," Flynn answered, his voice rusty.

"I'll give you some time," Dr. Carson said. "But you need your rest." He pointedly looked at Flynn, reminding him of my state.

With a final nod, Dr. Carson left. Ash came to my bedside, tears in her light blue eyes. "I'll come back later, okay?"

"Okay."

She made it to the door, but not before I heard her muffled cry. Flynn pulled up a chair next to my bed and sat down.

He took my hand and brought it to his lips. His mouth was warm, familiar. I would've cried if I had been able to feel any emotion. I hoped it was the drugs and nothing more.

"Where do I start?" he asked, still holding my hand in his.

"From the moment I dropped you guys off."

He nodded. "Andrew had men on his property. Duncan, Brad, and I were able to dispatch them fairly easily."

A small smile graced my lips.

"We got to the house and Katherine ran out the door. The big brute, John, followed her and managed to get off a shot and it hit Katherine. She's fine," he assured me. "Just a graze. But it was bleeding fiercely. Brad sat with her in the car and played doctor. Duncan went in search of John, and that's when I heard the scream from the side of the house." He looked at me in question.

I briefly told him what had happened with Andrew in the library, why he'd set out to destroy us, and how he'd expected me to die in the fire.

"I grabbed hold of the rain gutter because the fire had finally made it to the window. It wasn't strong enough to support me, and I fell backwards."

"Landing on your pelvis and back," Flynn finished. "So I got to you, managed to wake you up, and that's when Andrew found me."

"What happened to Duncan?"

"John clocked him in the ribs, basically rendering him useless. So I was on my own."

"I… Did I?"

"Aye."

I licked dry lips. "Good. How did you get away from John?"

"He was distracted by what you did to Andrew and I was able to take him out. Brad and Duncan cleaned everything up. Your house though… It's gone."

"Burned to the ground?" He nodded and I shrugged. "Hadn't been my home since my parents died."

His hand tightened on mine. "I asked you to be careful."

"Yes."

"You weren't."

I shrugged again.

"You might never walk again, love."

"I'll walk again. Stubborn, remember?"

"Barrett," Flynn began.

"Is Katherine safe?"

He frowned. "Aye."

"Is Andrew gone?"

"Aye."

I softened my tone. "Are we both alive?"

"Aye."

Finally, I smiled, feeling the faintest trace of emotion. Happiness.

I reached out to touch his cheek. "Then that's good enough for me, love. That's good enough for me."

Epilogue

One year later

"More bloody flowers?" Flynn growled. "That man is relentless."

My head peeked out from behind the bouquet of red amaryllis and I smiled. "They're not from Sanchez," I assured him.

Flynn raised an eyebrow. "No?"

I shook my head. "They're from Alia and Jake. Apology flowers that they couldn't make it." Their new restaurant was so popular they hadn't been able to take a vacation since it opened.

"Oh, well, that's all right then."

"The purple roses are from Sanchez," I said, walking over to the bouquet in the corner of the sitting room so I could lean down and smell their fragrance. "He wants to extend our business contract."

"Not going to happen."

"I told him," I explained.

"I'll tell him," Flynn growled, stalking toward me.

"Let's not start a war," I quipped. "We've had enough of that. I'm done with wars."

Flynn took the vase out of my hands and set it aside before dragging me to the carpeted floor.

"Here? Now?" I asked with a fluttering of my lashes.

"Woman, we have exactly," he looked at his Rolex, "thirty-three minutes before the castle is overrun with people here to celebrate."

"It was your idea!" I said with a laugh.

"We've had a hard year," he said quietly. "It's important to celebrate. And Scotland finally won its independence."

"Guess we're nothing more than scotch makers now."

"Successful scotch makers," Flynn corrected. "SINNERS was written up in one of those fancy American magazines."

"I don't care right now," I answered, dragging him closer. My lips found his, and I shoved my fingers through his dark hair. It was starting to go gray at the temples, and if it was possible, it made him look even sexier. I couldn't wait until he needed reading glasses.

We quickly shed our clothes, but I wasn't cold. The warmth of the fireplace a few feet away warmed even the coldest corners of the sitting room.

Flynn's hands roamed over my body, reverently, lingering on each scar. A few stretch marks from carrying our children and then the ugly red scar on my right knee from when they'd set my leg and had to go in and repair the damage.

There were pins in my hip, and when my body was tired, my lower back ached and I walked with a slight limp, favoring my right leg.

"You're beautiful," he whispered. "Strong, brave, stubborn as all hell."

I smiled softly, running a thumb across his lips. "A lesser woman would've given up."

The last year had been spent recovering, both emotionally

and physically. After I'd gotten out of the hospital, Flynn wanted me in Dornoch to heal. Those first few months, I could only watch from a bed. My sons had grown and changed so much in that time that I felt like I hadn't even been a part of it. They didn't understand why I was laid up in bed, unable to walk, unable to play with them.

When I was healed enough to move, I began physical therapy and then spent a lot of time in the scotch distillery, throwing myself into our deal with Sanchez. It was a good outlet for my grief and anger. Flynn had let me be.

"Hey," Flynn said. "Come back."

I smiled. "I'm waiting for you to take me someplace else," I teased.

He chuckled against my skin before moving lower, his mouth finding a pleasurable way to distract me. I erupted quickly, and before my last tremor faded, Flynn was inside of me.

We locked eyes and arms. I cried out, I cursed, I wept with the beauty of living—of being alive.

Flynn collapsed on top of me, and when he tried to move away, I refused to let him.

"I won't break," I whispered.

He smiled. "Promise?"

The faint slap of pattering feet echoed through the hall. A herd was headed this way.

"You better get off me," I teased. "Or our children will soon find out about the 'birds and the bees' with visual aids."

Flynn reluctantly moved off me and went for his shirt. I slipped into my dress just as the door opened and the troops rushed in. I sank to the floor, surrounded by my inquisitive and beautiful children. I looked at Flynn, my heart in my eyes.

It was good enough for me.

He smiled gently, reading the expression on my face. "Me too, love. Me too."

Additional Works

Writing as Emma Slate

SINS Series:
Sins of a King (Book 1)
Birth of a Queen (Book 2)
Rise of a Dynasty (Book 3)
Dawn of an Empire (Book 4)
Ember (Book 5)
Burn (Book 6)
Ashes (Book 7)

The Spider Queen

Writing as Samantha Garman

The Sibby Series:
Queen of Klutz (Book 1)
Sibby Slicker (Book 2)
Mother Shucker (Book 3)

From Stardust to Stardust

About the Author

Emma Slate writes on the run. The dangerous alpha men she writes about aren't thrilled that she's sharing their stories for your enjoyment. So far, she's been able to evade them by jet setting around the world. She wears only black leather because it's bad ass…and hides blood.

Printed in Great Britain
by Amazon